I0775549

A
Picture
PERFECT
Summer

BY JESSICA BOOTH

First edition: June 2023

Identifiers: ISBN 979-8-9870116-2-1 (trade paperback), 979-8-9870116-3-8 (ebook)

Dear Reader:
This book contains themes of grief, aging
parents, dementia, anxiety, and panic attacks.
While there is a HEA, our protagonists face
some of life's most difficult things.
Read responsibly.
<3 – Jessica

Chapter 1

KATIE

The light streaming through the window pane catches the vase of daisies at just the right angle, lighting up the white petals and casting long shadows on the table next to it. I'm framing it in my mind, placing the vase on the bottom right corner, allowing the lens to focus on the petals.

"Katie!"

I startle at Sadie's voice and drop the milk frother, its contents clanging against the counter and scattering.

"Didn't mean to startle you, love, but customers are waiting on their lattes. Let's pick it up a little, yea?"

Sighing, I look down at the mess of spilled oat milk in front of me and grab one of the damp cloths we keep on hand. I clean up quickly and force myself to focus on making a lavender latte. From the corner of my eye, I notice the long line of white cardboard cups, their future contents scrawled in sharpie on their sides. I groan inwardly. It's going to be a long day at Lattes and Lagniappe.

I lose myself in the work, switching to autopilot as I make specialty drinks, smile, and greet customers who come in and out of the coffee shop. This, at least, is easy for me. I've always been able to talk to everyone about anything and everything. When I was in school, my teachers constantly moved me from desk to desk trying to limit my conversations and make me focus on learning–but it never worked. I just struck up a conversation with the person nearest to me. There's something to be said about getting lost in other people's worlds. It's the comfort of an extrovert, I suppose.

When the morning rush eases to a lull, I grab my phone to swipe through everything I've missed. Hesitantly, I open my browser to the website for the University of Dallas and scroll through the photography graduate program requirements. My stomach immediately starts to flutter with the possibility and joy of something new and different on the horizon.

I've always been a bit of a raccoon when it comes to new things. "Oh look, shiny! I want it!" is my mantra. It's a blessing and a curse. I've never had problems trying something fresh and different… it's the deciding to stick with it and not getting distracted by the next pretty thing that's the problem. It's why I've flitted from job to job, never settling on a career. And it's also why my parents always graciously greet the boys I introduce them to, but never get to know them more than a passing hello–because, just like a raccoon, I'm always attracted to the next exciting man who enters my life.

And while my parents are too nice to say it, I know they think it's high time I made some decisions about my life and moved out of my childhood bedroom like every other normal, career-oriented 27-year-old.

The jangle of the bells above the door knocks me out of my reverie. I glance up and see him. Earth brown skin, wide grin, easy and confident nature. He's the only man I've never tired of daydreaming about–well besides Henry Cavill, of course–since I was seventeen. From the moment my brother, Rhett, first brought his best friend, Jacob, to our parents' house for dinner, my ultimate unattainable crush was solidified.

Not only is Jacob five years older than me, but he and Rhett are thick as thieves. He's been Rhett's one true constant throughout his nightmare of a relationship with his ex-wife, Chelsea. I love my brother way too much to ever do anything to hurt their friendship.

Not that Jacob is even interested in me. Why would he be? He's always seen me as Rhett's kid sister with frizzy red hair, a freckled smile, and an obsession with 90s boy bands. Plus, Jacob is sexy and charismatic. He's had his fair share of women over the years, and there have been many times that seeing him with them has made me want to lowkey fling toothpaste in their hair. And then brush it in until their hair becomes a white, chalky, tangled, unattractive mess.

Jacob glances toward the counter when he walks in. When he spots me, he unleashes that megawatt grin that plays a starring role in my fantasies. My knees tremble a little beneath the counter, but I play it cool. No way I'm ever going to let him know that I'm interested or, erm, fantasizing about how we will one day have a rock band together and travel the world making out in a tour bus.

I amp up my own smile to match his. *Play it cool, Katie.* He strides over to the counter, and I meet him at the register, all feigned ease and confidence.

"Hey, Kid," he says. I wince at the endearment Jacob has used since I first met him. But then I notice that he's staring intently at a spot just to the right of my eyes. My brows furrow as he extends his hand across the counter toward my hair. For a split second, I think he's reaching to brush a stray strand of hair away from my face, and all my fantasies leap to take a starring role in the forefront of my mind. *This is it.* This is the moment Jacob pulls a swoony move, brushes my hair out of my face, trails his fingers lightly across my lips, and tells me he's always wanted me. I prepare to be swept away.

Jacob's hand does, in fact, come into contact with my hair, but as he pulls it away, I notice something white on his fingertips. I stare in confusion as he grabs a napkin to wipe it away and laughs.

"You had some whipped cream in your hair," he says.

Well shit. I mentally douse the fires of my fantasies with a firefighter-sized water hose. *Keep it cool, Katie.*

"Hazard of the job," I say breezily. "What can I get you today? The usual?"

Jacob stares up at the menu for a minute, contemplating his order.

"I tell you what, why don't you choose something for me?" One of his eyebrows lifts slightly, already anticipating my response.

"Triple shot mocha with whipped cream and sprinkles coming right up!" I say with mischief, knowing it will irk him. Jacob is more of a plain coffee with one sugar and two creamers kind of guy.

He rolls his eyes before smiling wide again. "Lay it on me, Kid."

Damn this man.

With a wicked grin, I turn to the espresso machine and get to work making him a ridiculous beverage. I take my time, enjoying every second of his attention on me. I drag out the process, pretending my focus is entirely on my work. When I turn to face Jacob, I'm holding a mocha frappuccino topped with a mountain of whipped cream, chocolate syrup, rainbow sprinkles, and a striped paper straw. It's a beverage that would make any five-year-old's day.

I strut over to where Jacob waits at the counter, holding it before me like a prized trophy. I slowly, carefully place the concoction before him. I finally lift my eyes to his, and his grin has grown even larger as he stares back. I watch his tongue dart out; then he bites his lower lip. Jacob looks down at his prize, then slowly back up at me.

"This looks… *impressive,*" he says.

Do I imagine the heat filling his gaze? My mouth quirks in a devious, challenging grin. My eyes meet his, and I hold his gaze.

The bells above the door clang again, disrupting the moment. I am going to rip those damn things off and throw them in the garbage disposal.

"Hey, Jay! Sorry, I'm running late," a familiar voice calls out.

It's my brother. *Mood wrecker.* Jacob spins to face his friend, turning his back to me.

"Hey man," Jacob replies.

"Hey, Katie," my brother shouts over Jacob's shoulder.. I wave to him, smothering my disappointment.

Keep it cool, Katie.

"Hey, big bro. Need a triple shot mocha frappuccino, too?" I call out.

Rhett glances at the coffee monstrosity on the counter, then at his friend. "Did you really order that?" he asks skeptically.

In response, Jacob reaches for the ridiculous drink, places his lips on the straw, and sucks in a giant sip. To my surprise, he doesn't even wince.

"Ah, refreshing," he says theatrically, then lifts the drink as if in a toast before walking over to a table and sitting down.

Rhett shakes his head with a laugh. "You never do anything by halves, do you, Jay?"

Chapter 2

JACOB

I sit at the small table inside Lattes and Lagniappe and purposefully turn my back to Katie, hoping that will help keep my mind off her. But then I look down at this ridiculous drink she made me, and her defiant smirk flashes in my mind.

"Looks like someone had a good night last night," Rhett says from across the table, holding his perfectly respectable cappuccino in hand.

"Hmmm," I finally look up at him.

"Dude, I've been talking to you for like ten minutes, and I don't think you've registered a single thing I've said. Hot date last night?" he queries, lifting one eyebrow.

I shake my head no, attempting to brush *his sister* out of my thoughts.

Rhett's face turns solemn. "Oh shit, is it your dad?"

My stomach plummets with those words, but I refuse to think about how he's been acting lately. Not right now. I summon my public Jacob persona, ease back into my chair, take a swig of this awful sugar storm of a beverage, and smile.

"Just distracted with work," I say casually.

Rhett stares at me for a couple of moments. He knows me better than anyone and knows when I'm faking composure. But I'm not in the mood to be pushed on this, and he seems to realize it, so he lets it drop. Scrambling for a topic, I immediately pluck something out of the air that lets me deflect the attention away from the gorgeous redhead working behind the coffee counter.

"So, Rhett, I think it's time to plan your bachelor party," I say. These words have their intended effect.

Rhett immediately starts to stammer. "Oh no. I don't think. I mean, that's not something I... Um."

"Yea, so here's what I'm thinking," I say conspiratorially. "We drive to Shreveport and hit the casinos, then stop at the Hustler Club for a little strip show."

"Jay, man. I don't know...." He's beginning to squirm in the small, metal-framed chair.

I can't help it; I laugh. Rhett has always been shy when he's not railing on a guitar. And as much as I'd love to take him out for some fun, I think the man would honestly rather die than do any of those things.

"What are you doing to my poor brother?" a familiar voice chastises. Katie steps past me and slides her arm around Rhett's shoulders. I light up at the challenge in her voice. So much for blocking her out.

"Just planning a little bachelor party fun," I say.

Katie looks at me, and I swear I see desire flicker in her eyes when our eyes meet again. But then she turns her head down to look at her brother.

"Leave him alone, Jay. You know he's nervous enough about standing in front of all those people at his wedding."

"True," I concede. I see Rhett visibly relax, but I'm on a roll. "Surely you could rouse up a couple of your friends to put on a home strip tease for him," I suggest to Katie. Rhett coughs, then chuckles and shakes his head, rolling his eyes.

Katie cocks her head to the side, a cat ready to pounce. "Why Jacob Edwards. I do believe you're projecting your own fantasies onto my poor, dear brother." She lifts an eyebrow.

I snicker at her challenge. I love her fire.

I lean toward them, placing my arms on the small table between us. "Fine. Fine. Rhett, we are having a bachelor party, but we can keep it low-key. Margie says we can hang out in her she-shed and have open access to her beer fridge. We can watch the fight on her giant TV and have a couple of guys over."

Rhett nods. "Now that is a plan I can get behind."

"Sounds like my work here is done," Katie says, leaning down to kiss the top of her brother's head before sauntering back off to work. I try not to turn my head and watch her hips sway as she passes. Try… and fail.

Chapter 3

KATIE

"We can shove Brian into the cupboard under the stairs. He loves Harry Potter and would be thrilled to cosplay his life. He won't mind."

"He will, too, mind," a male voice calls from somewhere in the apartment.

I laugh as I hold my phone out in front of me. I'm Facetiming with my best friend, Celia. She peers over her shoulder, trying to catch a glimpse of her roommate, Brian, and grins with delight.

"It sounds like your plan to move me closer to you may not go over well with the person paying the other half of your rent," I say warmly.

Brian emerges from the hallway and walks over to the phone. As he leans in to say hello, his straight, jet-black hair falls into his eyes. "Hey, Katie," he says. "Listen, I'm fine with you moving in, but you and Celia will have to share a bed. I won't complain."

Celia elbows him in the ribs, and he falls onto his side, laughing.

"Seriously, Katie! There are so many more jobs in Dallas. We can figure out a place for you to stay. And we misssss you. Our friendship posse isn't the same without you here," Celia whines.

And she's not wrong. All through middle school and high school, Brian, Celia, and I were inseparable. But when it came time for college, they moved four hours away to Dallas to pursue their dream careers in finance and interior design, respectively. Struggling to decide where to go, I failed to turn in my college applications on time and only scrambled into Louisiana Tech by the grace of the admissions director being in a Zumba class with my mother. Once enrolled, I made it through college, okay, I guess. But I switched majors so many times that I ended up with a degree in general studies before hopping from waitressing to store clerk to librarian to barista.

As I peer at the small phone screen and into the perfectly appointed space of my two successful best friends, jealousy forms an ugly knot in my chest. I don't understand why I'm incapable of making the next step in my life like everyone else my age. But that's not their fault, so I shove down those feelings and keep talking.

"I don't even know what I would do if I moved there," I bemoan. "Moving to Dallas to be a barista seems kind of lame," I say, glancing down at my fingers knotting in my lap.

"I think it would be a great starting place!" Celia chimes in with her ever-present optimism. "I think being a barista gives you the perfect starving artist vibe. You just need some tattoo sleeves of wildflowers and a septum piercing, and you'll fit right in."

"Oh, Cee," I chuckle. "I don't know. Moving to Dallas is such a big commitment...."

"Just promise me you'll think about it," she pleads. "We could use some more fun around here. This guy is boring," she says, nodding at Brian, who has picked up his Nintendo Switch and tuned us both out.

"Katie! Come eat! Dinner is ready!" I hear my mom's voice echo outside my bedroom. I wince, embarrassed that I still live with my parents. They both know this already of course, but there's nothing quite like having it shoved blatantly in all our faces.

"Tell Mrs. H we said hello! Oh, and will you ask her if she'll make that pound cake when we visit this summer?" Cee asks.

"Noted. Talk to you soon, Cee."

"Love ya, Katie."

I end the call, then push myself up off the carpet and make my way downstairs to the kitchen. The heavenly smells of roasted chicken and mashed potatoes fill the room, making my embarrassment run away and curl up like a cat under a chair. This is, by far, the best part of still living with my parents.

Amelia, my brother's fiancé, is pulling rolls out of the oven. So the gang's all here tonight... Not that I'm complaining. I truly enjoy Amelia's company, and she's the best thing that has ever happened to my brother. She helped bring Rhett back to life after years of being under the thundercloud of his ex-wife, Chelsea.

When she turns, her face lights up. "Hey, Katie!" She walks over and wraps her arms around me in a tight embrace. I squeeze her back.

"Katie, grab the plates, will ya?" Mom calls over her shoulder. I get to work setting the table. By the time we're all seated and eating, comfortable conversation fills the room. Dad talks sports with Rhett while Mom quizzes Amelia about the upcoming wedding details.

"Have you gotten your bridesmaid dress yet, Katie?" Mom asks, pulling me into the conversation.

"Oh, um, no, not yet. I couldn't decide which style I liked." Mom frowns at that; well aware of the problems my indecisiveness usually causes.

Sensing the quickly forming tension in the room, Amelia chimes in. "What are you doing tomorrow? We can go to Minden together, and I'll help you choose one."

Mom visibly relaxes at the suggestion, so I jump on it. "Yea, sounds perfect."

"Oh, Katie, I meant to tell you," Rhett says. "My editor at work, Lauren, is looking for a freelance photographer to help with a special project she's working on over the summer. I told her how good you are at taking photos and that you might be a good fit."

Everyone at the table turns to look at me expectantly.

"Um, yeah, okay, I guess," I say with a shrug.

"And I may have told her that you could stop by the office on

Monday," he says like it's no big deal.

The thrill of something new and challenging ignites inside me, and my mouth quirks in a half smile.

"Do I need to bring anything?"

"Just your winning personality."

"Ha. How could she possibly say no to that?"

Chapter 4

JACOB

"Yea, I know Ollie. You can stop looking at me like that."

I stare into deep brown eyes full of longing. Sighing, I lower my sandwich and pluck out a small piece of bacon, tossing it in Ollie's direction. Despite his stocky bulldog frame and short legs, he scrabbles quickly, snatching up the offering with his oversized tongue and maneuvering it past his underbite before swallowing it whole. He looks back at me expectantly.

Ollie will never win a prize for his looks, but some days he is the only thing snapping me out of living on autopilot. I love my job as a reporter for *The Ruston Daily Leader*. It's what I've always wanted to do, but lately, the ins and outs of covering stories on small-town life have been… uneventful. Well, outside of my best friend Rhett nabbing the story of the year last year when he accidentally solved a decades long cold case. I'm happy about his newfound success. And discovering the love of his life. And his upcoming perfect marriage. Really, I am. It's just… I've been telling the same old stories, living the same old life, walking in and out of my childhood home every single day for, well, a really long time.

I hear coughing echo from the back of the house, and I get up to wander into the living room. My dad reclines in the old chair he's had for years, stirring from a nap.

"Hey, Dad. Need anything before I go to work?"

He stares at me bleary-eyed and seems confused for a moment, but then recognition colors and his features, and he straightens his posture.

"Pick up some peaches on your way home?" he rasps.

My shoulders sag slightly. Ruston is known regionally for its famous, delicious peaches, and there is always a long line at the Peach Orchard this time of year. But I know they are his very favorite thing. And my dad, who raised me on his own from the time I was ten, has always given everything to me. I certainly can't and won't deny him this.

"Of course. I'll grab a jar of Margie's jam from the Peach Store while I'm there, too."

He nods and flips on the TV, turning his attention to the latest updates on the Louisiana Tech Bulldogs and projections for the next football season.

I pat Ollie on the head as I walk out the door and climb in my rundown Honda Civic.

As I drive to work, I let my thoughts stray to a forbidden space, something I only allow myself to indulge in when I'm alone and need something to make me smile. Long, auburn waves. Endless legs to match. A soul of fire and a heart of gold. *Katie*. I know I shouldn't linger on these thoughts. She's so vibrant, so full of potential. And I'm… stuck in limbo, uninteresting. Not to mention, she's Rhett's kid sister. And something about that feels wrong. But still, I let myself imagine her strutting past me in the coffee shop again, a wide grin spreading across her face, curved hips moving with intent, and I sigh with contentment.

"EDWARDS, IN MY OFFICE." Lauren, our editor-in-chief, is used to her orders being followed. I close my laptop and follow the sound of her clicking heels down the hall. I'm not worried. After all, she usually only does this if something unusual happens that she wants me to cover—and I could go for something different right now.

"Sit," she says, nodding to the chair across from her desk.

I plop down and slide my casual smirk into place. I'm ready for whatever Lauren is about to throw at me. I'm kind of hoping it might even involve a little travel. Though at this point, I'm ready to take on anything that doesn't involve a senior citizen charity project–though those ladies do always thank me by making the best apple pies this side of the Mississippi.

"I've got a… project for you," she says, flicking her perfectly slicked-back blonde ponytail over her shoulder.

"Lay it on me," I say, beckoning the information from her with my hands.

She stares at me for a moment as if wondering where to begin. "You know a new lifestyle magazine is launching in town, right?" I nod. I've heard the news but haven't given it much thought. It's not the type of thing that really appeals to my interests. "Rumor is that they plan to launch in a few months, and already their appeal to women in the thirty-five to sixty-five age range is drawing off our advertisers in droves."

"Okay… And you want me to do what, exactly?"

"We need to get the advertisers back. And in order to do that, we need more content in the newspaper, and online that appeals to that demographic," she states plainly.

"Well, I am neither a woman nor quite in that age range yet. So I'm not sure where you're going with this."

"Jacob. As much as I am loath to admit this, you are charming," she says.

I smirk at that, sitting up a bit straighter in my seat. In my lowest, sexiest voice, I say, "Do you… need me to *seduce* someone for you?"

She rolls her eyes. "We aren't that desperate yet. I have a different sort of story I want you to cover for us. A series, actually. And I want you to use your creativity and ability to charm the pants off of everyone you encounter to write something that will appeal to a broader demographic of readers."

I sit back in my seat and lift one eyebrow. "So you do want me to seduce a story out of someone, or should I say someones?”

"Oh, knock it off. I want you to produce something that will lure advertisers back and new advertisers in, and I have just the thing. You're going to write a festival series.”

"Say again?”

"Louisiana has the most festivals out of any state in the country. Granted many of them are in the southern part of the state, but we have tons of them up this way, too. I want you to attend them, find out the little-known things. Talk to the people who have been there year after year. Participate in food-eating competitions—that sort of thing. I'll send a photographer with you. With your good looks and confidence, you'll help us blow up our social media feed.”

"I feel so... *Objectified*," I say with mock indignance. Lauren is like a sister to me, and I know she takes no sexual interest in me whatsoever.

"Good, then it's settled. You'll go to Mudbug Madness in Shreveport at the end of May.”

"But Rhett's wedding?”

"It's the weekend after the wedding. We'll foot the bill for your travel and call ahead to comp your food.”

I mull it over. Perhaps this is just the thing I need to shake me out of the mind-numbing sameness that's become my life. I nod.

"Sounds good. But you said 'festivals,' plural?”

"Right. You'll cover the local Ruston Peach Festival, of course. And then you'll go to the Farmerville Watermelon Festival and maybe something in Natchitoches. I think there's some sort of swine festival around here too. Let me think on it.”

"Thanks for the assignment, Boss.”

She nods. "Close the door on your way out, will you?”

Chapter 5

KATIE

Rhett opens the door to the newspaper office as I fidget, pulling my skirt down a little. I feel a little like Julia Roberts in *Pretty Woman* when she gets a wardrobe update she's not used to. The business professional look really isn't my thing, but I want to make a good impression. My big brother pulled some strings to get me this interview. And honestly, it's pretty exciting to think I might actually get paid to do something I love and that someone would value my photography that highly.

"We've had to keep the doors locked since the Jimmy Roberts story ran last year. Some crazy people have shown up at the office," Rhett says, ushering me in as he glances around behind me. I shudder. Hard to imagine people like that showing up in a town like this.

As I follow Rhett through the winding corridors and cubicles of his office building, I glance around, nerves dancing over tripwires in my body, hoping to spot Jacob's familiar grin or hear his booming laughter. But no luck. Not that it matters, though. Not really. I shake my shoulders, willing away nervous Katie and encouraging lead singer Katie to take the stage. By the time we make it to Lauren's office, I've evicted most of the nerves from my system, replacing them with smiles and confidence. Rhett knocks on Lauren's office door and opens it.

"Ah, you must be Katie," Lauren says, standing up and walking over to us to shake my hand. I greet her with a warm smile. I feel like I already know this woman by how Rhett speaks of her with the respect of a loyal subject.

"So great to meet you," I say warmly.

"I'll leave you to it, then," Rhett says. "Come find me before you go, Katie. We can grab lunch afterward." He winks at me as he closes the door behind him.

"Have a seat," Lauren says, gesturing to a pair of chairs in front of her desk. I grab the one closest, and she eases into the chair next to me.

"Thanks for coming in today, Katie. Rhett says you're a good photographer, and you're looking to get some experience under your belt. Can you tell me a little bit about that?"

Oh, Rhett, he's already oversold me. But I opt to step onto the stage my brother has set up for me. *Time to shine, Katie.*

"Everyone has something that calls to them, I think. For my brother, it's writing. For my friend Brian, it was a fascination with tinkering. Me? I feel like I have a gift for finding the *story* in things with my camera. When I take a photo, I like to try and capture a moment so other people feel like they are there when they look at it."

Wow, maybe I do love photography more than I realized, because all of that was one hundred percent true.

"That's beautiful, Katie. What are your favorite things to photograph?'" Lauren responds with interest.

I ponder her question, scanning through my favorite images on the slide projector of my mind.

"Beauty," I respond simply.

When her brows furrow, I expand on my answer. "I love to photograph people, but beyond just a face, I like to capture that moment when they greet a missed loved one or pull cookies out of the oven. Or the way the sun sinks below the trees and dances along the pine needles at golden hour."

This seems to satisfy her because she nods and offers me a small smile.

"And have you ever photographed an event before?"

I pause and chuckle a little, deciding to be honest. "Do you count my brother's band performances?"

She laughs a little, as I hoped she would. "I like you, Katie. Rhett has shown me some of your work, and I think you'd be a good fit for a special project we're launching this summer. It's a festival tour of sorts. Want to hear more about it?"

I nod my head with enthusiasm and lean in as Lauren shares her vision.

I SMILE BROADLY AT RHETT as I walk out of Lauren's office, giving him a discreet double thumbs up. He nods at me, silently communicating; I *knew you'd get it, Katie,* in that often indiscernible language only siblings possess.

"Ready for lunch?" I link my arm in his, and we walk out of the office together.

Once we're out of sight of the building's front windows, I leap into Rhett's arms and cling to him like an overly enthusiastic koala bear. I don't even care about my skirt anymore.

"That's enough, Katie," he says, not unkindly.

"Never, never, never enough!" I belt out in my best reenactment of *The Greatest Showman* as he tries to dislodge me.

"Keep acting like that and you won't make it past your first assignment."

"I think Lauren likes me," I tell him, slowly uncoiling myself from around him.

"Of course she does, Katie. Everyone likes you."

"You have to say that because you're my brother," I tell him, but he just smiles with warm affection and shakes his head.

This brother of mine. I know so many people fight with their siblings, but Rhett and I have always had an easy peace between us. I'm the rainbow sprinkle donut to his toasted wheat bread, the iced mocha frappuccino to his black coffee. And it works for us. We lift the other up when we need it. And even though he is often embarrassed by my antics, he tolerates them with affection.

"Yea, let's go. I want to sit on the patio at Portico and sample the menu so I know what to get at your rehearsal dinner," I say.

Chapter 6

JACOB

One Week Later

"Alright, fellas, listen up."

Amelia's Aunt Margie's distinct Southern cadence commands the attention of the room, or should I say shed. She-shed if we're being precise. At least that's what the sign that adorns the back wall says. Margie tosses her graying rusty brown hair back and pushes her impressive bosom forward, constrained only by her ever-present overalls.

She continues. "The fridge is stocked with beer. The cabinet has a variety of fine liquors. There are a whole host of munchies in the cabinet over yonder. And Katie is going to stop by later with food."

Margie takes a breath and looks each of us in the eye—a ringmaster with a captive audience. "A few ground rules, boys. First and foremost, drink whatever you want. *But I do not want to go to the emergency room tonight*, so let's at least be moderately responsible. Mmmmkay?"

She glares at us with all the authority of a queen, and our small group nods immediately.

"Next. I have everyone's keys, and I will not return them until tomorrow morning. Kapish?"

Another round of nods. She continues, "I ordered and paid for y'all to watch the fight on Dish. It comes on at 8:30." She motions at the TV as she says this.

I let out a "Whoop whoop." Margie eyes me and nods approvingly.

"But that is the only thing I'm paying for. I do not want to see any dirty movie charges show up on my account. Are we clear?"

I burst into laughter, and Rhett turns beet red. Rhett's dad and cousins look at each other uncomfortably. A couple of our coworkers, Carl and Ian, snicker.

"That, um, won't be a problem." Rhett murmurs.

"Does this mean you'll be giving us a show later, Margie?" I taunt.

She levels me with a gaze that would make paint curl off walls. "I think… not." A pause. "Finally, all these couches pull out into futons. There are air mattresses and extra blankets in the closet. Have fun at your slumber party, boys, and text me only if you have an emergency."

With her speech concluded, she turns and marches out the door without a backward glance. Talking to Amelia's aunt has always been like taking a shot of fire whisky. I love her.

"You know," I say to no one in particular. "I kind of like this she-shed thing. Maybe I need one."

"I'm pretty sure they call that a man cave," Rhett says.

"Yea, but I like the aesthetic of this shed better. Less dead, mounted deer heads, more cozy she-bear den."

They all stare at me.

"So, beer?" Rhett's dad, Ben, chimes in. Everyone turns to the fridge to grab their beverage of choice while I turn the TV on.

We settle in, keeping things low-key, exactly like Rhett wants for his bachelor party night. And I can't say that I mind too much. Although I've always gravitated more toward the bar scene myself, watching the fight with the guys allows me to zone out and decompress. I've been worried about my dad's behavior lately–how he seems more "out of it" and eating less. It nudges awake all my old fears that Mom's declining health spawned within me. I realize just how much the worry has been eating away at me as my third beer eases the tension out of my shoulders. I've sunk into the plush cushions of the couch, shouting with the guys as the boxers on the TV screen slam their fists into one another.

Carl, our lead photographer at the paper, grabs a beer and settles in next to me on the couch. He and I have worked together ever since I started with the paper a little over ten years ago, and his salt-and-pepper hair points to just how long he's been a photojournalist.

"Hear you got a new assignment," Carl says, leaning in a little closer so he can be heard over the fight.

I am not in the mood to talk shop, but I indulge him out of respect. "Yea… apparently, Lauren is spearheading a festival series and thinks I'm a good fit. It sounds pretty interesting."

"I hear she's still looking for a photographer. I could use the extra work. Put in a good word for me?" he asks as he sips his drink.

I pause. The beer in my bloodstream urges me to say things I'll probably regret. Carl is an old newspaper guy, and we are trying to compete with a flashy magazine. His work is good, but I think something fresh and new would be better. Fortunately, I'm not the editor, and it's not my decision. Relieved by that thought, I hedge, "Sure, man…."

The door to the shed clangs open, and a voice that sounds like warm sunshine echoes off the walls and ceiling.

"Feel the attraction! Color my hair, do what I dare. Oh-oh-oh, I wanna be free. Yeah, to feel the way I feel. Man! I feel like a woman!"

"Ow ow!" I call out in my best Shania Twain impression. Hands still raised, each holding a box of delicious-smelling tacos, Katie bows her head in thanks for the show of support. There's a reason we made Katie our little band's lead singer. The girl has a set of pipes on her and does Shania Twain justice.

"Tacos are here! Let's go, boys!" she calls out.

Ben rushes over to help his daughter set the food on the table and gives her a big bear hug.

Rhett steps past me to do the same. "Thanks for dropping these by, Katie."

"No problem. Always happy to help. Though, Rhett, this doesn't look like much of a bachelor party," she says, eyeing the subdued space.

"You're welcome to stay a while," I say before I can stop myself.

Everyone turns to stare at me. "What? She might liven things up a bit."

"As much as I appreciate the invitation, Jay, this scene looks a little drab for me. Enjoy your boys' night."

As Katie's dad hugs her again, I'm up and off the couch before I can think better of it. If they get a hug, then I want a hug. *That's not weird, right?* Beer fueling me on, I stride up to Katie with confidence.

"Thanks for dropping the tacos by, Kid. Be safe driving home." And then I lean in and scoop her up in a hug. Her arms fly around me in response, giving me a couple of pats on the back.

"Um, Jacob." Her muffled voice comes out after a couple of seconds.

"Mmm hmm."

"You can let go of me now," she laughs.

"You smell good," I say and squeeze her a little tighter.

"I think someone has had too much to drink," she says playfully, but she doesn't shove me away. "Jay, I smell like tacos, and that smell will linger after I'm gone. In fact, the real thing is even better because you get to eat the tacos."

I cough when she says this, trying not to let my mind wander to a place it shouldn't go to at those words. I feel her shake with laughter in my arms. Katie gives me one more tight squeeze and pulls away. I feel her loss like the blankets ripped off the bed on a chilly morning. Everything feels a little more stark, cold, and sober as she steps out of my embrace. And I still can't take my eyes off her, especially as her cheeks color slightly. Is she embarrassed or…

"Anyway. I'm going to go now. I have to be up bright and early for the morning coffee shop crowd. Love you, Dad. Love you, Rhett." And as Katie turns and walks out the door, her smell of coffee and vanilla lingers behind. I stare through the door at her retreating form, the beer urging me to pursue her.

"Let's eat!" I hear Rhett say.

I snap back to reality and try to shake Katie out of my system.

Chapter 7

KATIE

One Week Later

"You are breathtaking, Amelia."

We're inside the church's bridal chapel, and I can't take my eyes off the woman who is about to become my sister officially. The conversations of arriving wedding guests filter through the closed doors, alerting us that the ceremony is about to begin.

"We should have eloped," Amelia croaks out, hands trembling. Her best friend, Beth, and I wrap our arms around her in reassuring comfort.

"All you have to do is look at Rhett," Beth says. "Just keep your eyes on him, and you'll be fine."

The door creaks open, and Margie leans in. "It's time."

I give Amelia one more hug, then Beth and I walk to the door, sage green dresses fluttering around us, white rose bouquets in our hands. I hear the processional music in the church sanctuary, and my heart leaps at the thrill of walking down the aisle. When the doors to the church open, I step onto the center aisle and my eyes land on my brother. He can't hide his grin… or his nerves. He's fidgeting, but I know he's been hoping for this day since he was a kid and first laid eyes on Amelia. My eyes shift to the right, taking in my dad and… Jacob.

All my wildest fantasies of this man over the past ten years do not live up to the reality of seeing him in a suit and tie. I'm still staring dumbly at him when the photographer steps out in front of me to snap my photo. I pause, amping up my smile for the camera. Once he steps out of the way, my eyes find Jacob again, and he's staring at me just as intently. Is that a look of awe on his face? Or maybe he's just as overwhelmed by the day's events as the rest of us. At the end of the aisle I veer away from him to take my place on the bride's side.

All eyes return to the center aisle as Amelia makes her appearance. I glance at her, then turn to study my brother. Always quiet and unassuming, Rhett struggles–and fails–to hold back tears as he stares in wonder at the woman walking toward him. The emotion on his face filters into my heart. He deserves every single moment of happiness with Amelia. I feel tears well in my eyes and am momentarily surprised. I never thought a wedding would make me cry. When Amelia finally arrives to stand beside Rhett, he reaches out to cup her cheek, and my heart nearly explodes. He leans in and whispers something, then they both smile and turn together to face the minister.

As the ceremony begins, my gaze drifts past Rhett and Amelia to study Jacob subtly. His strong jaw is shaved clean, and his hair is trimmed tight to his head. I notice the way the overhead lights highlight his perfect bone structure. His gaze snaps up, snagging my own. I flush involuntarily. It feels intimate, despite the large number of people around us. Then, ever so slowly, he crosses his eyes at me. It takes me by surprise, and I have to focus every ounce of willpower I possess to keep my giggles at bay.

"You may kiss the bride!" the minister proclaims.

I snap back to reality just in time to watch my brother lean down and press his lips to his new wife's. "I now pronounce you Mr. and Mrs. Rhett and Amelia Hebert." Everyone claps and whistles. I grin broadly, my heart so full for both of them.

We swiftly exit the church and head off to the side to snap some family photos. The whole photo session is brief and unassuming, which is perfectly suited to Rhett and Amelia.

I'm relieved when we finally finish taking photos and make our way to the reception at the fall festival site, where Amelia and Rhett first reconnected a year and a half ago. She and her festival planning crew have been busy transforming the vendor barn into something spectacular. Twinkle lights crisscross the ceiling, and round white tables surround the perimeter of the open space. Everywhere I turn, there are white roses and sunflowers. The wedding cake has a rendition of the couple with a dog that looks very similar to Amelia's wild rescue, Tucker, atop it. It's simple, elegant, and meaningful.

Once inside the barn, I make my way to the bar and grab a glass of champagne, discreetly tossing it back and asking for another. It's been a long day.

"I always knew we were kindred spirits," a familiar voice says behind me. I turn to see Margie, cocktail glass in hand. Seeing her in a formal pantsuit, white rose tucked into the lapel is weird. Her hair is down and neat. Amelia's powerhouse aunt is usually clad in worn overalls or stained cargo shorts without a stitch of makeup.

"Cheers to that!" I say, clinking glasses with her. I join her at one of the tall cocktail tables nearby.

"He looks good," she says, staring out across the space.

"I know. Seeing my brother happy makes him look five years younger," I respond, watching as he holds Amelia close for their first dance.

"Oh, he looks good, too. But that's not who I'm talking about. She nods to the space across from us where Jacob lounges with his back against the wall. My cheeks warm as I drink him in, enjoying this moment of being able to stare at him unobserved.

"I see you agree," Margie says, smiling into her cocktail.

"Yes, I know he's handsome. But he's like a brother to me," I deflect.

"Oh, is he now?" she says, incredulity lacing her voice. "That's not what it seems like to me. Seems to me like the two of you have been flirting relentlessly since you formed that band for the fall festival almost two years ago."

I frown. "Margie, that's just how he is. Jacob flirts with everyone. He can't help himself." I can hear the bitterness in my voice.

"If you say so," she drawls, taking another sip.

Jacob's gaze snaps to us then, and he smiles as our eyes connect across the room. Pushing off of the wall, he starts threading his way through the crowd toward us. My heart rhythm ticks up a notch. He's stopped a couple of times along the way, so I toss back the rest of my second glass of champagne. I am just accepting a refill as he finishes making his way across the room to us.

"Margie," he says, inclining his head to her. "Looking good tonight."

"Same to you, Jacob. But I need some more bourbon," she says unceremoniously as she strides over to the bar, leaving us behind.

I'm two sips into my third glass of champagne on an empty stomach, and those bubbles are starting to rise straight to my head. The little devil that lives inside my mind is peeking out, ready to play. And as I stare at Jacob, her cheers to finally make a move on the man I've quietly fantasized over for years get louder and more insistent.

"Hey, Kid. You look. Wow." I hear Jacob say.

I do a slow turn and curtsey. "Why, thank you. You don't look half bad yourself." I stumble a little on my heels, and he reaches out, resting his hand on my arm to steady me.

"Must be some strong champagne," he says, hand lingering.

I gulp. "Yea, it's good stuff," I say, taking another sip. He lets go of my arm to grab a flute for himself off a passing tray and takes a swig.

"That is some good stuff," he says, impressed. "I guess I shouldn't be surprised that the booze is good since Margie is footing the bill for most of this."

"The woman does know how to prioritize," I agree.

"Twist and Shout" blares through the speakers, and Jacob tosses back the rest of his glass.

"Care to dance?" he asks, one eyebrow lifted and his full, magnetic grin is on display.

As if I could ever say no to such an invitation. I love that he's showering me with his attention, and my devilish inner cheerleader is tipsy and preening. I slap my hand into his and kick my heels off in the same motion. Those foot-devouring bitches can rest on the sidelines for the rest of the night as far as I'm concerned.

"Let's do this, Jay."

We hit the dance floor with hands raised in the air, bodies moving to the old Beatles tune. We're twisting our way down to the floor and back up again, laughing and soaking up the joy and energy of the people around us. And when we're dancing together, bodies casually touching, alcohol feeding our systems, it feels electric. My body is loose and warm as I move between dancing with Jacob to dancing with Beth and Amelia. We get carried away on the beat, laughing and celebrating in a way only wedding receptions allow.

When a slow song comes on, my shoulders dip in disappointment. I start to walk off the dancefloor for a break when I feel a light touch on my arm.

"Where do you think you're going?" a low, husky voice murmurs.

I turn to see Jacob standing close. "I've never thought of you as a quitter, Katie. Don't let a little slow music scare you away." His voice has turned from teasing to serious. A shudder runs up and down my body at his words. My skin heats like a smoldering ember where his hand still rests on the exposed skin of my arm.

I swallow and try for levity. "Challenge accepted," I say. andextend my hands as if we are going to waltz across the barn floor formally.

"Oh, we can do better than that." He says as he slides his hands around my lower back and pulls me in close. My arms rise instinctively to wrap behind his neck, and I press my cheek to his chest, resting comfortably in his arms. We begin to sway as Eric Clapton sings, "And my darling, yes, you look wonderful tonight."

We don't say a word, letting our bodies do the talking for us. I feel his nose press into my hair and inhale. "You smell amazing," Jacob whispers.

"Better than tacos?"

His low laugh rumbles through his chest and into my body. He has abandoned his coat and rolled up the sleeves of his dress shirt, exposing his muscled forearms. I feel the inside of his arm brush the side of my elbow as his fingers trace light circles on my lower back. I don't know what is happening right now, but I don't want it to stop. I trace the same light circles on the back of his neck in encouragement, and he pulls me in even closer. I breathe in his scent of champagne and sweat, covered only slightly by the smell of laundry detergent and cedar. It's warm and comforting, like a cozy cabin home in the woods. I long to hit pause and rest in Jacob's arms like this forever, soaking up his affection, confidence, and joy.

I let my arms drop from behind his neck and tuck them below his own arms, encircling his waist. I give him a little squeeze. This feels right, like the ultimate cuddle.

He chuckles. "That feels better, doesn't it snuggle bunny?"

"Snuggle bunny?" I scoff, pulling back slightly to look up at him. Laughter dances in his eyes as he raises a hand and gently urges my head back to his chest.

"What? You're totally a bunny. Always hopping around with her little tail on fire."

"Well if I'm a bunny, then you're a Tasmanian Devil."

"My thoughts certainly feel devilish right now," he murmurs into my temple, where I can feel his steady, warm breaths.

Did he really just say that? I think I've had too much champagne because my fantasies are starting to get confused with reality.

When the song ends, we linger together, neither wanting to break this moment.

"All the Single Ladies" suddenly blasts through the speakers like a bucket of ice-cold water landing directly on top of us. Before I can catch my bearings, Beth yanks me from Jacob's embrace. I'm stunned and irritated. But before I can register what's happening, I'm shoved into a group of women who are assuming a football defensive line stance. *Wait, what?*

The room is spinning around me—likely the combination of champagne, the crazed bunch of women bumping into me, and that intoxicating, torturous slow dance with Jacob. I'm shoved again and look up just as a bouquet plummets toward me and lands directly in my face, sending me windmilling backward. I trip over the hem of my dress and hit the floor. Hard. The breath is knocked out of me; I struggle to inhale, only to breathe in a mouth full of rose petals. *What the actual hell?*

"And Katie Hebert was quite literally knocked off her feet by the bouquet, ladies and gentlemen. Let's hope that's a promising sign for her future!" I hear the DJ, say as he laughs into the microphone. *I am going to unalive him.*

I push myself up, and the bouquet falls into my lap as I continue to sit on the floor and stare dumbly at the crowd around me. As the shock begins to wear off, I notice everyone staring and laughing. Warring with embarrassment, I decide to shove those feelings aside and just go with it. I am Katie fucking Hebert, after all. I grab the bouquet and thrust it into the air like a prized trophy, holding up a "number one" sign with my other hand. The room erupts into thunderous applause.

"You okay, Kid?" I turn to see Jacob watching me, concern darting across his features.

"Did anyone see my underwear?" I whisper loudly to him.

"Um. I think I would have remembered that" he says slyly. "You're in the clear…at least on that front. Or should I say, at least on that *bottom?*"

"Then yea, I'm fine. Wore my favorite dinosaur undies, and that could have been really embarrassing." I wink at him, and his whole face lights up like it's Christmas morning.

"Ready for some more dancing?" I say, lifting an eyebrow.

"That's my girl," he says. And before I can fully register that comment, he takes me by the hand and whisks me into the crowded floor to dance to an epic rendition of "Baby Got Back."

Chapter 8

JACOB

In the week since the wedding, I've been running around like a possum with its tail on fire. Between picking up extra story assignments at work while Rhett is on his honeymoon and constantly checking on my increasingly irritable dad, I've barely had a moment to breathe. But in those few moments I do—mostly on my drive to and from work and while cooking dinner—I'm obsessing over that slow dance with Katie. I can still feel the way her arms wrapped around me and how she rested so easily in my arms. When I close my eyes, I can smell her shampoo and that hint of champagne that rested over both of us. It's a treasured memory—one I plan to relive as much as possible.

But I'm also a realist. I know Katie had too much to drink at the wedding, and any touching—or tracing my neck with her fingers—was almost certainly a byproduct of booze.

I've seen Katie in passing a few times since the wedding. I stopped in to get a coffee and say hi while she was at work, but the little coffee shop was packed, and all she could do was wave as I grabbed my drink and headed to work.

I hoped we might cross paths as we took turns checking on Rhett and Amelia's dog, but no luck. It's finally Saturday, and all I want to do is lay down and take a break. But my new festival assignment is starting, and I have to knock this one out of the park. My first event to cover is Mudbug Madness in Shreveport, a bigger city about an hour west of us.

As I sit in the parking lot at work, I study the event brochure. Crawfish and beer. Okay, so maybe this one will be fun. Though I guess that depends on the freelance photographer assigned to go with me. I never did get a chance to talk to Lauren about Carl and his request for this assignment, so I have no idea who I will be partnering with today. I can get along with just about anyone, so it's not a big deal either way. But today will be far more enjoyable if my assignment partner is 55-year-old Frank, who currently holds the record for most beers chugged in one minute than surly Carl. Though if I'm stuck with oversharing Annie, I can always zone out to that memory of the slow dance while she prattles on about her most recent bout of gout.

I hear the crunch of gravel as a car pulls into the lot and parks next to me. Moment of truth. I look up expecting to see graying hair, but instead, I see... *Wait, what?* My heart starts salsa dancing in my chest as I spy a wavy, auburn ponytail climb out of the driver's seat. I begin to panic, thinking something terrible must have happened to Rhett or Amelia. But my fear eases when Katie looks through my passenger side window at me with confusion. I push the button to lower the car window.

"Hey there, Kid. What are you doing here? Everything okay?"

"Oh, hey, Jacob. I'm supposed to meet a reporter here. Rhett helped me get a gig as a freelance photographer for a few festivals in the area. But it occurs to me now that I forgot to ask who I'm supposed to meet. Any ideas?"

Well shit.

"Me."

"What?"

"It's me. I'm the reporter covering the festivals."

Her mouth drops open.

"Oh, um. I'll just... get my camera bag then."

She spins away from the window and heads to her car's trunk to gather the equipment she will need for the day. I'm dumbstruck, not sure if this is the worst or best thing to happen to me this year. The best, I decide as she opens the passenger door to my car and slides in. Any excuse to be alone with Katie is definitely the best.

"Well, this should be fun," she says, sliding her sunglasses into place. I can't tell if she's being sarcastic or serious, as I study her profile for a beat too long. Finally, I look over my shoulder and back out of the lot.

Katie is quiet, which is unlike her. I try getting her to talk by asking her about her brother and a few other inane things. She gives me clipped, one-word answers. I'm starting to think I have severely screwed something up. Was holding her at the wedding too much?

I try again. "So, first journalism assignment, huh? Want to talk about the game plan for today?"

"Yea. That would be good. To be honest, Jay, I'm pretty nervous."

I'm not sure if it's because she's in the car with me or... "Because this is your first assignment?"

She nods her head seriously. *Ah, so that's it.*

"Don't be nervous, Kid. You're with a long-time, award-winning professional. You literally couldn't be in better hands." Her cheeks warm, but she chuckles a little and slides her sunglasses off.

"I'm sure a lot of people *have* been in those longtime, award-winning hands," she says, glancing to where I hold the steering wheel.

There's my Katie.

I smirk at her. "It's true. I'm abundantly generous like that."

"I wouldn't want to overwhelm you. I'm pretty good with my own hands," she purrs.

I nearly choke on the swig of Diet Coke I just took. Coughing, I struggle to stay focused on the road. I hear her throaty chuckle.

"Looks like you're the one who needs a helping hand," she says, lifting one eyebrow.

I clear my throat.

"So, the game plan for today?" I'm desperate to change the subject because now I can't stop thinking about Katie giving me a "helping hand." And I definitely do not want my thoughts to stray further while I'm stuck in this small, overly warm car with her for another thirty minutes.

She smirks and picks up the brochure. "Well, let's hope all that talk about how good you are with your hands is more than just bluster because there is a crawfish-eating contest. You should definitely do that while I photograph you twisting off tails and sucking heads."

I cough again and keep my eyes focused straight ahead. *This woman is literally trying to kill me.*

Katie 3, Jacob 0. Well, this is certainly a change in how things usually go for me.

"Oh, don't worry. I am well-versed in peeling and eating crawfish. What else is on today's agenda?"

"Well, it's Friday, so it's $3 drinks all day."

"Are you sure you're ready for alcohol again so soon after last weekend's champagne palooza?"

"Oof, don't remind me," she says, looking green.

By the time we park in downtown Shreveport, Katie and I have assembled our plan for the day. First and foremost, we have to cover the infamous "mudbugs" themselves. That means I'm all in on the crawfish-eating contest. But I argue that I need at least one beer in my system so I'm limber and ready. Plus, a local brewer, Great Raft Beer, is launching a new beer named after the festival. We can't skip that detail.

We stride in together, get our 21+ wristbands, and head to the beer station. Katie shies away from drinking, insisting she needs to be one hundred percent sober for her first assignment. She clicks away as I try samples, finally ordering a large draft of Pale Tail, the new beer named for the festival.

Katie pauses to snap photos as we make our way over to the local business-sponsored cornhole tournament. The big plywood boards are set up, a large hole drilled in the top of each. Piles of small bean bags are stacked and ready for tossing. Proceeds benefit the winner's charity. It's fun to watch as participants don their team shirts and, with a beer in hand, fling the bags across the space.

I make my way over to some of the waiting teammates for an interview. I shake hands, ask questions, and try to get some funny stories–the usual. I like being able to have a beer in hand. It makes me more approachable, and people are opening up to me more about their stories and experiences.

After securing the interviews I need for this event, I realize I've lost sight of Katie. I walk through the crowd, looking for an auburn ponytail. I keep bumping into people I know from high school, so it takes me a while to spot her.

She's talking to a man. But not just any man, no. Somehow she wandered into the path of Shreveport reporter Brock Stephens. I use the term "reporter" loosely. Brock and I graduated with our journalism degrees from Louisiana Tech around the same time. But he was a bit of a Gilderoy Lockhart, "borrowing" other people's work and passing it off as his own. He got away with it, too, mostly because he had money and influence. Not to mention the man practically has a Ph.D. in charm, which he utilized to sell his lies.

When he stole a story from me, I reported it to the faculty, but Brock managed to convince the professors that he scooped me, and that was the end of it. I was forced to trash my piece and scramble for a new article only a few hours before it was due.

And now, he's standing there, golden hair catching the sunlight, *flirting* with Katie. I can feel my heartbeat inside my brain. Rage and jealousy, the twin instigators of bad decisions, have a vice grip on my heart. Katie is not my girlfriend. I know that logically, but logic isn't exactly the driving force behind my emotions right now. And I feel intensely protective of her. But more than anything, she will not be charmed and taken in by this *asshole*.

My legs are moving before my brain can catch up to them. I'm standing before them both in a blink, and I hear myself speak as if from a distance. "Hello, Brock, what a surprise to see you out here."

"I don't know why you're surprised," he quips as he slides his false grin into place. Each of his bright white veneers catches a glint of the sun, and I momentarily wonder if he's doing that on purpose to try to blind me and grab the upper hand. *Calm down, Jacob. Katie will not be impressed by how alpha male you think you are… nor any other response that resembles a gorilla beating his chest.*

"Oh, my bad," I say, sliding my own toothy grin into place. "I presumed you were actually attempting to do your own work for once. Should have known you were just out here playing."

"Bitter doesn't look good on you, Jacob," he says. "Still stuck at the Ruston paper, I see." His derision is practically dripping from his lips, a salivating hyena ready to strike.

"Ah, so you two know each other," Katie's smooth voice slices through our tension like a warm knife through butter.

I don't break eye contact with Brock. "You might say that," I say.

Brock turns to look at Katie, all signs of aggression sliding back behind his false mask. "You know this guy, do you, Katie?"

"He's my assignment partner. So I guess you could say we're both *stuck* at the Ruston paper." She says these words like she's declaring the forecast for the day is sunshine and rainbows.

"Oh I didn't mean it like that now, beautiful," Brock says leaning into her, inviting her to be wooed by his charm. "It's just that Jacob and I go way back. We went to Tech together. Same journalism program."

The way he is staring at her, like he would take a bite out of her if given a chance, has my hackles rising. *Do not throw this jackass into the food tent, Jacob. Lauren wants you to write the news, not create it.*

Instead, I step to Katie and slide my arm around her shoulders, pulling her in close. I'm surprised when I feel her arm slide around my back.

"Well, great to see you, Brock," I bite out. "But we've got more work to do today. I know you're not familiar with the time it takes to actually find a story. But let me assure you, we don't have any more time to linger."

He ignores me and pulls out his business card. "If you ever get tired of working with this guy, give me a call. I'd love to talk to you about some full-time photography positions in Shreveport." He sticks the card into the camera bag hanging from Katie's shoulder and winks. He actually *winks*. All he's missing is a gold chain and a sales pitch for a used car.

I turn us both and we quickly walk away.

"What's the story there?" Katie asks as she struggles to keep up with me.

"Later." I say. I know if I tell her the whole sordid tale now, I won't be able to stop myself from shoving Brock's head into a boiling crawfish pot.

Chapter 9

KATIE

I study Jacob's face, unused to seeing the lines of anger that trace his features and the tense angle of his shoulders. Sure, that Brock guy was smarmy, but he seemed harmless. Obviously, something happened between those two that Jacob does not want to discuss. A jealous part of my heart wonders if it has something to do with a woman. *Stop that right now, Katie Hebert.*

I clear my throat. "So, still up for the crawfish eating contest? I'm going to be really disappointed if I don't get to photograph you going face first into cayenne pepper."

He relaxes a bit at my question, and he smiles in a way that doesn't quite touch his eyes. "Wouldn't want to disappoint you, now would I, Kid?"

My heart wilts a little every time he calls me "Kid." It seems he will always only see me as Rhett's little sister. But I've got him talking to me again, and I am not going to lose this opportunity.

"Well, let's go get you one of those sexy plastic bibs then. I'll certainly be disappointed if you don't go for the title of Crawfish King with everything you've got."

His forced smile turns genuine. "You're on. Hope you have that camera ready for my crowning moment."

I WATCH THROUGH MY CAMERA lens as men and women line up down the long red and white checkered, plastic tablecloth. Buckets of boiled, steaming, bright red crawfish sit before a line of contestants, waiting to be consumed. The crawfish are weighed before being set before each contestant. They will have five minutes to peel and eat as many as possible.

But unlike other eating contests, crawfish come with their own special challenges. For one, you have to peel through their thick exoskeletons. Seasoned crawfish eaters know the trick to twist and crack them quickly. But that's just the first hurdle. The second is the Cajun seasoning. Most Louisianians can handle their spice, but when crawfish are eaten quickly, sometimes that yummy, spicy goodness can go straight into an eye and take you down for a good thirty minutes. I was even unfortunate enough to get a tiny piece of shell stuck in my eye one time and literally wanted to remove my entire eyeball to take the pain away. And while the competition allows for gloves, this group of contestants wouldn't be caught dead showing that kind of weakness.

A microphone squeals to life, and an old man approaches, ready to begin the event. His deep, booming voice sounds over the cheap speaker system. "At the sound of the buzzer, start peeling and eating. Toss the carcass in the buckets behind you. Tails only for this competition, though we'll let you save those heads for later if you want them," he says with a wink. This gets a chuckle from the crowd. "After five minutes, the buzzer will sound again, and you must stop immediately. No cheatin'. We'll calculate the amount of crawfish consumed and announce our winners shortly thereafter. Any questions? No? Well then, distinguished ladies and esteemed gentlemen, on your mark, get set, GO!"

And they are off. I'm both infinitely intrigued and slightly repulsed at the scene before me. Everyone is peeling and eating crawfish steadily, but Jacob is going at it like his life depends on this. I think he's got the win in the bag until I notice a tiny blonde woman in her early fifties sitting next to him. She's peeling and eating those mudbugs with so much efficiency that, I swear, not even one of the critters' legs hits the table. Twist, crack, peel, eat. It is mesmerizing.

Meanwhile, Jacob has thrust his whole body into the competition. I swear the man is using the entirety of his muscled arms to rip the crawfish apart, caveman style. The man lives by the motto, "Go big or go home," so I shouldn't be surprised. But still. Wow.

The rest of the competition slows down to watch these two: a tall, muscled Black man vs. tiny, efficient, white, blonde lady. Only a tween keeps peeling and eating his pile of crawfish like it's his job. When the buzzer finally sounds, Jacob slam dunks his last crawfish carcass into the bucket behind him, then turns to flex. Pepper and crawfish juice drip down his arms and mouth. I snap some photos of him grinning at his expected triumph. Meanwhile, his competition sits quietly next to him, completely unruffled.

"Well done, ladies and gents! Give us just a few minutes to weigh the results."

Jacob sits back down, relaxing back in the metal folding chair. His good mood is wholly restored now. He grabs a roll of paper towels, wrapping them around his hands and using them like mittens to take his plastic bib off. Finally, the announcer grabs the microphone, and the tinny speaker system comes back to life.

Jacob looks at me and mouths, "I've got this." I pull out my phone to record the winning announcement, a video to go along with our social media coverage for the day.

"In third place is Graham Jefferson!" The tween who hung in the competition pumps his fist and moves to collect his medal.

"The competition for the win was tough, folks. We had to measure everything twice, but the numbers don't lie. In second place is…."

Jacob leans forward, ready to jump out of his chair in celebration and claim his crown.

"Jacob Edwards!" He looks ecstatic, then bewildered.

"And first place goes to Kayla Connelly!" The small blonde stands and smiles, walking over to collect the crown and medal like she had expected it all along.

Jacob continues to stand there, gawking. He looks shocked but resigned. As he moves to collect his second place medal, a loud, calamitous sound rings out behind him. Everyone is scanning the area, trying to figure out where the rumbling sounds are coming from. That's when I notice a giant, gray *thing* flying toward Jacob. He turns and tries to leap out of the way. He almost makes it but trips over a metal chair in his haste to avoid being mowed over by what appears to be some sort of dumpster… and goes face-first into the table covered in crawfish juice.

Oh shit.

Chapter 10

JACOB

I have died and gone to hell. I am amid the demons, and they are stabbing me in the eyeballs with their pikes of hellfire, pain, and centuries of resentment. I can't breathe. I'm choking on pepper.I shove myself up and reach to free my eyes from this relentless torment, but my hands are also covered in the fiery embers of cayenne hell.

"JACOB!" I hear Katie yell from somewhere near me as multiple hands grasp my shoulders and pull me off the table.

"Hold still. I have wipes," Katie says, closer now.

I keep my eyes firmly closed. I am dying. No death is too easy. This is much, much worse. I'm being tortured. How in the hell did Mel Gibson yell out "FREEDOM" while his insides were being torn out in *Braveheart*? That was definitely less painful than this. One hundred percent. I feel a cold wipe swipe across what I can only imagine is the wasteland of my swelling face as Katie whispers, "I know it hurts. Hold still."

"Hang on there, sir!" a deep Southern voice calls out. Then an entire bucket of water hits me square in the face. I sputter, gasp for breath, and breathe in water mixed with pepper. Hell has apparently frozen over.

Paper towels find their way to my face. I feel as if I am, quite literally, being tarred and feathered.

"There is a bucket of clean water in front of you," Katie says soothingly. "I'll help you move to it. Dip your face in and open your eyes. You have to get that pepper and crawfish oil out of them as soon as possible."

I do as she bids, bobbing for eyesight. It helps, though, and once I pull my face from the bucket I can open my eyes some. Everything is still blurry, and my eyelids are swollen pits of fiery pain, but it's better.

"Sir, are you okay? It's EMS. Let us take a look." My hands are held to my sides as my eyes are pried open. Everything looks like it's being filtered through a snow globe, but I can make out a figure just before me. I feel a stethoscope press against my chest.

"On a scale of one to ten, what is your pain level?" a deep male voice asks.

"A fucking fifteen," I grunt out.

"Hmmm. Well, he's definitely aware and breathing okay, and his eyes seem to be tracking. You did the right thing by flushing his eyes, Miss. I would continue to do that several more times over the next hour."

"You got it," I hear Katie say with firm confidence.

"Sir, if your breathing becomes labored or the swelling gets worse, please seek immediate medical attention," the EMS person says.

I nod, and Katie guides me to a seat. "I have an ice pack," she says, gently lowering it over my eyes.

"Oh sweet, magical goddess," I whisper to her in appreciation.

"It's good to hear you recognizing my full potential finally," she says as she continues to press the ice pack over my eyes.

Despite the pain, the fact that I'm soaking wet from the water bucket, and the humiliation from the scene that just happened, I laugh at her words. I can't help it.

"Don't get used to it. I much prefer to call you 'bunny' or, even better, 'snuggle bunny.'"

I feel her squeeze my shoulder in response before saying, "Maybe it's best to stick with magical goddess. Do you think you can open your eyes? I need to flush them again, and then we can get you to the car. As part of our media swag pack, we got an event t-shirt that should fit you. You can change into it so you don't have to ride back to Ruston smelling like a boiled crawfish and looking like a drowned cat."

I ease the ice pack from my eyes, and the fire immediately comes back, but it has dulled significantly. I blink a couple of times and see Katie standing directly in front of me. She's close, staring into my eyes. I'm startled to see her this near, and it momentarily punches the breath out of me.

"Oh shit, is your breathing labored? Hold on, I'll call 911," she starts scrambling for her phone.

"No, no. Don't. I'm fine. I promise." She stops her frantic search and studies me, moving closer until I can smell her familiar scent, even over the crawfish boil that soaks my shirt.

"Your eyes are very red and… sort of look like they were stung by an angry pile of fire ants," she says with a grimace.

I stare back into her eyes, unable to break our locked stare.

"Let me go get that water so we can flush your eyes," she says. "Lean back. Keep your eyes closed. I'll pour the water on them. Then you can open them and let it flush more crawfish guts out."

"So very… nurturing of you."

"That's me. Nurturing to a fault. Probably should have been a nurse. At least that way, I'd have a career," she says with self-depreciation. But I can hear the bitterness creep into her tone.

"If you were a nurse, I'd feel an obligation to let your patients know they may want to seek out an additional source of care."

Water hits me square in the eyes. I startle. "What the heck? I wasn't ready."

"Hmm. Sounded like you were to me," she says. I can hear the smile in her voice. "So, want to change your shirt and hit the road?"

"I should make you sit in the car with me for an hour and inhale the tantalizing smell of dead crustaceans."

"Such a big word for you, Jacob. And I'm afraid that might backfire on you. I love the smell of crawfish. Instead of torture, I might just be tempted to take a bite out of you."

"I am rather tasty," I say, refusing to let her win this round.

"And then I'd toss your carcass in a bucket and ride off into the sunset," she continues.

"Like a mating praying mantis. So wicked of you," I say.

She coughs and laughs. Finally, one point to Jacob.

"Yea, let's get the hell out of here," she says. "Hopefully, you got enough to make a decent story out of the event. I know I certainly have the pictures to make for an, um, eventful feature," she says, trying to stifle a laugh.

"Are you laughing at me?" I say with a touch of humor.

"No," she gasps in mock indignation.

"You are!"

"Nooo," she says and then erupts into a fit of giggles. And damn if I don't love the sound of it.

Chapter 11

KATIE

I still cannot believe that just happened. I'm chuckling with shock and the general insanity of the day's events as we walk to the car. Now that I know Jacob is okay, all my emotions are bubbling up and out of me in fits of giggles. I kind of want to hit him in the face with water one more time. Not at all because I wouldn't object to seeing him in a wet t-shirt for a little longer. Shaking my head at myself, I toss the swag bag to Jacob.

"Here you go. Shirt's in there." I say.

I expect him to turn around, or duck into the car to change. I do not expect him to immediately pull his soaked, destroyed shirt over his head and toss it to the ground, leaving behind a rippling torso quite literally soaked in oil. Crawfish boil oil, but still. Damn. Unable to look away, I stare openly, fixating on every curve and turn of his muscled abs, eyes getting caught on the dip of his hips. My eyes track up his body until I'm staring at the tattoo of a ribbon curled over his heart. And then his arms flex.

"Like what you see, Bunny?" His voice comes out low and gruff but laced with his signature humor.

I turn the color of a pomegranate… a really splotchy pomegranate. And that is never flattering when your hair is rusty red. My hands dart up to cover my eyes, and I swiftly turn, placing my back to him.

"It's okay, Bun. I'm not embarrassed. You can look if you want to."

I know he's teasing me to ease the tension, but thoughts of Jacob's body are now swarming around in my head. And I do not want Jacob to see my raw desire mixed with embarrassment that is warring on my features right now.

"Nope. I'm good," I squeak out. Just like a damn little bunny. Ugh.

He chuckles low and deep. "It's okay. You can turn around now. I'm decent."

I turn slowly to find him standing there in a tight t-shirt that says "Crawfish Hero" on it. I burst into laughter, struggling to catch my breath.

"Please," I sputter. "Please tell me we got your second-place medal so I can take a photo of you wearing it with that shirt and your swollen face!" A cackle erupts from me. I have lost all control.

"Ha. Ha. Ha," Jacob says dryly. "You are so hilarious."

My laughter gets louder as I hug my stomach, struggling to get a grip on it.

"We're leaving now," he says as he climbs into the passenger seat. "And you're driving. The last thing I need is a police officer pulling me over and charging me with reckless driving because my face looks like this."

I walk around and climb into the driver's seat, still giggling, tears now streaming down my face. I am never, *ever* going to let him live this down.

I FACETIME WITH CELIA AND BRIAN that evening and relay the day's events in great detail.

"It was awful!" I say through bouts of laughter. "No, I mean it. It really *was* awful, but you should have seen his face!" I'm still in hysterics, and Celia and Brian are chuckling right along with me.

"You are awful," Celia says as she catches her breath. "But the absolute best kind of awful. And what did your man think of you laughing at him?"

"Cee, you know good and well that he is not my man."

"But he is the man *of your dreams*."

"Quit saying my secrets out loud like that. It feels weird."

"Hmmm. Weird or not, how did he feel about it?"

"He kind of just, I don't know, rolled his eyes and took it in stride. The whole drive back was pretty typical conversation for the two of us. We talked about how to showcase the story. I teased him about publishing the photos I have of him chowing down on some crawfish…"

"WAIT! YOU HAVE PHOTOS! KATIE! You are holding out on me! SEND THEM TO ME!"

"Now, Cee, I should not do that."

"Bitch, you better," she says eagerly. "I am your best friend. This is the kind of thing you share with your best friend."

I get up and grab my camera. "Listen, I'll show them to you over FaceTime, but I am not risking my new job by emailing them to you."

She leans in eagerly. I flip the camera around so she can see the screen. The first photos that pop up are shots I took earlier in the day around the festival. There are close ups of boiled crawfish and people mid-bean bag toss. A young girl reaches up to hug her mom, foam crawfish claw on her hand.

"Katie, these are amazing," Brian chimes from over Cee's shoulder. "I'm serious. We could really use someone like you at our company in the marketing division. So much of good marketing is about capturing the perfect moment, making people connect to the images they see so they will buy our products."

"You hear that?" Cee chimes in. "Maybe it's finally time for you to move to Dallas."

"I'm emailing you the job application," Brian says. "Just look at it. And think about it. You could have a full-time job paying you to do what you enjoy."

I pause at those words and look down at my digital camera screen. I allow myself to imagine it. Moving out of Ruston. Living in Dallas with my two best friends. Making a real salary and working with a camera every day. My lip quirks as I continue to flip through photos. Then a frame of Jacob pops up. He's standing with a beer in hand, sunglasses on, and looking out across the cornhole match in front of him. He looks content and happy. My smile fades as an anchor drops in my stomach. I'd have to leave him and finally give up on the romantic fantasy.

"Oh, girl. Your face. Show me what you are looking at right now," Cee demands. Reluctantly, I hold up the screen.

"Girl. He's fine. Here's a piece of advice from one best friend to another. You ready? *Ask. Him. Out.*"

"CEE! He's Rhett's best friend!"

"So what? You are both adults. What do you have to lose?"

"Um, one, my dignity. What if he straight up laughs at me? Two, my summer photography gig. Three, Rhett's respect."

"So what?" she quips. "Then you move here with us. I fail to see a problem with either result."

"Cee, right now, I have Jacob in my life. Yes, we're sort of friends, but that's better than being embarrassed around him and my brother for the rest of my life. I can't. *I won't.*"

"Suit yourself. But don't give me those puppy dog eyes when some other woman comes along and scoops him up. Because if that happens and you fall apart on me? I'm driving to Ruston, packing your bags, hauling that cute little behind to our apartment, and helping you start your life here with us. Hell, I'm tempted to do that now. What time is it?"

Brian eyes her. "Too late. It's like 9 p.m."

I chime in before Celia can talk Brian into driving four hours to collect me tonight. "Just, I don't know. Let me finish out this photo assignment with him over the summer. I need some more time. You know I hate to be forced into a decision."

She shakes her head. "Okay, deal. But if one of you hasn't made a move by the time summer is over, you're moving in with us."

"Okay. Fine. Deal." She grins, knowing that she's won no matter how this shakes out.

Chapter 12

JACOB

We publish the story about Mudbug Madness on Monday, less than a week before the annual Louisiana Peach Festival takes place in our own hometown. Knowing that our festival coverage will soon compete with a magazine, I took a more personal approach to my article. I even share what happened with the crawfish eating contest, face planting, and all. I got a little vulnerable, which feels strange, considering that I'm usually striving for unbiased journalism. I'm not sure if it was my stellar penmanship or Katie's photos that showcased the event's joy and my look of ecstasy as I lept in triumph after stuffing my face with a truly disgusting number of crawfish–but it works.

Our joint piece is the talk of the town, and Katie's video–yes, VIDEO–footage of me plowing face-first into a table might have gone slightly local Internet viral. We have had the PR people from every festival in Louisiana, Arkansas, and Mississippi call and invite us to their small-town festivals in hopes of a story and accompanying video. I'm not sure whether I should feel excited or humiliated, but my editor Lauren is calmly ecstatic.

"You'll cover our Peach Festival this weekend, of course." She says as Katie and I sit next to each other, across from her desk in her office.

"Well, um, our band is scheduled to play a set at the Peach Festival...," I start.

"Perfect," she quips. "Everyone loved that you took part in the Mudbug Madness events. I think that's our angle going forward."

Katie presses her lips together, shutting down the laugh I know is threatening to erupt from her. She glances at me, then tries, "I'm the lead singer, so it may be tough for me to get photos."

"So bring the camera on stage with you. That's a perspective of this festival we've never covered before," Lauren says without missing a beat.

And just like that, we've got our next assignment.

"Let's just hope there are no runaway dumpsters this time," I mumble under my breath.

"Maybe I should hire one. It made for a helluva video," Lauren says without irony. I look at her incredulously.

"What? A story's a story, and you weren't injured. Mostly." She lifts one eyebrow, daring me to argue.

Katie looks down, her whole body shaking to stifle her giggles.

"Please be aware that if a dumpster manages to jump off a flat surface and onto the stage, I know who to tell my injury lawyer to call," I tell Lauren.

Katie's cackle finally breaks loose, and Lauren joins her.

I throw my hands up in mock defeat. "The things I do in the name of reporting."

SATURDAY OF THE PEACH FESTIVAL dawns, and it is going to be a hot one. Already the viscous Louisiana sun is threatening to turn us into roasted roadkill. But ever since our band, The Graveyard Gators, debuted at the annual fall festival a year and a half ago, we've been in demand for everything from city events to wedding receptions. We're all busy, though—Rhett, Katie, their dad, and me—but we agreed we would make it work for something like the Peach Festival.

"Think we can get thirty to fifty box fans rigged up to blow directly at us while we play?" Rhett asks. He steps up next to me, shielding his eyes with his hand as we stare at the stage. It's covered, fortunately, but that's about all it has going for it.

"I'm trying to decide if fifty box fans aimed straight at Katie while she sings will make her look more like a model or a tornado victim," I say with skepticism.

Rhett chuckles. "Maybe some rain will blow in and cool things down."

"More like turn it into a sauna." I grunt in reply.

"There you two are." I hear Katie before I see her, and my whole body lights up like a pinball machine. I make myself count to five before I turn to greet her. She's dressed for summer today in a tank top, denim shorts, and a ponytail. So much of her creamy, freckled skin is on display. I drink her in, trying to hide how much I enjoy looking at her. She takes a sip from the straw of her iced coffee and holds a camera in her other hand.

"Hey, Jay. I know Lauren wants us to cover the festival from the stage point of view, but I am going to wander around and take photos of some other things first. Want to join me and see if we can dig up any other stories?"

Do I imagine the hope I see in her eyes? Regardless, it's the perfect, innocent excuse to spend some time with Katie. I practically fall over myself to move to her side.

"I'm in. Let's walk," I say, trying to sound casual.

Her smile is wicked as she says, "I'm ready and able to protect you if any dumpsters or food carts come barreling your way."

"Yeah, right. Where were you when I needed you to jump in front of a speeding train last time, supergirl?"

"Recording it," she says, biting on her bottom lip. My eyes catch on the movement.

"See something you like?" she quietly echoes my own words from last weekend back to me.

This woman is my personal kryptonite. I amp up my smile and look around us. "I see lots of things I like."

"Hmmm," she hums and smiles.

"So, where are we wandering to?" I ask her.

"You know how famous Margie's gotten with her YouTube

channel? I thought it might be fun to check out her vendor booth and see if any out-of-town fans have stopped by."

As we walk into the town convention center, I see makeshift booths filled with everything from Christmas wreaths to t-shirts with "Blessed" scrolled across them. There are homemade candles, soup mixes, custom-carved name plaques and children's clothes. And at the far right, there's a long line of people.

"I think we found her," Katie says.

We wander over and take in the sight of Margie meeting and greeting a whole host of diverse characters from across the Ark-La-Tex. Over the past two years, Margie mixed her hobby of creating booze-infused jams with local peaches and her eccentric personality to make extremely popular, viral YouTube videos. They started out pretty basic–how-to's, tips and tricks–and evolved into a channel that now boasts half a million followers and climbing. Rumor has it that Margie is even being courted for a cookbook deal. And, it appears, her fanbase has shown up to get some of her famous Zingy Peach Jam.

Katie pulls out her camera and snaps photos of Margie rubbing elbows and offering up a bit of her wisecracking wisdom. I wander over to the line and start interviewing people about their visit to Ruston and why they follow Margie. I see Carl walking around and taking photos, too, and wave at him. He nods his head and gets back to work. A twinge of guilt nags at me for never bringing his name up to Lauren, but he appears to have plenty of work still. That eases my conscience some

"Hi there!" a perky voice chimes from behind me. I turn to see Kylie Jefferson, one of my college buddies, standing behind me.

"Oh, hey there. Good to see you, Kylie."

"It's good to see you too, Jacob," she says warmly and gives me a hug.

"I'm surprised to see you working today. I saw on the event calendar that your band is playing tonight," she says.

"Eh, I don't mind so much. Any excuse to get out and have some peach ice cream," I say with a grin. She blushes in response. "So, out shopping the vendors on this sweltering day?"

"Oh, I'm working too!" she says cheerfully. "Did you hear about the new magazine I'm launching? It's all about local events, lifestyle, and things that appeal to young families." Pride and joy are pouring out of her like sunshine as she talks about her project.

My smile freezes as my brain connects the dots. So Kylie is our competition at the newspaper. Interesting. But she doesn't seem to be threatening or concerned about us interacting. I wonder if Lauren is just overreacting to all this. But Lauren didn't restore the paper from the brink of extinction by having poor instincts. Still, no way am I going to be rude to my old friend.

"Jacob? Did you hear me?"

I snap out of it and shake my head. "Oh, yeah, sorry. I was just racking my brain, trying to remember if I'd heard about the magazine."

Her grin falters a bit. "We're new, so you probably haven't heard of us yet. But Jacob, you are an awesome writer. If you're ever looking for freelance work or, um, want to hang out and catch up, give me a call or shoot me an email. Here," she says, handing me her card. I hold it in my hand, studying its neatly printed text and fine details.

"Thanks, Kylie. And good luck with the new magazine," I say with sincerity. After all, we are different formats. Surely there can be room for both of us.

"Back to work, then," she says cheerily. "Good luck with your performance this evening. I'll stop by for a bit!" And then she's retreating to the booth I now notice has been set up to display information about the new magazine. *The Ruston Review* does have a good ring to it.

"Who was that?"

I turn to see Katie eying Kylie.

"Just an old college friend."

"She gave you her number," Katie says, looking at the business card in my hand.

"Correction, she gave me her business card," I say.

Katie studies her again, then looks at me. "Our competition gave you her business card?"

I wince. "It's not like that. She's got a new business. We're friends. It's no big deal."

Katie shrugs. "I just want to be a fly on the wall when Lauren finds out. Maybe a little bird will tell her." Her voice is laced with its usual playfulness again.

"You wouldn't dare."

She just arches an eyebrow at me. "Time to get ready for the set," she says simply. Then walks toward the convention center exit.

AS KATIE AND I WANDER over to the music stage together, I walk a little closer to her than strictly necessary, but she doesn't pull away. I don't know what's going on between us exactly. A lot of flirting, yes, but the need to be physically near her is almost painful. I wish, more than anything, that I could whisk her into another slow dance.

"There you two are," Ben calls out. "Time for a sound check."

I take my place behind the percussion set and grab a cool pack to wrap around my neck. I'm glad I get to sit for the show because it is still mind-meltingly hot outside. I close my eyes and listen to the sounds of my fellow band members warming up around me. Ben is on the keyboards, Rhett is on guitar and singing backup, and Katie is front and center. She's the star of the show, exactly where she should be.

Lost in the rote movements of our band warm-up, I let my mind wander to my dad. He's still acting strangely and has refused all of my attempts to get him to the doctor. "I'm just tired," he growls at me when I ask him if he's okay. But an ember of fear ignites in my gut as I think about him. Just imagining that something might be wrong, that he could be taken from me like Mom was, is enough to make me nauseous and jittery.

"Hey, Jacob? You okay, man?" Rhett's staring at me like I have a spider on my head. I realize that I paused in my warm-up and am staring at nothing.

"Hmm? Oh, yea. Just hot. I'm good." I grab my phone and set it up to record the audience in front of us. Lauren wants us to report from this side of the stage, but honestly, when I'm playing, I get lost in the rhythm of the drums. It's ecstasy in its own way—an opportunity to shut my brain off from spiraling fear and… I see Katie bend over and stretch. And unrequited lust for my best friend's little sister. I grab the cold pack and put it directly on my face. *There will be none of that tonight, Jacob.*

"How are y'all doing tonight?" I hear Katie call out over the microphone. The crowd cheers and claps, ready for the show. "Before we get started, can y'all do me a favor? My fellow bandmate Jacob and I are not only performing tonight, but we're covering this for the paper. And we need a photo! How about a selfie?"

Everyone cheers. Katie motions for us, and we all crowd around her. "Get in tight," she says, sliding her arm around my waist and pulling me into her. "On the count of three, everyone yell 'Graveyard Gators!'" she calls. On the phone screen she holds in front of us, I can see the large crowd gathered behind us, their hands raised in excitement.

"One, two, three!" she shouts, and my hands slide to the curve of her hip. I squeeze her closer for the photo, and she leans into me. I am a masochist, I decide. But dammit, I'll take my hits wherever I can get them.

The crowd yells, "Graveyard Gators!" and she hits the button quickly, snapping one photo after another. We pull away to start the show, but I turn my head to stare at the side of her face for just one extra moment. I'm a starved man hungry to study every freckle, every eyelash. I wrench myself away and head to my drum set.

"Let's get this party started!" Katie cries into the microphone. The crowd joins in with their excitement.

Rhett strums the guitar for the opening notes to "Low Places" by Garth Brooks.

"I got friends in low places…" Katies husky voice purrs. It's an easy song to hook the crowd with. They all join in and start singing along. Katie scoops up her camera and moves around the stage as she sings, photographing us and the crowd around her. I'm mesmerized by how she moves around the stage, taking time to frame every shot and occasionally pulling back to adjust her aperture and white balance. She turns to me. I haven't stopped playing, but I also haven't taken my eyes off of her. I see her finger hit the shudder and realize that her camera now holds a photo of me looking like a lovesick puppy.

She returns to the mic stand and continues singing, hips moving in rhythm to the music. Just as she leans into the microphone again, a loud boom sounds from our left, and sparks fly from one of the speakers, startling all of us. Katie jumps back and trips, falling onto the stage. A collective scream sounds from the crowd, and all the stage lights cut out.

I jump up from where I'm seated behind the drums and run to Katie, anxious to make sure she's okay, but Rhett and her father are already there. Suddenly sparks erupt from the right speaker. One of the embers lands on Rhett's setlist taped to the wooden stage, and a small fire ignites. Before I can rush to put it out, more sparks shoot from the rear speaker. Screams and yells sound around us.

"We have to get off this thing!" I yell over the building noise. We move to the front of the stage, and all four of us jump off. Rhett reaches back to grab his guitar as the fourth and final speaker seems to explode. We hear sirens in the distance, and in the chaos of the crowd around us, I feel Katie's hand latch onto mine and hold fast. I squeeze it in return, pulling her away from the exploding speakers and the fire that's starting to spread.

"What in the hell is going on?" she calls out over the noise. But panic urges me away from danger. I continue to pull her away from the chaos as my mind fixates on images of the stage going up in flames and Katie getting caught up in the inferno. I won't let anything bad happen to anyone else I care about.

Chapter 13

KATIE

"Jacob. Stop. We're far enough away and we will need to be close when the police arrive to get eyewitness accounts." I tug on his hand as he continues toward the parking lot.

"Katie. It's not safe. What if something explodes, or the stage erupts in flames or…." He's not joking, I realize. Traces of panic line his features, and his hand is trembling.

"Hey, hey, Jay. Calm down. It's okay." I say and slide my arms around his waist. I'm trying to ground him, hoping it works. Thinking about how much comfort my weighted blanket brings me, I sort of climb up his body, pressing all of my weight onto him and hold on tight. I feel his arms wrap around me and squeeze. We stay like that as the minutes tick by, and sounds of panic and sirens echo around us. Finally, his breaths and heartbeat slow.

"I didn't know bunnies could climb," he manages to croak out. I laugh and try to untangle my legs from around his waist, but he holds onto me, needing me.

"Well, to be fair, it was more of a hop and grasp," I say into his chest. His body vibrates as a low rumble of laughter sounds through his body.

"Aren't bunnies supposed to run from fires?" He asks.

"Jay, there wasn't really a fire. Look." I reach up and grasp his face with my hands, turning him to look back at the stage. Police now surround it, but all traces of the small fire are gone. His body relaxes, and he allows me to slide out of his grip. I feel his fingertips brush along the back of my arms as I step back.

"Are you okay?" I ask, studying his features.

"You're making me look bad. I was just trying to rescue a damsel in distress," he says, aiming for levity and falling short.

"Hmm. You should know I'm no damsel Jacob Edwards," I say, lifting an eyebrow, trying to push away the ghost of fear still lingering around us.

"No, you're more like one of those Monty Python bunnies, ready and able to decapitate unsuspecting knights," he says.

I chuckle at the thought. And with that comment, I know Jacob is back in the present, the ghosts of fear pushed firmly back into the shadows where he likes to keep them.

"Come on. Let's go talk to the police," I say. I slide my hand around his again, relishing in its warmth and size. It feels like a comfort sandwich for my hand. But as we get close and I see Rhett and Dad, I pull my hand from his. I'm not ready for an inquisition from either of them. Jacob is a good guy–they both know it–but I've always been daddy's only girl, and I know he will tell mom if he sees us holding hands. I don't need that kind of pressure, especially when nothing is going on between us besides maybe a growing friendship and coworker relationship.

"There you are," Dad says. "I was worried when I couldn't find you."

"We were just getting out of the way," I say.

"Ma'am, you were on stage when everything started sparking?" An officer asks me.

We each take our time, answering questions. It becomes quickly apparent that they believe someone tampered with the speaker wires, especially because there were firestarters near where they sparked.

"But why in the hell would anyone want to set fire to a stage at the

Ruston Peach Festival?" Rhett voices what we're all wondering.

"Well, it will make for one hell of a story," Jacob says quietly to me, echoing Lauren's earlier words. I nod, then reach for my camera that's still sitting on the stage. Sneaking away, I snap photos of the scorched stage, the blown out speakers, the police officers lingering around the scene.

It's all eerie, like I'm watching an episode of *Cops* play out in real time.

"Katie," I hear Jacob's voice behind me. I turn to him. "I have to go home and check on my Dad. He's been home alone for a while. I just want to make sure you're okay before I go."

"I'm fine," I smile and nod reassuringly.

He lets out a long breath and nods his head. "See you at the office tomorrow?" he asks.

"Yea, I'm sure Lauren will want a full debrief," I say.

"Oh, no doubt," he says, then turns and walks through the dusky light to his car.

Chapter 14

JACOB

"Dad! I'm home!" I call out as I walk into my house.

I can hear the evening news blaring through the house, already reporting on the evening's exploding speakers at the Peach Festival. Great, he's probably worried I'm hurt. I should have called him. But when I step into the living room, I see that he's sleeping soundly in his recliner. His head is tilted to the side, snores echoing out across the room. Ollie is nestled at his feet, letting out equally loud snores, woofs, and whimpers. *Great guard dog he is.*

I open the fridge and dig around for something to eat. I notice there are no leftovers and I turn to look at my dad again. *Did he skip dinner? Or maybe Mary, our next door neighbor, brought something by. But then there would be dishes…*

My phone vibrates. I look down and see a text.

KATIE: Make it home okay? Didn't run into any dumpsters on the way?

JACOB: I think the joke is dead.

KATIE: Not possible.

JACOB: You worried about me, bunny?

KATIE: Nah, just looking to make my next viral video.

I laugh.

KATIE: Seriously, though. I can bring dinner by if you need some company.

Every square inch of my heart yearns to say yes. But as I look around our messy, old house, all I can see are all the repairs that need to be made. The patterned linoleum floors are torn and curling. The carpet is stained, and the dark wood wall paneling has never been updated. Plus, I don't want Katie to meet my dad like this. I get lost in staring at him, noticing the wrinkles that line his face, his bones beginning to protrude more in his forearms. When did Dad start to wither? It seems like yesterday he was holding me in his arms, throwing a baseball with me in the yard, keeping us both going after Mom was gone.

KATIE: I'm sorry. I didn't mean to overstep. I'll make myself some ramen noodles and leave you to your evening.

I realize I waited too long to respond.

JACOB: Sorry, was just cleaning up a bit. I think I'm just going to lay low tonight. Did you see the email from Lauren?

KATIE: About covering the Peach Pageant tomorrow? Yea. Think she wants us to participate in that too?

JACOB: You would make for a lovely Princess Peach.

KATIE: Peach dresses and red hair do not mix.

JACOB: Ariel pulled it off.

KATIE: Did you just make a Little Mermaid reference?

JACOB: I know my Disney movies, Bun.

KATIE: Maybe you should enter the pageant.

JACOB: I do look dashing in a pair of heels.

I see the reply dots pop up and disappear three times before a GIF from RuPaul's Drag Race pops up on my screen.

I burst out laughing and then hear my dad grumble awake.

JACOB: I think I'll leave this contest to the real queens. See you at 3:00 tomorrow?

KATIE: See you then.

I set my phone down and wrap myself up in the warmth of Katie's humor. I pull a couple of cans of beef stew out of the pantry and start heating them up on the stove. A cold, wet nose pushes into my leg, and I peer down to see Ollie looking up at me expectantly.

"Someone coming into the house won't wake you, but food will?" In response, a line of drool makes a slow descent from Ollie's mouth to the floor. I reach into his treat bag and toss him a snack. I can't help it. This stinky, fat dog gets me every time.

While the food heats, I walk into the living room to check on Dad. His eyes are closed, fingers lightly twitching on the recliner's arm rest. I kneel down a bit to check his breathing, my paranoia always on high alert. Losing a parent at a young age left a deep scar on my soul. A scar that twinges with pain every time my mind wanders to the trauma of losing Mom.

"Dad," I say quietly and rub his leg. He moves around a bit before finally cracking open his eyes and looking at me. "Hey, Dad. I'm home. Have you eaten anything?" He stares at me in confusion for a beat. I feel my heart plummet in fear. But then he seems to come back to himself.

"Hey, Jacob. Hmm. Not hungry. Just tired." Relief courses over my body. I must have imagined it.

"Did you eat anything for dinner?" I press.

"I'm not hungry," he says again, closing his eyes. I shake his leg again.

"Dad, did you eat anything?"

"I had a sandwich earlier, but I'm tired. Help me up? I need to get to bed."

I do as he asks, relieved to know he ate something. I feel guilty that I wasn't here tonight to make sure he had dinner, but then again, he's never needed me to before. Maybe he has a virus. I make a mental note to call his doctor tomorrow, whether he wants me to or not. I'll get Mary to stop by, too, I decide.

Dad reaches forward to hold onto my forearms, and together we get him to stand. He shuffles off to his bedroom, and Ollie and I follow him. Once I make sure that he's securely in bed, I head back to the kitchen and pour up my beef stew. Even with Dad and Ollie here, the house is uncomfortably quiet.

I allow my thoughts to linger on Katie, the feel of her as she leaped onto my body and hung on for dear life to comfort me. Only she would do something like that... but it worked. I wish I wouldn't have been so wrapped up in my personal panic and actually been able to enjoy the feel of her body pressed into mine. I growl out loud in frustration, mad at myself for acting so unreasonably. I'm Jacob Edwards. I'm easy-going, laid back, and always have everything under control. But just the thought of Katie getting injured was enough to allow fear into the driver's seat of my brain.

But the whole exploding speaker thing *was* really strange. All of them igniting like that. And the cops seemed to think someone did that on purpose. First, that damn dumpster hurdling toward me, and now the speakers blowing up. Maybe they are a sign from the universe that I'm on the wrong path. Or maybe I just need some sleep.

Finishing my dinner, I rinse my bowl and put it in the sink. I pull up the Peach Festival schedule of events on my phone for tomorrow and smile. I open my texts.

JACOB: Ever seen a calf scramble?

Her text reply comes almost immediately.

KATIE: Is that some kind of new fancy brunch item?

I bark a laugh.

JACOB: Not quite. Have time to meet me a little sooner tomorrow? Say 12:00? We could grab lunch and then watch some epic entertainment.

KATIE: I'm in. :)

Chapter 15

KATIE

I must have seemed desperate when I offered to bring dinner over to Jacob last night. My mind has concocted a whole scenario where Jacob saw my text, cringed, and thought about deleting my number. Then he probably texted his friends–ie, my brother–and told him I'm a stage five clinger.

But then he texted me later and asked to have lunch today. In a public space. I am definitely being placed firmly in the friend zone. Of course, I am. There is nothing between us romantically. I know this. Anything I thought I felt was a result of my years-long fantasies.

Before I head out to the festival site to meet Jacob, I open my laptop and pull up the application that Brian sent me for the photography job in Dallas. I read through the job description and try to imagine it. I picture myself walking into a high-rise building and getting on an elevator in Downtown Dallas. I'd wear professional clothes daily and probably see Brian fairly often. I'd have a desk and amazing photography equipment. I'd photograph electronics, gadgets, and models with said electronics and gadgets. At the end of the day, I'd fight my way through the abysmal Dallas traffic, but maybe Brian and I would carpool. I'd get home to our shared apartment, hang out with my besties and laugh, or maybe retreat to my own room and unwind. It sounds pretty good, actually. Well, minus the whole Dallas traffic situation. But if Brian and I travel together, we can utilize those HOV carpool lanes and make better time.

I allow myself to sit with this idea and then try to assess my feelings. I've always been anxious to move to the next exciting thing. Right now this festival photography gig is perfect because it's different every day. In a way, it makes my soul sing. I don't know if photographing for a corporate technology company will be the most exciting thing, but it won't be the same thing *every* day, right?

The thrill of moving to Dallas and seeing Celia and Brian is enough to motivate me to download the application and pull up my resume. I work on both for a bit, then save them. I think about it for a minute, then send drafts to Celia and Brian and ask them to look them over and offer suggestions. I know this may be leading them on, but they also know how squirrely I am about decision-making.

My mind wanders back to Jacob. His smile, the warm feel of his body when I jumped into his arms. Ugh. I need to put those thoughts to bed. Friendship is the only thing in our future. I close my laptop and pull on my shoes. I guess it's time to see what this calf scramble thing is all about.

"HOW IS THIS LEGAL?" I ask Jacob as my mouth hangs open in fascination and horror.

"Their parents sign waivers," he says simply. "Also, maybe close your mouth. You do not want to inhale that dirt they are kicking up. There's probably poop in it."

My mouth claps shut, but my eyes don't leave the scene before me. "Those poor baby cows," I say, hand moving to cover my mouth.

"Oh, they're fine. They are used to being around people," Jacob says easily as he reclines back in his stadium seat.

"So am I, but I would be upset if thirty kids came charging at me, screaming at the same time. And then imagine if they were trying to jump on top of me, tie a rope around my mouth, grab me by the tail, and drag me into a square with even more people waiting to tie me up!" I shudder.

Just as I say this, one boy, age ten or so, makes a running leap for a calf. He misses and falls face-first into the dirt of the rodeo floor. I chuckle.

"Told you this was good entertainment," Jacob says, stretching his arm around the back of my seat.

Don't do it, Katie. Don't. I ignore my inner voice and lean back into his arm. He put it there, so he can deal with me leaning against it.

I continue to stare ahead of us and let out a squeak as children trample one another to get to the calves.

"What is this, some modern-day version of *The Hunger Games*?"

"Something like that," Jacob says. "Want some nachos? They have the chili cheese ones."

"You can eat beef nachos while watching–and smelling–this? What is wrong with you, Jacob Edwards?"

He shrugs. "Be right back."

As I continue to watch, one kid grabs a calf by the tail to slow it down. This is too much for me. All I can think about is how much that must hurt the poor baby cow. The boy slips a rope around the calf's muzzle, and my heart shreds a little inside my chest. Then, with renewed burst of energy, the little cow takes off with the boy still holding the rope. The kid goes face down into a dirt cloud but doesn't let go. I can smell the cow dung from here, so I know that can't be a pleasant experience.

I cheer loudly as the cow drags the kid behind it. "Go, little cow, go!"

"Are you cheering for the cows?" Jacob's warm rumbling voice says from behind me.

"Hell yea, I am." I say, taking the beer he offers. I sit it in the cupholder, then grab my camera. I must capture this great moment of retribution and justice.

I look across the arena and notice another roped calf refusing to budge. Its feet are planted firmly, and the little girl attempting to move it across the space is basically running on a dirt-covered treadmill.

Anxious adults pace the parameter, waiting for kids to give up out of sheer exhaustion. I pump my fist as I watch the calf victoriously hold its ground.

"You are something else, you know it, Kid?" Jacob says.

I wince a little. "Kids are baby goats. Is that how you see me? As something to throw a rope around and tackle?" I nod my head to the poor calves in the arena.

He guffaws at that. "Katie, I would never dare try to rope you in and tie you down. You are too much of a free spirit. I would never try to take that from you."

Shit. Things just got serious. Time to fix this.

"Oh, is that why you call me Bunny, then?" I crook a smile. "Because I'm a free spirit?"

"And cute and snuggly," he adds with a wicked grin.

Those words make me want to crawl into his lap, tuck my face into his chest and fall asleep surrounded by the scent of laundry detergent and his woodsy shampoo. And I'm staring. At his chest. Like some kind of weirdo. I shake my head and turn back to the pint-sized gladiators in the rodeo arena.

Jacob's hand brushes my shoulder. At first, I think I imagined the touch, but no, there it is again. His thumb lightly traces the outline of my shoulder muscle as his bicep presses into my shoulder blades. I subtly shift, pressing my back a little more into his arm. I feel the weight of his whole hand come to rest on my shoulder.

I turn my head to see his gaze locked on me, eyes intent. I stare back, suddenly oblivious to the chaos unfolding in front of us. We search each other's features. I study his defined jaw, the hint of stubble on his warm brown skin. My eyes linger on his full lips, and I bite my own in response. He lets out a low sound of appreciation and lightly tugs me closer to him. I press my thigh into his, relishing his warmth so close to me.

A loud buzzer echoes through the stadium, and we both startle.

"And the winner of this year's Peach Festival Rodeo Calf Scramble is Rochelle Valentine. Rochelle has won a $1,500 scholarship to help fund her future college career!"

The crowd cheers and I stand up quickly, suddenly very aware of the building sexual tension between Jacob and me. I'm hot and bothered. Confused. I can't do this, not with him. Yes, we have chemistry. That's undeniable at this point. But I'm sure Jacob uses these moves on everyone. It's no wonder women practically throw themselves at him. I mean, that girl Kylie yesterday looked like she was ready to drag him into the nearest corner and have her way with him. And I will not be the next girl to fall to his charms, especially when I'm thinking about applying for a job in Dallas. I start making my way out of the stadium, wishing desperately that I could pick up the old woman in front of me and toss her out of the way. I need to get out of here.

"Katie, wait up." I hear Jacob call from behind me. I stop, taking a slow deep breath. I turn to him, false smile plastered across my face.

"Sorry, that whole calf scramble wasn't really my thing, and it stinks in here. Ready to head over to the pageant?" Before he can answer, I spin on my heels and start walking again.

"Katie." I feel him grab my hand, and I steel myself.

"Hmmm?"

"Did I do something to upset you?" he asks, confusion lacing his voice.

"Hmm? No, just ready to get out of here. Need to use the restroom," I say, knowing I sound like an idiot.

"Okay… Because Katie, if I did something wrong…."

"You did nothing wrong, Jacob. We've got a lot to cover for work today, and I'm anxious about it, okay?"

He finally nods his head and follows me out of the stadium. We step outside, and the day's heat nearly knocks me to the ground.

"I almost prefer the cow poop to this suffocating heat," I mumble.

"Good thing the pageant is indoors," Jacob says in agreement. "I think it's supposed to hit one hundred and two degrees plus heat index today."

We walk in awkward silence toward the convention center. I'm kicking myself for making this weird, but I had to put a stop to, well, whatever that was.

"Oh my gosh! Jacob! Is that you?" a high feminine voice cuts through my thoughts. We both look up as a gorgeous Latina woman, all curves and crop top, comes bouncing her way through the crowd to us.

"Bianca?" Jacon says, a grin slowly creeping across his face. She throws herself into him, wrapping her arms around him like some kind of face-hugging alien. His arms rise, and he squeezes her back. *What is this? Jacob Fan Club Weekend at the Peach Festival?*

I am seized with the urge to grasp her long, flowing black waves and pull her to the ground. Maybe I could grab a bottle of ketchup and squirt it all over those perky dimples. I didn't even know dimples could be perky, yet here we are. I could start a brawl that would rival those on *The Jerry Springer Show.*

"What are you doing in town?" Jacob asks through that perfect, gorgeous smile of his. Maybe I should just sink my teeth into him. I'll go for his throat. Like one of those Monty Python bunnies he compared me to.

"Here visiting Mom. She asked me to help judge the Peach Pageant," she says. Why does she have to have adorable dimples and perfect boobs? Some people get all the luck.

"Oh wow! That's great. Katie and I are just heading there to cover it for the newspaper," Jacob says, turning to me.

Breathe, Katie. Do not rip into throats or pull hair. We have had enough crazy, near-death experiences so far. You do not need to add to it.

"Hi," I say through gritted teeth. "I'm Katie. How do you know Jacob?" It sounds more like an accusation than a question.

Her grin turns wicked as she slides her arm through his like they are some sort of cute, perfect couple. *I will cut a bitch.*

"Oh, Jacob and I go way back. We dated on and off when we were at Louisiana Tech together." I swear hearts appear in her eyes like some deranged anime character as she says this and swoons into him. "But then I moved to Florida for work, and it got too difficult to keep our relationship up." She squeezes his bicep. "But wow, Jay. You look great."

"So do you, B," he says warmly. She practically purrs and rubs against his leg like a cat in heat. I guess I was right about his willingness to flirt with anyone and everyone. Thank goodness I pulled away back in the stadium. But that doesn't mean I have to like this... *predator*.

I clear my throat. "Well, I'll let the two of you catch up. I'll see you at the pageant," I say, tone clipped.

I turn and bolt, needing to separate myself from Jacob and all these feelings he stirs up in me. Jealousy forms a dam in my throat while anger threatens to spill out and turn my hands into heat-seeking cat claws aimed directly for Bianca's face.

Chapter 16

JACOB

Well, I royally fucked up this entire day.

That's all I can think as Katie scorches a path to the convention center. I can practically see flames shooting from her heels like she's wearing rocket-propelled roller skates. Bianca's arm slips from my arm to rub my back, and I tense.

"Are you two…?" she asks suggestively.

I cough. "No, no. Just coworkers." Even I can hear my disappointment as I say it.

Bianca lifts an eyebrow at me. "Well, I can't say I'm mad to hear it. You and I should catch up while I'm in town." She bites her lip suggestively.

Bianca is gorgeous, and when we were in college, we had a lot of fun together. But now? I look back to Katie's quickly disappearing form and wilt. I feel Bianca's warm hand reach up and turn my face to her. "Just think about it. My number is still the same." Then she locks my arm with hers, and we walk to the convention center.

I'm dazed as I try to figure out how I went from touching Katie, the air sizzling between us like the sidewalk on a Louisiana summer day just thirty minutes ago, to walking arm in arm with another woman while Katie looks like she wants to punch me in the balls.

No wonder I've never been able to manage any kind of meaningful relationship. I suck at this.

When we walk into the convention center, a gaggle of senior citizens greets us with pageant programs and points to the stage area where the event will take place.

"I've got to head over to the judging panel," Bianca says. "Let's catch up later." She presses a lingering kiss to my cheek, and I nod my head. When I turn, I see Katie staring at us, her gaze practically burning a tunnel straight through my sternum. I rub my hand over the phantom pain and wince. I start walking toward her, but Katie turns from me and stalks off, camera in hand. *Fuck.*

Maybe I just need to give her some space to let her work through whatever the hell is going on. But the longer I sit here, the longer *she ignores me*, the more irritated I get. Katie is the one who pulled away from me at the calf scramble like I tried to steal her virtue or something. She's the one acting like I contracted the bubonic plague. She has no right to be treating me this way.

Now thoroughly convinced of my own innocence, I decide to ignore Katie and focus on work. But I swear I can feel the emerald daggers she's thrusting at me with those gorgeous, furious eyes of hers. I stare straight ahead as tiny toddlers with big hair and even bigger personalities strut around the stage. I chuckle as one clings to her mom's leg, refusing to walk out with everyone else. I try to focus on taking notes for a story, thinking that I can chat with Bianca for an interview.

I spy Katie from the corner of my eye. She's near the stage, capturing the frills and twirls the little girls are making. *She's a natural at this*, I think idly. My gaze keeps drifting to her, despite my resolve to keep my eyes away. I force my head to turn to Bianca. I watch as she waves at the little contestants, giving them a thumbs up. She's gorgeous and sweet. Maybe I should try to make something work with her, distract me from my fucked up obsession with Katie. She obviously doesn't want me, not like that. And Bianca made it abundantly clear what she wants...

A shout echoes across the large space. I turn just in time to see Katie's arms pinwheel as her camera flies across the room and lands with a devastating crunch on the concrete floor. People start jumping up, blocking my view. All my resolve to ignore Katie crumbles as I jump up and push my way through the crowd to where she sits on the ground, holding her ankle. Tears stream down her face, and it cracks something inside of me.

When I kneel next to Katie, she looks up at me, pain dancing in her features.

"The camera," she chokes out, looking at the fragments of metal and glass scattered across the floor.

"Don't worry about that right now. Are you okay?" I ask her, reaching to touch her shoulder. She flinches back, and it's like a slap across my face.

"I'm okay…" she whimpers out and tries to stand. But her ankle gives out, and she falls back down.

A man steps forward and offers to help her stand, but I put my body between her and him. My protective hackles are up, and I can't bear for anyone else to touch her right now. I wrap my arm around Katie's waist and lift her to stand beside me. "Put your arm around my shoulder. I'll help you out of here. I can drive you to the hospital."

"I don't need a hospital," she gasps out as she hops along next to me. "I just sprained it. I need ice."

"Come on then. I'll take you home."

She leans into me, allowing me to absorb her weight as we slowly make our way to the car. As she holds one injured foot in the air and hobbles along, I chuckle. The laughter vibrates through my body and into Katie's.

"What's so damn funny?" she growls at me.

"It's just that…" I laugh again, unable to stop myself. "It's just that you're hopping like a little bunny."

For a moment, I think she's going to slap me. I brace myself, but then I feel the tension leave her body, and she leans her forehead on my shoulder. Her body starts to shake. I freeze, thinking she's crying.

But then Katie looks up at me, and I realize she's laughing.

And just like that, we're back to being Jacob and Katie, good *friends* and coworkers again.

Chapter 17

KATIE

I sit in Lauren's office, head held high and mock confidence draped over me like a queen's mantle. I can do this.

"So, do you want the good news, or the bad news?"

Lauren studies me. "Give me the bad news," her eyes dart to my foot, which is currently in one of those medical-grade boots.

I grimace. "Yea, um, that happened at the Peach Pageant. And, well, there's no easy way to say this. The camera was completely destroyed." She blinks at me. "And so was the lens," I say.

"And so was your foot, apparently," Lauren says dryly. "What could possibly be the good news?"

The camera's memory card survived, so we still have all the day's photos." Lauren looks only slightly mollified at this revelation.

"Do the two of you have some sort of hex on you or something?" Lauren asks.

"It was weird, actually. I was photographing the pageant, and this little girl was having a helluva meltdown. It was sort of adorable with her hair all teased and in that dress that might have actually been cotton candy. I was 'in the zone,' you know? And then an extension cord literally pulled taut behind me like a tripwire. I went down, and it wasn't pretty. The camera went flying and hit the concrete. I am really sorry that happened, by the way."

Lauren levels her gaze at me. "Do you intend to sue us?"

I sputter, "What? No!"

Lauren's shoulders sag just slightly. It makes me realize she has seen some shit in her days as editor. "Well, the camera is certainly a financial loss that I'm not thrilled about. But you got the photos, and you're okay?"

I nod my head in the affirmative.

"Okay. Well, we have a backup camera you can use for Dugdemona Fest this weekend. That should hold you over until we can get a new one."

I bow my head in relief, then look back up again. "Wait, what the heck is a Dugdemona?"

She grins. "Buckle in, Katie. You and Jacob are heading to Winnfield."

"WELL, LOOK WHAT THE CAT dragged in," Jacob says as he watches me hobble along in my medical boot.

"I hate this damn thing. It's already a hundred and fifty-seven degrees outside, and now I've got this thing strapped around my ankle like my own personal heating device. By the time I can finally take this thing off, it's going to stink to high heaven," I grouse.

"Just make sure you coat that thing in bug spray. You don't want mosquitoes nesting in it," Jacob says, eyeing my boot wearily as we climb into his car.

"What the hell is a Dugdemona, anyway?" I say, buckling my seatbelt.

"Katie Hebert. Are you telling me you didn't do any prep work for this? Shame, shame," he says.

"Now, why would I do that when I know you'll brief me on the drive over," I say, batting my eyes at him.

"There's not too much to this one. There's a watermelon eating contest, a key hunt, some live music, and fireworks. I think the key hunt is probably the most unique angle out of all those things," he says thoughtfully.

"Wow, look at you getting all serious," I quip.

He shrugs. "I like my job. Mostly. This assignment has been nice, different—a way to shake things up. Only so much news happens in Ruston, you know? Plus, my photographer's not too bad," he says with a wink.

I flush at his words. Staying in the friend zone with this beautiful man is like death by a thousand mosquito bites.

"Thirsty?" I blurt out and fling my torso into the second row of his car, digging around for the water bottles I tossed in the back before we left. I shift things around, my hand landing on a leather journal with the initials JAE embossed on the cover. I turn back around, lifting it up.

"What's this?"

He glances over and... is that a blush on unflappable Jacob Edwards' face?

"It's nothing," he demures. "Just something I doodle in."

"Can I look?" I ask.

A million emotions run across his face before he finally settles on his decision. "Yeah, I guess. But keep it to yourself, okay, Bun?"

I smile at the nickname and crack open the pages. I'm expecting to find notes on stories, maybe song lyrics from our work together in the band. What I don't expect to see are some of the most detailed and exquisite drawings I've ever seen. My eyes nearly jump out of my head as I bend my face closer to take in the detailed line work that graces the pages of this private notebook.

"Jacob. You... you *drew* these?" I ask, disbelief coating my voice.

He shrugs and says, "It's nothing. Just something I do to help me relax."

I stare at the sketch of a dog that could be mistaken as a photograph. I hold it up to him. "Who is this handsome fella?"

He glances from the road to look and laughs. "That's my pal, Ollie. Had him for a long time. Though I think handsome is a stretch to describe those big jowls and impressive underbite."

I laugh and keep turning the pages. The subjects are as varied as they are intricate. There are trees, storefronts, leaves, and cats. I turn another page and halt, startled by the portrait of an old man in profile. He looks a lot like Jacob.

"My dad," Jacob says.

I study the drawing, noting the line of his jaw, and the set of his smile. I glance up to study Jacob's profile.

"So this is who your good looks come from," I say absently.

Jacob laughs. "I'm sure he would love to hear you say that. He's always told me the apple doesn't fall too far from the tree."

"I can't wait to meet him–and your mom–in person. I need to see how much of your mom you have in you, too."

Jacob's smile disappears immediately, and he clenches his jaw.

"Oh no, what did I say? I'm sorry, Jacob. Whatever it is. I didn't mean to upset–"

"My mom is dead," he interrupts.

My stomach plummets. "Oh, I'm sorry for your loss. I didn't know, Jay."

He nods his head and clenches his jaw again. "It's okay. It's been a long time. But, God, I miss her so much still." He swallows and refuses to look at me. So I slide my hand over to his hand and squeeze. He returns the gesture. The heat our hands create together is a balm to my soul.

"Do you want to talk about it?" I ask, studying him.

He shakes his head no. "Maybe another time. I need to focus on work today."

We sit there like that for the rest of the drive, hand in hand. The silence should feel awkward, but it doesn't. Maybe he'll open up about his mom one day. That's what friends do, after all. But right now, I know he just needs the comfort of a hand in his.

Chapter 18

JACOB

I can't stop fixating over how I reacted to Katie bringing up my mom in the car. Mom died nearly twenty years ago. I've struggled with it over the years, sure. But I haven't reacted like, well, like *that*, in a very, very long time. I vaguely wonder if it's because I'm worried about dad, but no.

Head in the game, Jay.

We park in a small lot in downtown Winnfield for the Dugdemona Summer Fest.

"Well, this is… charming," I say. I stare at the pop-up canopies in the lot in front of us.

"I think Lauren may have missed the mark sending us to this one. This must be punishment for breaking the camera," Katie says.

"Eh, I've covered worse. Come on. Let's go talk to people." We both climb out of the car. The smell of funnel cakes and corn dogs fill the humid air. Despite the heat, the scent of it feels nostalgic, exactly how a Southern summer childhood should smell and feel.

"WELL, HOWDY! Y'all ain't from these parts!" I swing my head around and see an older couple. He's got a too-tight shirt pulled down over his bulging belly that says "Down on the 'Dug," the festival's slogan. And she is wearing a tank top that says, "Kiss My Grits." I do love it when an interview presents itself so easily.

The man, who probably passes for the local Santa in December, walks up to us and shakes our hands with a warm smile. "Y'all look like newspaper folks," he says, nodding to Katie's camera. "We are so happy y'all came out to our festival. I'm Doug–like the shirt says–and this is my wife, Betsie. We've been helping with this here event for nigh on ten years. What paper y'all from? Shreveport?"

I shake my head and grin. "No, sir. We're from Ruston."

"Ah, the peach place! Very nice, very nice. Can we show you around?"

I look at Katie. Mirth lights her features, and I can tell she's struggling to keep the words in. "We'd love that," she says, grinning wide. "I'm Katie, the photographer. And this is our reporter, Jacob."

"Just delightful," Betsie says. "Come on now. I'll walk you around."

She turns on her heel, loops her arm through Doug's, and the two walk off.

"I guess we follow them," Katie says. She gets her camera ready, and we follow behind the apparent leaders of this shindig.

"Hey there, Claudia," Betsie calls out. "Got some newspaper people here. Let them try some of your cracklins."

"Oh, welcome, welcome!" Claudia calls. Much like Betsie's, her hair is a poof of white curls that no wind or movement could shake. She dons a grease-spotted blue apron and scurries back to the fryer under her designated canopy. I glance at the framed sign that says "Claudia's Crunchy Cracklins."

Alright then. So maybe this event is a little different. It's certainly more… friendly.

Claudia turns, cardboard baskets stacked high with fried pig skins. The heavenly smell radiating from them nearly takes me to my knees. It reminds me so much of my Mama. I swallow the lump forming in my throat and reach for the offerings.

"Cheers!" I say, tapping my container with Katie's. We each grab one and pop it into our mouths. Oh, sweet heaven in a fryer. The serotonin shooting through my brain right now would rival that of a two-year-old in a cotton candy factory.

"This is magic," Katie says, eating another.

"You betcha!" Claudia says. "I make the best cracklins this side of the Mississippi. Don't forget to include that in your article, now."

"I think she might be right," I lean in and say to Katie. Her eyes are closed, and she looks like she's in a state of pure bliss. *Well, that look will haunt my waking hours for the rest of my life.*

I clear my throat. "Um, maybe we should check out the rest of the festival?"

Her eyes snap open. "As long as I can take these with me," she says. Then looks down at her camera. "Probably shouldn't handle that with greasy fingers. Shoot."

She pops the last three into her mouth and tosses the container away.

"I've got you covered, darlin'," Betsie says. She produces a container of wipes from the depths of a fanny pack wrapped around her ample waist.

"My hero!" Katie shouts. *Why is Katie so damn cute?*

"Next stop: roasted pecans!" Betsie calls out.

"I'm going to gain fifteen pounds before today is over," Katie says quietly to me.

"Worth it, though," I say.

"Oh hell yes," she says, lifting her camera up to begin documenting our day.

TWO BEIGNETS, A SHARED SLICED boudin, a handful of roasted cinnamon pecans, and a couple of crab cakes later, we are seated in a couple of Doug and Betsie's extra chairs, listening to live music and stuffed.

"I'm so full I can't breathe," Katie says, leaning back into her chair. "I know I need to photograph some more, but ugh."

"I can roll you around if you want. Like one of those hot dogs on the heated rollers over there."

She chuckles, then groans. "Oh, don't make me laugh. It hurts." She rubs her stomach in misery.

"You have to pace yourself, woman."

"Didn't want to. Too good." She keeps her eyes closed, allowing me to study her features, imprinting them perfectly on my mind so I can think about them again later.

"Hey there, folks. Having a good time?" It's cheery Doug again, white cotton beard waggling as he smiles at us.

"An excellent time," I say.

"Good, good. We could use a good write-up in the paper," Doug says. "I appreciate y'all coming out to Winnfield. You'll stay for the fireworks, won't ya?"

I look at Katie and wonder if she'll make it that long.

"Definitely. I need time for my body to digest the five thousand calories I consumed today," she says, making Doug laugh.

"My wife and I brought you a little something to thank you," he says, offering up a foil covered tray.

"What is it?" I ask, taking it from him. Whatever it is, it smells delicious.

"Oh, just a little something she cooked up for you. A little something to, uh, help us with our glaucoma, if you know what I mean." He winks. "Well, enjoy!" Then he walks back to his wife about ten chairs down. Betsie waves to us. I wave back, then turn my attention to Doug and Betsie's gift.

I peel back the foil. Inside lay a pile of brownies. I sniff one and take a bite. They taste amazing, actually. So I take another bite.

"How can you eat those after everything we ate today?" Katie moans.

"I paced myself. They're good. You should try one," I tell her, offering them up.

"Are you trying to put me in a food coma?" she says.

I shrug and polish one off and reach for another.

As we sit there, listening to the band, I start to relax and enjoy myself. *How are these folding chairs so comfortable?* I think as I lean into it. When I close my eyes, I can somehow see the music dancing on the back of my eyelids. I start giggling.

"Jay, are you… okay?" I hear Katie ask as if she's far away.

"Oh yea, I'm good. Just relaxed and kind of… hungry."

"That's hilarious."

"No, I'm serious," I say.

She stands up and hobbles over to me. *That damn boot.* I start laughing loudly.

"What's so damn funny?" Katie demands.

"You and that fucking bunny hopping boot," I say, gasping out laughs.

She folds her arms in indignation and starts to walk away. Impulsively, I reach out and snag her rear shorts pocket and tug her back to me. I slide my hand around her waist and pull her into my lap.

"Woah, Jay. That was… unexpected," she says.

"But I want to pet you, Bunny."

She turns and stares at me then, eyes hard on my face. She's adorable, especially when she's indignant. I start laughing again, giggling, really.

"Jacob… you look high," Katie says.

"High on you, Bunny," I say and press my nose into the crook of her neck. She freezes like a rabbit in a trap.

"Jay, what are you doing?" she says cautiously.

"Just relax. I just want to hold you. You're so pretty." Those words dance out of my mouth, and they feel so utterly right. This woman is gorgeous. *Why have I been punishing myself by staying away from her?*

She turns in my lap to face me, rubbing against my crotch. I groan.

"Jacob, you are high." She reaches for the pan Doug brought over. "Are these *pot* brownies?" she says incredulously, sniffing them.

"Doug did say his wife makes them for his glaucoma," I say, then start giggling again. "Please, Katie, just sit with me for a while. I promise to be a good boy."

She looks me up and down. "But you are not of sound mind."

"But my body is sound with you on it." She tenses, pressing harder into me. I know she can feel just how much I want her to be in my lap–what it does to me. I lift my palm up and cup her cheek, staring into her eyes, silently begging her for more.

"Katie… please," I moan.

She pulls back slightly, and I drop my hand. Even stoned out of my mind, I'd never make a woman stay close to me if she doesn't want to.

"All right now, all you guys and gals, time for a little slow dancing!" the band's lead singer calls out.

"Oh, hell yes!" I say. I stand with Katie still in my lap, and she stumbles a little. "Oh shit, I forgot about the bunny boot. I'm sorry, Katie. I just wanted to dance with you like at the wedding."

Katie hesitates, then nods. "Yea, that sounds nice."

We make our way over to where all the older couples sway slowly around in front of the stage. For once, we both sidestep the spotlight, opting to dance on the edge of the main lights. She slides her arms around my neck, and it scorches my skin like napalm.

I let out a groan. "Katie, you are setting me on fire."

"No, Jay, those are the brownies setting you on fire," she laughs.

"But they make everything feel so good. And you make everything feel so good. It's like an explosion of good feelings." I tell her, pulling her tight to me, wishing I could somehow meld our bodies together. I wait to see if she will pull away, ready to let her if she does. When she doesn't, my mouth keeps moving without any filter.

"You smell as good as you feel. I wonder if you taste that good, too?"

I distantly realize I should probably be embarrassed at saying this to her, but right now nothing really bothers me. I lean closer to her as we dance and rub my nose against hers. Fire is dancing in my face, my hands, my soul. I stay like that, soaking up the intense sensation of her skin on mine, her lips so near. I inch a little closer, trusting that she will pull away if it's too much. But she doesn't. Her breathing is loud and ragged. I can feel her heart pounding against my chest.

"Can I taste you?" I ask her.

"That is a really weird question," she says breathily. The music lulls us into an easy sway, and everyone dancing around us fades into the background.

I chuckle, but then she nods, giving me permission, and I fall into her. I press my lips to hers, and, I'm not sure if it's the THC or just everything that is Katie Hebert, but I feel like I'm falling down a waterfall. Sound, smells, and sensations woosh around me. I move my lips against hers and feel her respond in turn. Katie's hands slide to my face, pressing a hand on each of my cheeks, and she pulls me down to her. I'm fascinated by the way her lips feel, obsessed with the light taste of beignets that lingers there. I pull her bottom lip into my mouth, tasting the sugar. She gasps, then her tongue moves into my mouth. This could possibly be some brownie-induced hallucination, but I don't want to wake up from it. *Ever.*

I kiss her back fiercely, our tongues dancing together as our bodies sway. I have dreamed of this moment for years, ever since the day Katie showed up in that hot dress at the college frat party Rhett and I were at. I shouldn't want my best friend's sister like this, but damn. She is sweet and spicy and tastes even better than she smells.

"Thanks for joining us tonight, folks!" the lead singer calls out as the song ends. We pull apart, and, as I take in the stage lights, I realize I have forgotten where I was. I was so completely wrapped up in this stunning woman in my arms that I didn't care who or what was around us. I stare at Katie, her lips swollen from our kiss.

"I..." she stutters. "I shouldn't have done that." She glances down, embarrassed, I realize.

"What? Yes you should have. And you should do it again." I lean forward, desperate to feel her lips on mine again.

She holds her hand out and steps away. "Jacob, you are high. I... I took advantage of you." The look of remorse that fills her face doesn't fit with the explosion of feelings and sensations that are still coursing between us.

"Oh, Katie, no. It's not like that. I wanted to kiss you. I wanted to taste you." I start laughing again, hard. The THC is driving my emotions like a court jester. She shudders and turns.

"I'll meet you at the car," she calls over her shoulder. And once again, I find myself staring at the woman I want, walking quickly away from me.

Chapter 19

KATIE

I can't believe I did that.

That mantra repeats over and over in my head with varying degrees of awe and horror.

When Jacob sobers up, he is going to feel humiliated. It's all my fault, but everything just felt so right. We were like two magnets. He wanted to kiss me, and saying no was impossible. Everything worked to lure me in: the feel of him pulling me into his lap, his hard body underneath mine. I should not have enjoyed that. He was out of his mind. I was, obviously, out of mine. But that kiss. I trace my bee-stung lips, still feeling his mouth on mine, his tongue sliding against my own.

Doug and his fucking brownies.

I'm standing by the car, fuming and embarrassed. When Jacob walks up, I can't even look at him. I hold my hand out for the keys. It looks like I'll be driving our return trip again. He hesitates, then drops them in my hand. I open the car door and climb in, then shut it.

He slides into the passenger seat next to me. "Katie, I… um, I'm sorry?"

I sigh and press my forehead to the steering wheel. "I'm the one who needs to apologize. I got caught up in the dancing and the atmosphere. I kissed you, and you are high. That was awful. I feel awful."

"No, Katie, I mean, obviously I kissed you, too."

"Yea, but you weren't, aren't, in your right mind," I protest. No part of me can believe that he would actually want to kiss me that way. Not in the way I so desperately crave to kiss him. "Just, please. Please accept my apology. I feel awful, and I can't stand the thought of you sobering up and looking at me like I'm a terrible person."

"Katie, stop. It's okay. We're okay. I promise." He slides his hand over mine and squeezes. I turn to look at him. It's dark outside, but I can still see the concern on his face and feel the worry that radiates from him.

"I'm sorry. You're sorry. We're both sorry. See? Everything is fine," he says. I relax, but inside, my heart squeezes in pain. I wanted so badly for it to be real, for that kiss I've dreamed of for years to mean something. It was amazing, delicious. I'm going to crave that kiss for the rest of my life. But that's the punishment I deserve for taking advantage of this situation, so I nod. "Yeah, okay. Let's go home."

He squeezes my hand again, then lets go as I place them both on the steering wheel and pull onto the interstate.

"YOU FILLED OUT THE JOB application!" Celia squeals through my phone screen.

"But I didn't send it to them. Not yet," I say, feeling self-conscious.

"Katie, it looks really good," Brian says in that quiet, certain way of his. "I'd be happy to submit it to the company for you and make a personal recommendation."

Panic erupts like a kicked anthill in my stomach. That is a huge commitment... one I'm not sure I am ready to make. "Not yet," I rush to say. "I want to finish out this summer festival assignment first. Build up my portfolio." It's a convenient excuse, and we all know it.

"What is going on with you tonight?" Celia says, cutting right through all the awkward tension weighing heavily on my shoulders.

"Hmm? Nothing. Just tired. Working two jobs is exhausting," I say.

"No, it's not that. Something is bothering you. Don't lie to your best friend, Katie." She studies me through the screen as I remain quiet, mentally fumbling with something, anything I can offer her that she will actually believe. "Oh shit. Did something happen with Jacob?"

My head snaps up, and I start turning red. "Ohhhh. Oh! I thought something bad happened, but this looks like it was something *goooood*," she says, stretching out the word with meaning.

"No, it was bad, awful, actually. I mean, no, it was good, really good. But awful," I ramble and cover my face with my hands.

"Leave us, Brian," Celia says. "We need to have some girl talk."

He shrugs and obeys, picking up his Nintendo Switch and heading down the hall. Celia watches him. When I hear a door close, she turns back to me.

"What *happened*? Did you finally confess your undying love to him? Are you a thing?" she asks with excitement.

"No," I huff out. "I sort of kissed him." I wring my hands.

"About damn time," Cee says. "Tell me everything. That man has some beautiful lips. How did they feel?"

"Cee! It was awful!"

"Oh no! He's a bad kisser? I would have never guessed. This *is* awful," she says.

"No, that's not what I mean. He is an amazing kisser, actually. That was probably the best kiss I've ever had in my life," I say, and I mean it.

She blinks at me. "So the problem is…?"

"He was high on redneck pot brownies," I wail.

"Say what? Is that some kind of new drug the meth heads are cooking up that I don't know about? Because I gotta say, Katie, if the man is into meth, you need to run, not walk, away as fast as you can," she says.

"No, nothing like that. This old guy, Doug, his wife, Betsie, made brownies with pot in them and gave them to us. I don't think Jacob realized that's what they were when he ate them. But then he was all relaxed and smiling. He pulled me into his lap and practically inhaled me. And I was so, so into it. And then I realized that the only reason he was behaving that way was because he was *high*. I tried to pull away, but then he asked me to dance. Harmless right? At least, that's what I thought. But then we were slow dancing and it brought back all these feelings of how we danced at Rhett's wedding. And then Jacob asked to kiss me, and I was like, I don't know, high on *him*. So I said yes. And then the next thing I knew, we were making out while we danced in freaking *Winnfield*, of all places. Also, I'm pretty sure a hoard of mosquitos ate me alive, because I'm covered in bites, but I didn't even notice because that was the hottest kiss ever. But did I mention that he was high?"

Celia is speechless—a rare thing.

"See. Awful. I'm an awful person," I say and then hide my face in my hands again.

"But he asked to kiss *you*, right? You didn't like jump on him, hold him down, and assault his mouth with your tongue while he bellowed in protest?"

"Um, what? No. Definitely not," I say.

"So he liked it?" she says.

"Yea, but Cee, he was out of his mind on pot brownies," I protest.

"Katie. Pot makes you feel good, yes. But it also amplifies natural feelings. No, do not ask me how I know this. I plead the fifth. But that boy is into you. And you are into him. Why are you talking to me instead of kissing him right now?" she demands, one eyebrow lifted.

"Because I made him accept my apology for kissing him," I say weakly.

She throws her hands up. "Girl! What am I going to do with you?"

"Not like any of this kissing stuff matters if I go for this job in Dallas, anyway," I murmur.

"Katie, you don't have to do that. I mean, yes, Brian and I both want you to. We love you and want you here with us. But above everything, we want you to be happy."

"Cee, I can't. He's Rhett's best friend. It's…complicated."

"You are both consenting adults. You can't live your life for someone else. Katie, you have permission to pursue Jacob if he is who you want. And I'm practically your fairy godmother, so I have the power to grant you absolution from your guilt."

I shake my head and smile at my best friend. "I think I messed it up. What if it's too late? Or what if the high made him act that way, but he's uncomfortable when he's sober because of Rhett?"

"Only one way to find out, my dear. Time to make a move," she says.

"I don't know," I demure.

"Promise me this. If the situation presents itself again, don't think about what anyone else wants or how they will react. Think about what the two of you want and go for it. That's the only way you'll know if it's right," she says.

"When did you get to be so wise?" I ask her.

"I was born this way, Katie." She winks at me. "Now, go rest that pretty head of yours and get ready to woo your man."

Chapter 20

JACOB

"I hear you finally made it through a festival without injury," Carl says with a laugh. He settles in next to me in the break room at work and starts unwrapping a sad, droopy turkey sandwich.

I manage a short laugh. "Unless you count overeating?" I say with a smile.

He smiles and takes a bite of his sandwich. "So, Lauren didn't want me as the photographer on the festival assignment, huh?"

And... we're going there. The awkwardness is so painful that I swear I can hear crickets chirping in the heavy silence now standing between us. I take a moment to rally. This isn't the first time I've been thrust into an uncomfortable situation, and I'm certain it won't be the last. I can usually maneuver through them like an eel in water. *Time to start swimming, Jacob.*

"She already had someone else in mind," I say easily. *There, that wasn't a lie.*

He slumps his shoulders. "I guess I wouldn't protest either if I got partnered on an assignment with a little hottie like that," he says. Inwardly my hackles raise, and I sit up, straightening my posture.

"Don't talk about her like that, man. Katie's a good photographer," I say.

"Yeah, okay," he says dismissively.

"I'm serious. She's great at what she does. You should know that by how much Lauren likes her work. She doesn't coddle anyone," I hold my ground. Carl is my friend, but I will not let him demean Katie like this to make himself feel better.

He struggles with what to say for a moment before finally dropping his shoulders. "You're right. I'm sorry, man. I shouldn't have said that. I guess I just feel washed up like I don't have any value anymore with all the young talent around here," Carl says.

I relax and place my hand on his shoulder. "Look, I'm sorry this assignment didn't work out for you, but you're staying busy. I saw you photographing stuff at the Peach Festival, and I've seen lots of your photos printed in the paper and online. Don't be so hard on yourself. Maybe it's time to rise to the occasion and push yourself. Show Lauren you've still got it, you know?"

Carl nods his head slowly as if unsure if he should truly consider what I just said. "Yeah, man, yea. You're right." He smiles weakly. "We good?"

"Yea, we're good," I say. The awkwardness lingers between us, so I decide to shove it aside and try to take the high road. "So, how do you think the Bulldogs will fare this coming football season?"

We fall back into our regular, easy, noncommittal lunch chat. I'm glad I made Carl feel better, but his words nudged at something uncomfortable inside me. *Is this what my future looks like? Am I destined to spend the next decade—or two—in this lunchroom, staring at the same coffee-stained counters under the same flickering fluorescent lights? Doing the same old thing as newer, fresher talent comes in and makes me irrelevant?* I shudder.

I managed to compartmentalize most of these thoughts with Katie dancing through my life in a tornado of color and passion. She has pulled me into her vortex and I thanked her for the privilege. And that kiss on Saturday. *Damn.* I'm still not one hundred percent sure it actually happened. It turns out Winnfield pot brownies pack a powerful punch. But that kiss… it felt real.

I am desperate to feel her mouth on mine again, to feel more of her body pressed into my own. But as I stare at Carl, fluorescent light glinting off the top of his balding head, I can't help but think that any relationship with Katie would be the equivalent of tying a cinder block to her ankle and tossing her into the ocean. She is talented and brilliant. Katie won't stay in Ruston forever. Why would she? She has the whole world ahead of her. And as much as I would love to chase her flame across the world, I won't leave the man who gave up his life to raise me on his own. Dad needs me now. He sacrificed any free time he had to go to my baseball games or pick up extra shifts at work. He will need me for the rest of his life and I am not anxious for that to be over anytime soon.

I sigh, attempting to resign my heart to a place of contentment. I'll allow myself the fun of this summer assignment with Katie, but I can't let it grow into anything more. I won't do that to her.

"WATERMELON SUGAR!" KATIE CROONS OUT.

"Harry Styles, really?" I ask.

"What's wrong with Harry Styles?" Katie says with indignation.

"Nothing is wrong with Harry Styles… I just thought you were more of an old soul when it comes to music," I tell her.

"I like any music with soul, old or otherwise. Plus, this is *the festival* I have been waiting for!"

We are about to drive thirty minutes to the Farmerville Watermelon Festival, and Katie has dressed the part. She's in a cropped green top, just a hint of her stomach peeking out from beneath it. She's also wearing cutoff denim shorts, and I momentarily forget my resolve to keep things strictly friendly with her.

Katie is acting like everything is normal between us, and I'm relieved. Though I can navigate awkwardness with Carl and story interviews with the best of them, when it comes to Katie, all bets are off. I'm also now convinced that the whole making out with her while dancing thing was, in fact, a pot brownie-induced hallucination. Maybe I should call Doug and ask him for some more of those suckers. I wouldn't say no to those kinds of hallucinations. No wonder his wife keeps baking them.

"Okay, Jay, listen up. You are driving us there *and back* this time. There will be no diving face first into crawfish juice or getting high on pot brownies," Katie declares with all the authority of a monarch.

"Oh, excuse me, Miss High and Mighty. There was the whole flying through the air thing at the Peach Festival that required me to be the day's driver," I say pointedly, eyeing her still-booted foot.

"Please. That was *in town*. I am always exhausted after these festival events and tired of driving at night. That means no alcohol and no food from unreliable sources. It's your turn," she says with finality. She opens the passenger door to my car and sits, cranking up the a/c to try and ward off the triple-digit temperatures.

"Good Lord, it's hot. You could bake cookies on your car dash in this heat. Should make for a fun day at the festival," she says sarcastically.

"I'm sure we could enter you in a wet t-shirt contest to cool you down," I say, flirtation inching into my voice. I need to stop, but Katie brings it out in me. I can't help myself.

"Please, like the women of Farmerville Baptist Church would ever allow something so scandalous to take place on their fair streets," she quips back.

"Might be just the thing the paper needs to get more readers…," I start.

"That's very sexist of you, Jacob. Here's what I suggest. Let's have a contest where we shove all *the men* into Lake D'Arbonne and then rate them based on how they look when they emerge. Sounds fun, doesn't it?"

I beam at her. "You know, that's not a bad idea. I'm sure there are some rock-hard farmer bods around here. At the very least, we can probably dredge up a mean beer gut from the crowd."

We continue our conversation, passing quips back and forth like we're playing a well-honed, evenly matched tennis game. The jabs flying between us only stoke my feelings for Katie, but I keep them under lock and key–where they belong.

We're only a mile or so down Farmerville Highway when we hear a loud pop followed by a slapping noise that makes me scared that I ran over some sort of critter. Katie and I stare at each other in horror as I pull over to the side of the road. Once parked, I open the car door and walk around its perimeter, looking for the source of noise. I check under the vehicle, then eye each tire—and there it is. The rear right tire is flat. The sun is now directly above us, with temperatures soaring past one hundred. The heat index is somewhere between sauna and boiling soup. Sweat coats my brow and I can feel moisture forming beneath my arms.

I pop the trunk and start shoving notebooks, drawing pads, and blankets out of the way to get to the spare tire compartment. I really should clean this thing out sometime.

Katie steps out of the car, walks around to where I stand, and leans down to look at the tire. "Huh, that's strange. It looks like you hit a curb or some sort of hard object. Remember anything like that happening?"

"Not unless you took out a boulder with my car while I was high on redneck brownies," I say, but my usual playfulness is beginning to fade in favor of simply breathing through this heat.

Finally, I manage to pull the spare out, only to see that it is nothing but a sad, deflated pancake. *Well shit.* I feel Katie move to stand beside me and take in the sad sight.

"I guess I'll call my brother," she says, sounding defeated. Just as she pulls out her phone, I hear a rumbling engine turn onto the road. Shading my eyes with my hand, I squint through the heat waves rising off the asphalt. As the vehicle nears, I recognize Margie's vintage Ford truck. Finally, a stroke of luck. When she spies us, she pulls over.

"Fancy seeing you here," she says from her rolled-down driver's side window. "Need help changing a tire?"

"If only. Spare is out of commission, and we are going to be late to the Watermelon Festival," I tell her.

"Well, get in then. Let's go to my house, and you can take the truck for the day," she says.

I don't stop to argue. Katie simply grabs her camera bag and climbs onto the truck's bench seat, squeezing in next to Margie. I slide in next to her and heft the truck's heavy door closed behind me. Vintage though Margie's truck may be, she has made sure her baby has air conditioning and that it is turned up to full blast. I reach out and angle the vent on me, soaking up its blustery cool air like it's the last drink of water on earth.

"Margie, my savior," I say.

"Remember that next time I need help cleaning out my chicken coop," she says.

The truck engine revs and Margie pulls back onto the road. It's bumpy, so my body sways with the motion of the truck. I slide into Katie multiple times as we make the two-mile drive to Margie's country home. I try to pretend like I'm unaffected by the contact, but with both of us wearing shorts, our sweat-coated legs keep bumping into one another. I should probably be more self-conscious after standing out in the heat, but all I can think about is her close proximity.

Margie has country music cranked up, making it too loud to have a conversation. Instead, Katie joins her voice to Dolly Parton's blaring through the truck's speakers. The two croon "Jolene" in perfect harmony and lull my soul into a place of homey comfort. When we make it to the turn off into Margie's gravel driveway, the truck's tires crunch and slide, tossing Katie forcefully into me. When Katie tumbles halfway into my lap, I have to force my thoughts into a platonic and *friendly* place. Margie lets out a low chuckle. I swear this woman is swinging this truck around on purpose.

"I didn't realize you drove like real-life Mario Kart," I mumble.

"Watch it now, or I'll throw a banana peel at you next," she says in that dry way of hers.

"Margie! You know what Mario Kart is?" I ask with a laugh.

"You forget that I practically raised Amelia. Who do you think was playing Nintendo 64 with her? I was a damn good Princess Peach," say says with a huff. She parks the truck, and we all climb out.

"I need to call someone about my car," I say.

"I'll take care of it," Margie says. "I'll call Rhett, and we'll get a tire on her and bring her to my place. When you're done in Farmerville, just come back here, and we will swap vehicles."

"You're a lifesaver," Katie says and wraps Margie up in a hug.

"Go on now, you two. And take care of my truck, or I'm going to slash the rest of your tires, Jacob." She tosses the keys to me, and Katie and I climb into the old vehicle. Her comment rings through my head, reminding me I have no idea what happened to my tire.

"Well, at least we'll fit right in with the Farmerville crowd," Katie says, taking in the truck's interior and grinning. I stare at her for a beat too long, before backing out of the driveway and getting on the road.

Chapter 21

KATIE

I'm beginning to wonder if every one of our festival trips is doomed. Maybe it's a sign from the universe that being romantically involved with Jacob is a terrible idea. So far we've had to seek medical attention twice, spoken to the cops once, been stranded on the side of the road, and I'm still in this damn medical boot. Should I really tempt fate by trying to make things more between us? After all, just as I was thinking about sliding my hand into his in the car, the damn thing got a flat. I don't know. I think about the job in Dallas and wonder if that's what I'm supposed to be doing. Do I have this all wrong? Maybe it's time to just go for it and let the cards fall where they may.

"Where did you disappear to?" Jacob asks.

"Hmmm?" I muse.

"'N Sync just came on the radio, and you haven't sung a single word. Is your foot bothering you?"

I bring my focus back into the present, taking in the glorious boy band song bursting through the old truck's speakers. I look at Jacob, noticing how his jaw clenches as he drives. *Could I walk away from this?*

"Jacob, this is the Backstreet Boys, not 'N Sync," I say.

He smiles. "I know. Just wanted to make sure you were paying attention."

"Just tired. Working two jobs and all," I murmur.

"Maybe it's time to ditch the coffee shop job? You're working a lot on this photography gig."

"Nah, it's really only weekends. Plus, I need to save up extra money so I can get my own place soon."

"Oh, fair. Where are you looking at? Somewhere close to Tech?" His hands tighten on the steering wheel. Why is he asking me this? Maybe it's polite small talk? But Jacob and I don't really do small talk. We do flirting and banter and impulsive slow dancing with suggestive touching and making out, apparently.

"I don't know. But I'm twenty-seven. Probably time to move out of my parents' home. It's kind of embarrassing," I say, trying to change the focus of our conversation.

Jacob stares intently at the road and says. "I live with my dad in my parents' home." He says it simply, with no tone, no inflection. *And I am an ass. Shit.*

"Oh no, I didn't mean. I mean, I just. I'm ready to be on my own a bit." I finish lamely. "I'm an idiot," I mumble under my breath.

He does laugh at that. "There's nothing wrong with wanting your own place, Kid. But there's nothing wrong with staying with your parents until you're ready. Don't be so hard on yourself."

I grind my teeth at the endearment. "I told you, I'm no baby goat. Quit calling me that."

He turns his eyes from the road to look at me. He must see something in my face because he nods and seems satisfied.

"Oh, there's the turn up ahead," I say, pointing to the Downtown Farmerville sign. I hate the awkwardness that's sprung up between us. *And why is he asking me where I'm going to live anyway?* The paranoid rabbit that lives inside my brain wonders if he somehow knows about Dallas.

"Okay, so game plan?" He asks, pulling into the small downtown area.

"There's a watermelon eating contest," I begin.

"Nope. Not doing an eating contest again. What else?" he says.

"What? Scared? There's no crawfish oil in this one," I taunt.

"I think I've already proven to the world, or at least a significant portion of the internet, that I'm a champion eater. Next?"

I skim the itinerary. "Oh! Perfect. How about watermelon seed spitting? You're bound to do well with that gigantic mouth of yours," I say with doe-eyed innocence, but his mouth quirks a smile.

"I am good with my mouth," he says, laying on an extra helping of sultriness and raising one eyebrow.

"Perfect. I'm sure the photos I'll take of you spitting seeds will win us top journalistic awards," I say.

I continue to scan the itinerary, noticing that the evening closes with a street dance. The image of us making out in Winnfield immediately springs to mind, and I decide not to mention it.

"Let's go hit up the tricycle races," I say decidedly. "Then we can get to your seed spitting."

"You know, seed spitting really is an unfortunate name for it," he says.

"You stop it right there," I say, cutting him off and laughing. He chuckles and climbs out of the truck.

I wander through the festival set up, camera in hand. We have our press badges displayed and it feels so fun, so professional. I snap photos of kids with sticky, red, watermelon-smeared faces, black watermelon seeds clinging to their cheeks. I frame up shots of old couples sitting in the shade, holding hands. It makes me long to experience these kinds of family moments in my own life one day, but it all feels impossible. After all, I can't even decide what I want for dinner, let alone contemplate a serious future life plan.

"Well, fancy seeing you here, beautiful," a male voice attempts to croon from nearby. I turn and see Brock. *Damnit.* Not this guy again. I look around to see if Jacob is nearby, anxious to prevent another fight. But when I finally spy him, I see that he's cozied up and chatting with… Bianca. My heart clenches with jealousy, so I turn my focus back to Brock. It's the attack of the "B's" today apparently. Maybe it's time for my inner B to come out. At least trying to talk to this tool will burn all this weird, tangled energy out of my system. Maybe.

"Brock," I say, all teeth. "What are you doing all the way in Farmerville?"

"Same as you, I imagine," he says. Then he turns, spreading his arm out as if to say, "*Taking in all this.*"

"Didn't realize the Shreveport paper had an interest in the Farmerville Watermelon Festival," I say, attempting to be cordial.

"They didn't until my friend Jacob over… *there*," he says pointedly, taking in the beautiful Latino goddess standing next to Jacob. "Until he went viral with that little video clip you took. Now my editor is on my ass to chase the sudden surge of interest in Louisiana festivals. Speaking of, any chance you've thought over my proposal to work in Shreveport? Bigger paper, larger reach. " You could start today," he says, staring pointedly at my camera.

"I appreciate it, but I'm not interested," I say firmly. Though the little indecisive voice inside my head peaks her naughty little head up and whispers, "*Are you sure about that, Katie?*"

Brock must see me hesitate because he continues. "Oh, come on. Photograph the watermelon eating contest, and send me the photos. We'll pay you better than whatever the Ruston paper is offering. You're already here, after all. The extra money couldn't hurt."

What he's saying does make a strange sort of sense. Whether I pursue Dallas or try to move into my own place in Ruston, I will need the extra cash. Wait, what am I even thinking? Lauren would be so disappointed in me.

I feel Brock's arm slide around my shoulders, a boa constrictor ready to pull me into its death squeeze. I tense, my fight or flight instinct surfacing. I try to step away, but his grip tightens. "Oh, come on now, beautiful. Just think. You and I could be a team… in more ways than one."

Bile rises in my throat. I try to slow my wild heartbeat and think.

"Please let go of me," I say as calmly and firmly as I can manage.

"Relax. We're just having a little fun," he says as he presses his nose into my ear. "Let's go grab a beer. We can talk more about my proposal. I have a hotel room in Ruston tonight. Luxury suite. You're welcome to join me."

I lift my foot, then slam my heel down on his toes. Hard.

"Mother fucker!" He yells. I pull away from him. "You crazy bitch. What's your problem?"

"You are my problem, asshole!" We are drawing a crowd. Old biddies titter around us as they look on with mixed expressions of horror and fascination.

"Are you okay, Ma'am?" a deep male voice asks. I turn as relief floods my body, expecting to see Jacob. But instead, a tall man with hair so dark it's nearly black stands next to me. He's wearing a cowboy hat and a pair of dimples so deep that I could stick a penny in them. I stare at him, confused.

"Is this guy messing with you?" The stranger asks.

"It's okay. I handled him," I say, turning back to look at Brock, who is staring murderously at me.

"Sir, I think it's best if you got the hell out of here," he says with measured calmness.

Brock eyes us both before turning and murmuring curses as he storms away.

"Well, that was awkward," I say to my would-be rescuer.

"I should have stepped in sooner," Mr. Hottie McDimples says. "But I couldn't tell if you two were friends from a distance."

"No, it's okay. I handled it," I repeat, voice quivering. I let my eyes flit over him, taking in his muscled biceps and bear paw tattoo that graces one of them.

"You certainly did," he says, admiration coating his deep Southern drawl. "I'm Josh."

"Katie."

"Nice to meet you, Katie. Though I admit, I regret it was under such unfortunate circumstances."

Is he flirting with me? Because Cowboy Josh is a tall drink of water on a hot day. He's almost enough to make me forget about...

"Hi, Josh, did you say?" Jacob says, stepping up behind me and reaching out his hand to take Josh's in an overly firm handshake.

"Oh, um, hi," he stumbles. "I'm sorry, didn't realize–"

"No!" I blurt out. "No, it's not like that. Jacob is my coworker." A pang of guilt pricks my conscience. But Jacob was flirting with Bianca. *Again.* I'm obviously not who he wants, and Cowboy Josh looks mighty appealing right about now.

Josh's smile drifts back across his face. "Say, want to join me at the street dance in an hour? I have to meet my mom for dinner in a few minutes, but I'd love to see you again."

I'm tempted to turn to Jacob to see how he feels about all this, but no. He certainly wasn't thinking of me with that curvy sex pot clinging to him a few minutes ago. I won't pass up a respectable invitation from a beautiful man for someone who is interested in someone else.

"Yeah, sure, okay," I say. And the wide smile that crosses my face is real. Maybe the universe is looking out for me after all.

AS WE APPROACH THE AREA where the watermelon seed spitting contest will take place, any ground I'd gained with Jacob is gone again. We speak in clipped, short sentences—just enough to convey the work we need to get done for the day. I can't stop thinking of the way Bianca leaned into him. Maybe all of Jacob's feral energy toward Cowboy Josh was just big brother protectiveness. After all, to Jacob, I'm just a "Kid."

Jacob storms off to the sign-up station, and I pick up my camera and get to work. I allow myself to get lost in the framing and shooting, checking the white balance and f-stops on my camera to set up the perfect shots. While I can definitely learn more when it comes to photography, as I flip through the screen to see what I've taken, I give myself a little pat on the back. These really are pretty good.

I watch as the seed-spitting contestants line up, and despite my resolve to be angry at Jacob, I can't help but stare at him. Even irritated, he's grinning and chatting with his fellow contestants, laying on his infamous charm. He's a beacon in the dark, a siren drawing in boats of little old ladies—and not-so-old ladies—-everywhere.

Unlike the crawfish eating contest, the watermelon seed spitting goes off without a hitch. The top prize goes to a woman named Ethel, whose deep wrinkles and curling white hair put her age somewhere close to ninety. But even Jacob's competitiveness can't stop him from celebrating this year's champion. He pulls her aside for an interview, and I sidle up to them to snap some more photos and take some video.

The evening is starting to set in, and my stomach rumbles. Jacob hears it and eyes me. "Hungry?" He raises one eyebrow.

It's a one-word question, but at least there's some emotion in his tone. I nod. "Starved." Two can play at this game.

"Barbecue?"

"Delicious."

His lips quirk, and he extends one arm out for me to take. I take it, and together we march off to the food tents.

Chapter 22

JACOB

Today should have been perfect. I had Katie to myself for hours. And even though I resolved to keep things friendly, I was looking forward to this time together. Why, then, did it all go up in a flaming pile of poop? That cowboy guy—John? Jeff?— immediately flashes into my mind. He was putting the moves on Katie, and she seemed to *enjoy* his attention. Irritation, hot and thick, rises like volcanic ash in my throat as I remember the scene. I force it back down. I have no claim on Katie's affections.

"Jacob? Are you… are we okay?" Katie asks.

I snap my focus back to the present. Katie is seated across from me at a picnic table, and we are eating pulled pork sandwiches, barely acknowledging one another. I'm a jealous SOB. I know it. I need to pack that shit up and put it away.

I inhale and exhale slowly. "Yea, Bun. We're okay. Weird day."

She starts to speak but hesitates. Finally, she nods. "Okay. Good." Then she takes another bite of her sandwich.

"I guess we need to make our way back to Ruston soon," I say. Maybe an evening ride back in Margie's rumbling truck will help settle the mood between us.

"Oh. Well, I kind of promised Josh I'd meet him at the street dance in about fifteen minutes. I'd like to at least stop by. I don't want to be rude," she says cautiously.

I feel my hackles rise but force them back down. "Yeah, okay. But I don't want to stay too late. I don't like Dad to be home alone for too long."

"Oh, of course. I'm sorry, Jay. I didn't think about that. Let me just find Josh, and I'll tell him we have to leave," she says.

Guilt rears its ugly head as I study her disappointed face. I may be jealous, but making Katie sad is an even worse feeling.

"We can hang for a little bit," I say, hating the words. "Let me see if my neighbor can check on Dad."

"Jacob, you don't have to," she says, but I can see the hope and excitement in her eyes.

"It's no problem," I say. Let's go on over there, and I'll try to get her on the phone.

We get up and walk our cardboard trays over to the trash can. When we make it over to the street dance area, the music is loud, and people are moving with all the joy and enthusiasm of kids on Christmas morning. The sight pumps nostalgia through my veins as a memory I didn't realize I still possessed rises to the surface. Mom and me, out in the backyard. We had the radio turned up and the grill going. She was drinking a beer, and her internal sunshine was on full display. She grabbed my hands, and we danced together, just the two of us, on the back patio. The warm glow of the memory fills my veins. I look to Katie, seized by the need to share, but she's not there.

I scan the scene before me and finally spot her auburn ponytail. She's dancing with Josh. He must have snagged her while I was lost in the memory. My heart lurches, but I decide to turn from the scene. She doesn't need jealous, angry Jacob. She needs to be happy. I walk away from the music to call my neighbor.

After a couple of rings, Mary picks up. "Everything okay, Jacob?"

"Yea, yea. All good. I'm still on a job. It's running a bit later than I planned, and I was wondering if you could stop over and check on dad for me? He hasn't been himself lately, and I'd feel better knowing someone has eyes on him tonight. Maybe just make sure he's eaten, and he's okay?"

"Sure, Jacob. No problem. My son is over right now. Okay if I stop by in about forty-five minutes?" She asks.

I sigh in relief. "Of course, thank you, Mary. I owe you one."

"You owe me nothing, Jacob. I'm happy to pop in and say hello to your father. You have a good night now, and be safe driving home."

When I hang up the phone and turn back around, I see that a slow dance has started, and Cowboy John-Jeff has Katie pulled in close. I feel physically ill watching her so near to him. Just last weekend, she was pulled in close to *my* body, kissing *me*. A hand slides over my shoulder, and I turn to see Bianca.

We talked earlier in the evening, catching up on each other's lives. She made it clear that her invitation to hook up still stood, but I told her now isn't a good time. She turned to look at Katie with a knowing smile, and only then did I see Brock and Cowboy Joe. I shake off the memory.

"Seems your girl found a different piece of arm candy for the night," she says with a playful taunt in her voice.

I turn to her. "Want to dance?"

Her beautiful, maroon-painted lips twist into the smile I fell for back in college.

"Why, yes, I would."

I grab her hand and pull her out into the crowd. She moves against me, pressing her curves into my chest. It should be an answer to a prayer, but all I can think about is how she doesn't feel like Katie. Bianca leans in and presses a kiss on my cheek.

"I know you're not into this," she whispers into my ear. She's always been direct, and it's one of the many things I like about her.

"Is it that obvious?" I say reluctantly.

Bianca lifts an eyebrow. "A woman knows when a man isn't into her." She turns and looks at Katie, who is staring at both of us over Cowboy Joey's shoulder. Bianca nods her head in Katie's direction. "You've never been one to let someone else stop you from getting what—or who—you want. What's changed?"

I sigh. She's right. But, I realize, for once in my life, I'm more worried about what someone else wants than what I want.

"I don't think she's into me," I tell Bianca. It's weird to say the words out loud, to acknowledge my interest in Katie after trying to hide it for so long.

"Oh, trust me, Jay. She's into you," Bianca says with certainty.

I peer over her shoulder, watching Katie dance with her cowboy. She suddenly locks gazes with me, the air crackling between us. Maybe Bianca is right. The song ends, and Bianca pulls away from me.

"See you around, Jacob," Bianca whispers. "And, for what it's worth, she's a lucky girl."

She walks away, and I'm left alone and cold. I turn to watch Katie again, and her face is an odd tangle of emotions as she leaves Cowboy John to walk over to me.

"Ready?" She asks.

"Yea, let's go."

She starts walking away, and I follow her lead through the crowd until we're both standing next to Margie's truck. True to my word, I pull out the keys and make sure I'm the driver tonight. The tension between us is as taut as a bowstring, and I don't know how to fix it. I fire up the engine and pull out of the parking lot.

The awkward silence permeates the truck as I drive. I wrack my brain for a way to ease the tension. An idea pops into my head, and I clear my throat. "Before we go back to Ruston, can I show you something? It's a place my dad used to take me after... well, after Mom died."

Katie's posture softens slightly, and she nods her head in agreement.

I turn off Farmerville Highway and make my way through a winding corridor of dirt roads, the memories leading me along the unmarked paths. Dusk is beginning to settle in, and the song of cicadas drifts through the cracked windows. When I spot the old boat house, I pull up behind it and park.

We both stare quietly out at the lake before us as I search for the right words to explain why I wanted Katie to come here with me, why it might help.

"Dad and I used to fish here when things were hard on both of us. I thought it might be a good place to just sit for a few minutes. I've always done my best thinking out here," I say.

Lake D'Arbonne stretches across the horizon, dotted with cypress trees. The dusky pinks and pops of orange are painted across the sky and reflected in the water as the sun makes her final descent for the day. There's a small dock with a gazebo at the end of it that I spent countless hours sitting on, cane pole in hand. Maybe bringing Katie to a place so full of emotion and memory wasn't a good idea, but it felt right in the moment.

"Jacob," she says, breaking the heavy silence. "What are we doing?"

A hot knife of anxiety lances my stomach. "What do you mean?"

"I mean… is there…" she takes a deep breath, steadying herself. "Is there something between us? More than just friendship, I mean?"

I cough a laugh, then turn and stare at her. The two of us still sit in the truck, and it feels like its own protected space. In here, it's just the two of us, no one else to stomp on this fragile thing we're trying to balance between us. The magic of the lake sunset fills the cab, and I feel like it might be safe to place my heart in Katie's hands.

"It's okay if you don't feel that. I don't mean to be weird or awkward. It's just that we kissed, and then, well, I don't know," she stumbles. She's staring down at her lap, hands twisting.

I reach over and place my hand over hers, and my veins light up like the fireflies starting to emerge around us. I crack open the truck door.

"Come out here with me," I say. Katie looks as anxious as a cat who consumed two cups of espresso. But she follows me, opening her door and climbing out. I go to her and take her hand again. She looks at me, questions dancing in her eyes as I gently pull her toward the dock.

"I really hope this isn't the part where you let me down gently, then toss me in the lake," she says nervously.

"Katie," I finally say. "You have to know I'm into you."

Her eyes widen. "Jacob, you had that curvy goddess pressed up against your body on multiple occasions tonight," she says with an edge in her voice. I wince.

"Bianca is an old fling, nothing more," I tell her. Katie folds her arms and turns from me. "Besides, you looked mighty comfy with Cowboy John tonight," I jab back.

She swings back around and her brows furrow deep. "It's Josh. And that was because you were so into Miss Hips and Lips that I thought I might as well find someone else who wanted to give me—and only me—the time of day."

Her verbal slap lands soundly. I flinch back, realizing that she's right. I've been nothing but mixed signals with her. Though, to be fair, she's been the same with me.

"Katie, I can't get a read on you. First, you dance with me at your brother's wedding like we're about to go on our own honeymoon…" Her jaw drops in indignation, but I'm not done. "And then you're cold, then hot, then cold, then freaking kissing me. And then there's Rhett." I sigh.

"You kissed me, you ass. Or did you forget that because you were in a THC-induced feel-good high? Why do you think I pulled away? I didn't want to *finally* kiss you when you were under the influence of mind-altering drugs. Talk about a blow to my ego." The pitch of her voice has risen, and this conversation is not going how I hoped.

"Katie! I wanted to kiss you. Couldn't you tell by the way I basically pulled you into my lap and dry-humped you in public?"

Her cheeks flush a brilliant red. "Then why do you flirt with every woman who crosses your path? How in the hell am I supposed to realize that you want me when your focus is on me and then immediately on someone else? How am I supposed to know—"

But I can't take it anymore. Her words are ripping my heart out. I know she's right, but I'm desperate to show her that she is the only person I want. I step in close, bend down and press my lips to hers. I kiss her desperately, sucking on her bottom lip, pressing my tongue against the seam of her lips. She opens for me, and I rush in to fill the space. Our tongues tangle as the chemistry that's been building between us for months, maybe longer, finally ignites. I pull her closer but then feel her hands press between us and she shoves me back.

"Jacob. What in the hell? You can't just end this conversation with…with…" she gestures in the general direction of my face. "Is that what you do with Bianca?" She demands. "I saw her kiss you tonight."

"Katie. She kissed my cheek and told me that she knew I was hung up on you." Her expression twists from anger to confusion. "And she asked me why I was letting some other guy go for you. She verbally kicked my ass and woke me up to what a dick I've been."

"Oh," she says. "Oh." Then she bounds across the distance between us and presses her lips to mine.

Chapter 23

KATIE

Jacob's arms envelop me as I press my mouth to his, devouring him. I'm a woman starved. His five o'clock shadow scrapes against my cheek, and he slides his lips down to press kisses along my jaw, and my neck. It's every fantasy from the past seven years come to life, and I briefly wonder if I'm fantasizing right now. *Are we still in the truck? Have I fallen asleep and into a dream?* And then I feel Jacob press his teeth against my ear lobe and growl out, "Finally."

Awake, I'm definitely awake. I tilt my head, inviting him in closer. Every part of my core has turned into liquid heat, and all I can think about is how I need to be closer to him. I reach my hand around to grab Jacob's ass, pulling him into me. His deep chuckle rasps against my ear.

"I like a woman who goes for what she wants," he says in a low voice, then presses his hips harder into my body. I can feel just how much Jacob wants me. His hands move down my back and grab my ass, pulling me into him. I let out a low chuckle. Even in this, it seems, we have to meet each other move for move.

"Is there any question who I want now?" He asks teasingly, pressing his arousal into me as he continues to kiss my neck.

"I'm not convinced," I manage to squeak out.

"Hmmmm, I guess I'll have to do better."

His mouth moves back to mine, his tongue finding my own. One hand leaves my bottom and moves to my front, lightly massaging my breast. A gasp escapes me at the touch. "You like that, don't you, Bun?"

In response, I pull his body closer and drag my mouth away from his and plant it along the side of his neck. It's my turn to explore. He groans as my mouth brushes along the tendons of his neck. I graze my teeth along the sensitive spot where his neck meets his shoulder. He grinds into me harder in response.

My wicked streak rises to the surface. I love how much Jacob wants me, and how he responds to my touches and my sounds. I want him to keep wanting me. To chase me. I pull away from him, taking in his lust-filled gaze. I know my eyes must look the same, half-lidded and full of desire. I take off half running, half limping down the dock, struggling to move quickly with the damn medical boot still weighing me down. I laugh as I'm caught up in the absurdity and joy of the moment.

I hear Jacob following down the old wooden boards. "Come here, little bunny. The big bad wolf is going to get you." It's so silly, and so us. This dock dead ends at a lake, and I can't wait to see what he will do when he catches me.

When I reach the end of the dock, I turn just as he reaches me. I think he'll grab me and pull me in for a kiss, but instead, he leans down, scoops me up, and tosses me over his shoulder. He starts walking back toward the land and playfully slaps my ass. "That's for running from me," he says.

"But you liked it, you big bad wolf," I yell back. I reach down from my position over his shoulder and squeeze his ass.

"Oh, you're in trouble now," he says as he swings me down and stands me in front of him. He lifts an eyebrow, waiting to see what I'll do next. Impulsively, I jump up and into his arms and plant a kiss on his lips. My momentum makes him lose his balance. He stumbles but manages to catch himself. He glances at the dark water behind him. "That was close," he says, then leans in and starts kissing me again.

That's when I hear a loud crack. Then we're tumbling off the dock and plunging into the lake. Cold, dark water fills my senses, and I'm momentarily disoriented as I attempt to adjust from hot makeout mode to cold lake water. I push to the surface and gasp in air. Jacob bobs to the surface beside me, looking equally shocked.

"What the hell?" He says, staring at the place above us on the dock where we were just making out.

"I think we put too much weight on a couple of those old boards," I say pointing to the splintered wood.

"You're so vicious, Bun," he says, laughing.

I splash water at him, and he immediately goes into play mode, using his whole arm to throw a wave of water back at me. I jump on him and dunk him under the lake's surface. He pops back up and grabs me, running his fingers up and down my ribs, tickling me. I squeal and try to retreat, but he won't let me. I turn to push off his chest and swim for the shore, but once I face him, he leans in and says wickedly, "I can see through that wet shirt of yours."

I blush and try to push away again, but he leans in and kisses me. I stop all protests and lean into the kiss. This is fun and spontaneous, and everything all my previous relationships were not. Just as I slide my tongue into his mouth again, I feel something bump my toes in the water. I freeze.

"What's wrong?" Jacob asks, pulling back from me.

"Nothing, I just thought…" but something bumps me again. I flail and start screaming like one of those YouTube goats. I do not do dark water and creatures of unknown origin touching me. "Something bit me!" I screech, continuing to swing my arms around like a Kraken devouring a ship as I move toward the shore.

"Oh right, I think there are alligators in this lake," Jacob says a little too casually.

"JACOB! Get out! Come on!"

He laughs. "What's wrong, Bun, scared?" He's all wicked delight.

"Hell, yes, I am. And if you have half a brain cell in that head of yours, you would be, too," I yell as I finally drag myself out of the water, soaked boot dragging behind me. "I rather like your body and would prefer you not to lose an arm to a gator out of pure stubbornness."

He grins and begins to make his way toward me on the shore. As he emerges from the water, though, all I can manage to focus on is how the soaking wet t-shirt hugs his body, clinging to his well-defined pecks and sculpted arms. I've seen him shirtless before, and it's nearly dark outside. But I hadn't made out with him then. This is wholly different, and… wow.

"I guess you got your way, after all," he says, his gaze full of fire.

"What?" I blink, confused.

"Well, you did mention a wet t-shirt contest," he says, raising an eyebrow.

"You win," I blurt out.

"Oh yes," he says, eyes drifting down from my face to my shirt clinging to my breasts. "I definitely won."

My blood heats at his perusal, and I am desperate to feel his body on mine again. He stalks with the feral energy of a wild wolf toward me. I push up to meet him, my body a magnet to his. He places a hand on each of my cheeks and tilts my head back, staring intently at my mouth.

"You are gorgeous, Katie. Gorgeous and absolutely delicious." He presses his mouth to mine and kisses me thoroughly, leaving us both breathless.

Distantly, I hear a phone ring inside the truck behind us, an alarm reminding us the outside world is probably wondering where we are.

"We should check that," I say, eyes never leaving Jacob's mouth.

"Let it go to voicemail," he says, pressing his lips gently to mine. I pull back.

"My parents are probably worried about me," I say. "I really need to get my own place to make them stop treating me like a teenager."

"Go check it then," he says, pressing his forehead to mine. I pull away and limp over to the truck, water trailing from my soaked clothes as gravel clings to my squishing shoe and water-logged boot. I lean in and grab my phone, but there are no missed calls.

"Not mine!" I call out. Jacob, who followed me to the truck, opens the driver's side door and grabs his phone. He stills, his breath catching.

"Jacob?" I say, worry coating my voice.

He presses a button on his phone and holds it to his ear. "Mary?" His voice is strained. He pauses. His whole body tenses as the woman on the other line speaks. The air is suddenly stifling as I try to discern what's being said on the call.

"Which hospital?" He finally asks. My heart drops and waves of fire and ice race through my body.

"I'm on my way." He hangs up and turns to me. His face is taut with worry. "It's my dad."

Chapter 24

JACOB

"I'll drive," Katie offers, reaching for the keys. My brain is like an electric bug zapper, thoughts hitting it and disintegrating into a fiery oblivion.

Dad. Dad. Dad. His name is the only thing I can focus on.

"But I can't navigate us out of here. You're going to have to help me with the back roads," Katie says, pulling the keys from my hand. "Jay? Can you do that?" Her voice is calm, and steady. It soothes something inside my soul, and pulls me back from the brink of despair. I nod my head in the affirmative and climb into the passenger seat.

The truck's old engine revs, and Katie turns on the brights, helping us find our way through the now-dark woods surrounding the lake. I try to focus on the roads, the landmarks, and the turns. But my conversation with Mary is drowning out all my conscious thoughts.

Dad collapsed on the floor, unresponsive. Mary calling an ambulance. Unconscious. Hospital.

And all of this happened while I was making out with Katie and splashing in the lake like some sort of irresponsible teenager when I should have been home checking on him. The guilt is paralyzing. Its tendrils snake through my body and wrap tightly around my heart. I lost my mom, and now I might lose my dad… and it's all my fault. A sob clogs my throat, but I refuse to let it out. I have to be strong for him.

Once we get to the main road, Katie turns on her GPS, and we head straight to the hospital. She attempts to ask me if dad is okay a few times, but I don't know the answer, so I just shrug my shoulders and swallow the pain down. She finally gives up trying to talk to me and focuses on getting us there as fast as she can.

I spy lights of the hospital ahead of us and immediately unbuckle my seatbelt and reach for the door handle. Katie places her hand on my leg.

"I'm going to park. Just hang on a second. We don't need you to barrel rolling onto the road."

As soon as she parks, I leap out of the car and rush toward the hospital. Katie runs up beside me and grabs my hand. Emotions rip through me. I want her here, her comfort, her affection. But my obsession with her is the whole reason dad is here to begin with. I can't focus on, well, whatever she and I are doing right now. My dad *needs* me.

I turn to her before walking into the hospital. "Katie, I–"

"Don't you dare tell me to leave," she says, cutting me off. I blink at her.

"You don't need to be here for this," I say, but I still can't bring myself to let go of her hand. Selfish. I'm so selfish. I brush my thumb over her knuckles.

"Jacob, I want to be here for this. For… you," she says.

I feel a tear trickle down my cheek. "I need to focus on my dad right now, and I'm not sure if I can do that with you here." She flinches at the words but grips my hand even tighter.

"Jacob, I don't know what we're doing right now. But we are friends. And no friend would let another friend go into a hospital alone. I'm going with you. If you need some alone time with your dad once we're in, that's fine. But quit trying to be so damn noble."

She turns and walks through the hospital doors, and I follow behind her. Part of me wishes that this stubborn woman would listen to me, just this once, but my heart wants her here, supporting me. *Selfish. I'm so selfish.*

We stride up to the front desk and give the receptionist dad's name. She tells me he's in the ICU and directs us to the correct floor. When we arrive, we learn that he can't have visitors at the moment. I feel utterly helpless, like a drink of water offered to a drowning man. Katie seems to know what I'm feeling because she tugs at my hand and leads me to the waiting area.

"I know you're feeling useless right now, Jacob. So here's what we're going to do. We're going to make a list of all the things we *can* do right now," Katie says.

She opens the Notes app on her phone. "Okay, let's start with number one. Who's taking care of your dog?" I blink at her, startled out of my spiraling thoughts. "No one. Got it. That will be the first item on the list. I'll text Amelia. Where's your spare key?"

And on it goes. Katie asks questions and demands answers. I fall into a rhythm of answering her questions, focusing on the sound of her voice, and the way her fingers glide across the phone screen. It's easier than the horror scape my brain paints as I imagine my dad in the worst-case scenario. Our clothes are still wet from the lake and I shiver as the cold air condition blows down on us. I know Katie must be freezing too, but the only indication are teh goosebumps that trail up and down her arms.

Finally a doctor comes out and asks for the family of George Edwards. I leap to my feet and walk to him. Katie trails behind me.

"I'm Jacob. I'm his son," I tell him.

"I'm Dr. Gifford. I've been overseeing your father's care since he arrived. George has had a stroke."

Fear lances my stomach, bolts of fiery cold punch into my shoulders. My legs start to tremble, and I fight the urge to collapse at his words. I feel Katie's hand press against my shoulder in comfort and support.

"Is he?" I gulp, and swallow down the tears. "Is he going to live?"

"Yes. But his recovery will be difficult. We don't know the full extent of the damage the stroke caused yet, but he is experiencing some paralysis on his right side."

"I need to see him," I tell the doctor, desperation filtering into my words.

"You can go back for twenty minutes," he says. "Are you family, too?"

I realize he's talking to Katie. She shakes her head no. "I'm sorry, but it's family only until he's able to leave ICU."

Katie's hand drops from my shoulder, and she nods her head. "Of course. Jacob, I'll wait out here for you."

I should tell her to go home, to rest. But I don't have it in me to send her away. Instead, I nod my head. She wraps her arms around me, embracing me in a tight hug.

"I'll call Rhett and get him to bring us some dry clothes," she says. I'm suddenly seized by the fear of Rhett finding out I kissed his sister.

"I don't know if that's a good idea," I mumble.

"Not something you need to worry about," she tells me. "Now go." She nods at the doors that lead to the ICU rooms. Seeing my damp shirt, a nurse offers me a hospital blanket to wrap around my shoulders and I accept it, creating a light blue cape around my shoulders.

I follow the doctor along the white corridors where patients are housed, passing the nurses' station and bowing my head away from the fluorescent lighting above us. Dr. Gifford pauses at room eleven and opens the door. I'm greeted by the sight of my dad in a hospital bed.

He looks shriveled, a husk of the man who cared for me on his own most of my life. There's an oxygen mask over his face, and he's hooked up to beeping monitors measuring his heart rate and oxygen levels. His eyes slit open as I enter the room, and I'm relieved to see that he's conscious.

I stalk over to the bed and reach for his hand, squeezing it tightly, but he doesn't squeeze back. Panic ripples through my body again as the worst-case scenarios roll over me again and again, threatening to crush me beneath them.

"Come over to this side of his bed," a nurse says. He pulls a chair up, and I stumble numbly to it. I take a seat and grab dad's left hand and squeeze. Nothing. I squeeze again, willing him to respond. I hang in the stillness of the moment, my vision tunneling to our clasped hands. Finally, his hand lightly squeezes mine in return. I exhale in a loud whoosh.

"Hey, Dad, it's Jacob. I'm here. You're going to be okay." I try to keep my voice strong and reassuring, but emotion makes it quiver. "I'm sorry I wasn't at home when this happened. That's on me. I promise I'll be here for you like you always have been for me. I won't mess up again."

He squeezes my hand in response and mouths something through the mask, but I can't make it out.

"Rest now, Dad. I love you." I tell him as I study his face, wondering if he even knows how bad things are right now. I hope not. I want him to have at least a few more hours of ignorance before facing the reality that some parts of his body seem to be paralyzed.

"It's time to go now," the nurse says gently. "Your father needs to rest. Go home for a bit, and try to get some rest. Visiting hours won't start back again until 10:00 a.m."

I stand slowly, clasping my makeshift blanket cape around me, and lean in to press a light kiss to his temple. "I love you, Dad. Stay strong." I ease away from him and make my way to the door.

"Thank you for taking care of him," I tell the nurse.

"He's got a lot of fight in him. Take comfort in that," he says. I nod and return to the waiting room.

When I emerge through the doors, Katie jumps up and runs to me, wrapping me in her arms. Rhett and Amelia are there, too. They offer me hugs in turn.

"Brought you a shirt," Rhett says. "Katie said you two fell in the lake while fishing."

I realize that Katie lied to her brother about what we were doing at Lake D'Arbonne, but I don't have the mental capacity to unpack that right now.

"Thanks," I murmur. "I'll just go change."

When I return from the restroom, they're waiting on me. The sympathy in their eyes is a lead weight on my shoulders, and I can't take it anymore. I need to be alone for a while to process things and figure out what the hell I'm doing.

"Can you give me a ride home, Rhett?"

Katie flinches slightly. "I can take you," she volunteers.

"It's on Rhett's way," I say firmly.

"Yeah, I got you, man," Rhett says. "Come on."

I follow him out of the hospital as Katie trails behind us. Once we're out in the parking lot, I feel her hand tug mine.

"Jacob, did I do something, or?" She asks, questioning. I hate the pain in her voice, but I hate myself more for creating this whole situation. I know better.

"No, it's not you. It's me." I wince at the words, and Katie reels back as if I slapped her. "It's just that, Katie, Dad needs me now more than ever. He's fucking paralyzed on one side, and I left him at home alone," my voice cracks on the last words. Katie reaches up to rub my shoulder, but I pull back. "Katie, you have your whole life ahead of you. I can't, I won't hold you back while I focus on the man who gave his life to take care of me."

"Shhhh," she says, pressing a single finger to my lips. "This is not your fault, and I won't watch you shove me out of your life because you're feeling guilty and grieving. Go home. Get some rest. I understand that you need to process things. But tomorrow, you better bet your ass that I will be there to take you to visit your dad."

"Katie, don't," I say against the finger still pressed to my lips.

"Jacob, you coming?" Rhett calls from somewhere in the dark parking lot.

"Yea," I call back. Then I turn my back on the woman who stormed into my life and took my heart prisoner, embracing the pain it causes. *She deserves better.*

Chapter 25

KATIE

Katie: I'm not up for FaceTiming tonight.

Celia: WTF not?

Katie: Jacob's dad is in the hospital and... I don't know. I think I'm a burden to him.

My phone starts ringing. Sighing, I pick up.

"What happened?" Celia demands.

Resigned, I tell her the whole story beginning with the flat tire and ending with Jacob leaving me behind at the hospital.

"So he kissed you. Again. And you think you're a burden on him?" She says.

"I don't know," I confide. "Cee, that was one of the hottest make-out sessions of my life. And we didn't even take off any of our clothes! But then he got that phone call and disappeared on me. I know that he's worried about his dad. He should be. I know he's processing what all of it means. But, Cee, you didn't see him when he walked away from me this evening. It was like he was saying goodbye," I choke on the last word.

"Maybe you're right," she finally says.

"Wait, really?"

"It's just. Katie, caring for a parent with a serious medical condition is a lot to handle. And it's going to take all of his attention. I don't want to see you cast your heart on someone who can't take care of it. You are so passionate and joyful, and I want you to have all that in return and more."

I pause and think about what she's saying, but it doesn't sit right with me.

"Look, just take some time and think about it. You said yourself that he asked for some time, so you take some of your own. Think it through. And don't just think about that hot kiss. Think about your future. It's okay to do that, to weigh everything and figure out the best option for yourself," she says.

"Cee, you know I'm the worst decision-maker on the planet," I tell her.

"Oh, Katie, I know. Speaking of..." she trails off. "Now, Katie, don't get mad."

"No good statement ever follows after those words," I say.

"Well, the thing is. I know how much you struggle to commit to a decision, so I did a thing."

"A thing?"

"Yea, well, Brian and I did a thing, really. He talked me into it."

"Ceeeee?" I say dangerously. "What did you do?"

"I might have submitted your cover letter and resume for that job at Brian's company. I might have also pretended to be you in an email and agreed to a phone interview."

"You *did what?*" I demand. This seems like a lot, even for Celia. "You did not."

"I... we... did. Yes. And they are very interested in you!" She says with forced enthusiasm.

"Why would you do that?" I ask her, irritated.

"I already told you. You're terrible at making decisions, and I wanted you to have another option. If things had worked out there, I would have canceled the interview. But seeing how things are sort of rocky, maybe you should do the interview. Besides, it's just over the phone. You don't even have to dress up for it'"

"I… don't know what to say," I tell her, shocked.

"Say you'll seriously think about it. I know you're still figuring this thing out with Jacob, but I wanted you to have another option. Just imagine it. You could come live with us. Start your life and your career in Dallas. How many times have you told me that you can't decide on a career, stick with a job, or find your own place? What do you have to lose by doing the interview? You can always say no if they offer you the position."

"Now's not a good time to be making decisions about this," I say, irritation lacing my voice.

"That's the beauty of it. I made the decision for you. I'm forwarding you all the details, including the information for the new email I set up for you."

"Isn't impersonating someone illegal?" I squeal into the phone.

"Meh, I'm giving all the info to you and telling you about it. No harm, no foul."

"Celia. I don't know."

"Just look at it, Katie. Get some rest. Think about it tomorrow," she says.

I sigh in defeat. There's no changing Celia's mind once she's set on something, so I let it go.

"I'm going to bed."

"Perfect, darling. That's exactly what you need. Talk to you tomorrow!"

I end the call and stare at my phone screen. Pulling up the text app, I find my text thread with Jacob.

Katie: How are you holding up?

I wait. And wait.

Nothing.

He's probably already asleep, but insecurity worms its way into my stomach and I begin to wonder if Celia's right. I know I've been hot and cold with Jacob, but he's been the same with me. Was tonight really something more, or was he using his charisma and inherent sexiness to try to mend the fence between us? My mind replays the many times this evening he pushed me away this evening, and the pain of rejection fills my chest with searing pain. *No, he's grieving. That wasn't really him. But was it?*

Tomorrow. I'll think it all through tomorrow. I crawl into bed and attempt to sleep, but I'm plagued by confusing dreams of Bianca working as my new boss in Dallas, telling me that I'm not good enough, that Jacob deserves better, and that I abandoned him.

Around five a.m. I can't take it anymore. I get up and check my phone again. Nothing. Growing in frustration, I grab my laptop and open my inbox. I quickly find the email Celia forwarded me and read through their correspondence. My eyes catch on words like "innovative," "opportunity," and "creativity." I allow myself to mull over that future. Tentative excitement lights my senses as the thought of a wholly different life unfolds in my head.

But as I imagine my new, idyllic life, Jacob strolls into my imaginings unbidden. He's flashing his warm grin and staring at me like he did yesterday evening: eyes full of lust and mischief. I see the dog he drew in his journal walking into our apartment and… I slam the laptop closed. What am I thinking? Jacob won't, can't, leave his dad. There is no future where I'm working some kickass photography job in Dallas with Jacob by my side. I have to make a choice, and that terrifies me.

Glancing at the clock, I notice that it's nearly nine. I promised Jacob I'd take him to the hospital to see his dad this morning. I grab my phone and text him to let him know I'm on my way. He doesn't respond, but I don't let that deter me. I hop in my car, noticing Margie's old truck still sits in my driveway.

The whole drive over to his house, I panic over how he'll treat me. I had to get his address from the company intranet, so I'm not sure he believes I'll actually show. I pull up in the driveway of the old house and look around. Everything is a little too worn, in need of repair and a fresh coat of paint. But that doesn't matter to me. I stroll up to the front door and knock. A dog barks enthusiastically, and I smile, picturing the old bull dog from Jacob's sketchbook.

I wait and wait. Finally, I knock again. I pull my phone out of my pocket and text.

Katie: I'm here. Where are you?

Jacob: Caught a ride with Rhett. Don't worry about me.

My temper flares as hurt brands itself into my chest.

Katie: Don't worry? Are you kidding me right now?

Three dots appear as he texts his response. I wait. And wait some more. They disappear, but no more texts appear.

Katie: Look, I know you're hurting, but you can't just disappear on me like this.

Nothing.

Growling in frustration, I slam my foot down on the concrete of his front porch. I knew yesterday was too good to be true. For one hour, everything was perfect, and then it was ripped away, leaving me bleeding out.

Why do I care so damn much? I stomp back to my car, tears of hurt and fury making hot tracks down my face. I slide into the driver's seat and slam the door behind me. Pulling up my phone, I log into the email Celia created for me and respond.

Hi Mr. Garfield,

Thank you so much for your response and additional information about the position. I'd love to schedule a phone interview. What is a good day and

time for you?
Sincerely,
Katie Hebert

I fire off the email before I can think better of it. I lock my phone and toss it to the passenger seat. Then I slam my key into the ignition and drive. I turn up the radio as Nine Inch Nails blares through the speakers, feeding my anger and hurt. I don't know where I'm going; I just know I need to get out of here for a while. My conscience pricks at the back of my mind, but I squash the tiny voice down. I don't want to hear it, not now when it's easier to be hurt and angry.

Chapter 26

JACOB

Don't worry? Are you kidding me right now?

I re-read her text. I've started to respond to Katie and stopped a dozen times. The first time I wanted to beg her to forgive me, but then the doctor came into the room, and I never sent the text. When I picked my phone back up, I typed out a response that told her she was better without me, but I couldn't bring myself to send that one either. Finally, I put my phone away and focused entirely on my dad. He needs me right now.

I look at him in the hospital bed and see him smiling at me. He's awake, and his oxygen saturation has improved, allowing the doctors to remove the mask.

"Hey, son," he says, voice slurred. The right side of his mouth droops, a side effect of the stroke.

"Hey, Dad. How are you feeling today?"

He raises his left hand and turns it side to side, indicating that he feels "so-so." I nod.

"You're doing great, Pop. The doc says they will have you back up and in rehab in no time. Get ready to be fawned over by hot nurses."

His short laugh comes out in a wisp. It's crushing my heart into dust, but I refuse to let it show. Instead, I plaster on the smile I've spent years cultivating for conducting story interviews.

"Dad," I pause, trying to figure out the best way to approach this. "Do you remember what happened? Before you went to the hospital?"

His vision seems to glaze over. I'm not sure if it's the medication they have him on, the stroke, or something else that I'm too scared to think about too deeply right now.

"Dad?" I try again.

He turns his head and looks out the hospital room window, gaze unfocused. My heart starts pounding in my chest, anxiety a helicopter blade slapping me over and over again in quick succession.

I get up and walk over to where he looks, trying to snag his gaze. I kneel down and peer into his eyes, but they continue to look past me, blinking every so often. Chills ripple up and down my body. Until now, I've been coasting along on cruise control, ignoring the signs that Dad has been in physical and mental decline. Even the call from Mary and seeing Dad in the hospital all felt like I was watching someone else's life from a distance. It's not until now, as I silently beg my dad to lock his gaze on mine, that the full force of what has happened plows into me like an eighteen-wheeler on ice. Our lives have changed irrevocably, and there's no going back to how things were ever again.

Waves of pain begin to pound into me at the realization, first at my knees and then at my back and shoulders, as memories of my mom in the hospital crash over me, threatening to pull me under.

I feel physical pain as the old memories crack open the folds of my brain and come rushing out, a kicked ant hill flooding my entire being. My hands begin to shake, then my shoulders and my knees. My vision tunnels, closing in around me, trapping me. My heartbeat thunders inside my head, and I can't breathe. Desperately I try to suck in breaths as I wonder if this is what death feels like. I want to call out for help, but I can't talk.

My knees fold, and I hit the hospital floor, shaking. I hear footsteps, then someone calls for help—but it sounds far away. My vision shrinks to a pinpoint, and everything turns black.

Chapter 27

KATIE

Once I start driving, I can't decide where to stop. Do I go home and listen to my parents ply me for answers on what's wrong? Hell no. I'm twenty-seven, and that is the last thing I need. I think about driving to Rhett and Amelia's, but I can tell that they suspect something is going on between Jacob and me after asking them to bring us both clothes—and I don't want to answer those questions right now. I growl in frustration in the car. This is why I don't commit to anything. It's easier to move onto something new when things start to get too hard, to let the feelings roll off me.

"Hey, Siri. Play Foo Fighters," I say, then turn up the car volume. "Learn to Fly," comes blasting through the car as I pull onto I-20 West. I coast down the interstate and try to let the music push out all the bad thoughts. My head suddenly clears, and I know where I need to go.

"Hey Siri, call Celia."

The phone rings twice before the sound of my best friend's voice fills the car.

"Katie! Please don't be mad at me about the job application. I did it because I love you. Please forgive me." All the words come out in one breath, and it's just what I need to break through the rager going on in my head.

"Celia. It's okay."

"Whew, thank goodness. Now, did you look at the emails I sent over?" She asks, curiosity lighting her voice. She accepts forgiveness so easily, my Cee.

"I did, but let's talk about it later. In person," I say.

"You mean like on FaceTime?" She asked, confused.

"No, I mean, in person. Things have been… difficult over the past twenty-four hours, and I need to get out of town for a bit, clear my head."

"Oh, you're coming to see me!" She squeals delightedly into the phone. "About damn time. When should I expect you?"

"Depending on traffic, about three and a half hours," I say.

"Okay then, girl. You're on your way. I approve of this decision. I'll have drinks and dinner waiting on you when you get here. You going to stop at Buccee's on the way?"

"Not really in the shopping in a sea of beaver-obsessed motorists mood," I say dryly.

"Okay, but they have some good stuff," she says.

"Cee!" But I'm chuckling, the thrill of seeing my bestie already beginning to ease the tension in my body.

"Alright, alright. Be careful. I'll let Brian know you're coming."

I hang up the phone and crank the music back up, cruising toward my escape.

WHEN I ARRIVE AT CELIA and Brian's apartment, she comes running out, hands in the air like she just found out she won the Miss America pageant. She's wearing bright yellow, which compliments her light brown skin. That's my Cee, a ray of fierce, delightful sunshine. And oh, how I've missed her.

"Katie! You're here!' She yells loud enough for the entire apartment complex to hear before wrapping me up in a tight embrace and rocking us from side to side, a couple of buoys on a stormy sea. "I missed your face," she declares before pressing a kiss to each of my cheeks.

She pulls away. "Let's get your bag and get you inside. I've got Chardonnay chilling, and Brian is making spaghetti."

Well, you see, I didn't actually bring a bag." I tell her. She stares at me in confusion, so I continue. "This is a bit of an impulse trip, and I may have driven here in response to being caught up in a feeling tornado of indignation and hurt."

"Oh, Katie. Come on, baby. You can wear some of my jammies, and we keep extra toothbrushes in the apartment. You can sleep in my bed with me or on the couch, wherever you feel most comfortable. But first, let's get some wine and food in you so you can tell me the whole story."

I follow Celia up to her apartment. She opens the door, and I take in the space. It's bigger than I thought it would be. It may only be two bedrooms, but the large open kitchen and living room space are warm and inviting. Cee has definitely styled the apartment with her signature flourishes of color and joy. She points to the kitchen bar and says, "Sit."

She opens the cabinet, pulls out two wine glasses, then moves to the fridge to grab the bottle of Chardonnay. She doles out two liberal pours before returning the rest to the fridge. Sliding a glass my way, Celia holds hers up and says, "Cheers to two fabulous ladies!" We clink our glasses.

"And one very dapper gentleman!" A voice calls out from down the hallway. Brian emerges, wearing the same soccer shorts and worn t-shirt he's owned since his Freshman year of high school. "So good to see you, Katie," he says quietly before sliding an arm around my shoulder and giving me a squeeze.

"Would you like a glass of wine?" I ask, starting to get up. But he nods his head no.

"Someone has to keep things under control tonight," he says with a wink and moves into the kitchen to start working on dinner.

I am instantly comforted by the sense of normality around me. Back in high school, the three of us would sit in Brian's living room, eating popcorn and playing video games while his mom flitted around us. Cee and I have always been big talkers, but Brian's quiet one-liners kept us laughing. We were a strange group, but we worked. Still do.

As the wine begins to settle into my bones, I'm finally able to relax. Cee grabs my hand and pulls me over to their well-worn couch, a hand-me-down from Brian's parents. We sink into the cushions, carefully avoiding spilling our wine.

"Katie, I'm so happy to see you, you know that. But what, or should I say, who spurred you to leave town?" She says a little too innocently. She knows what happened at the hospital with Jacob, but she's giving me the space to think through it all and tell her more.

"Jacob…" I inhale. I don't know where to go from there.

"Well, obviously," she says. "What did the man *do?*"

"I told him I'd pick him up and take him to see his dad at the hospital. But when I got to his house, he was gone. He's ignoring my texts. And look, Cee, I know this is difficult for him. But I can't help but think that I read way more into making out with him than he did. And I kind of feel like an idiot."

"Did he ask you to pick him up and take him to the hospital?" She asks.

"Well no," I allow.

"Did he say, 'Okay, see you in the morning,' when you told him that you would pick him up?"

I feel the slight heat of shame color my cheeks. "No."

"I see. And he gave you his address so you could come on over?" She asks deliberately.

"I had to look it up on the company intranet," I say with a wince.

"Katie," Celia says. "You have a big heart, but maybe the man just needs some space to worry about his dad. It doesn't mean he doesn't like you."

"I thought you were supposed to be on my side," I say with a pout.

"Oh honey, I am. I always am. And believe me, my selfish heart wants to tell you that he is an ass, and you need to take the Dallas job immediately. But I love you, so I'm trying to actually help."

"Speaking of the Dallas job," I hedge.

"Yes?" She says, her full attention blazing into me.

"I emailed them to set up an interview," I tell her.

"You didn't!" She says with excitement.

"I did. But I kind of did it when I was feeling sorry for myself. I don't know if it was the right decision," I say, biting my lip.

"Well, you have to do the interview at least, now. Just see where it goes," she says.

"But, what if I messed up? With Jacob, I mean?"

"It sounds like he needs some time and space to figure things out right now. You said his mom died when he was a kid. After coping with something like that, I can't imagine seeing your only parent in the hospital under such dire circumstances. Jacob wants space? Give him space. Check on him if you want, but don't overstep. Stay here a couple of days, take some time for yourself, and think things through."

I nod my head. It's a good idea.

"Dinner's ready!" Brian calls out. "Can one of you set the table?"

We both stand at the same time and move to prep the small wooden table. Already the hurt isn't quite as sharp. I check my phone one more time, but there are no new texts from Jacob. There's just one from Mom telling me to tell Celia and Brian hello.

Chapter 28

JACOB

I squint at the fluorescent lights blinding my vision and turn my eyes down to stare at the clean white walls around me, struggling to figure out where I am.

"Jacob? Jacob? Are you back with us?" A low male voice asks.

A man in scrubs I vaguely recognize hovers over me. I stare at him, brain full of cobwebs as I try to figure out what's happening.

"I'm going to help you sit up slowly," he says.

As I do, I notice the hospital bed next to me. My awareness clicks into place. *Dad. Hospital.*

"Good, good. That's great, Jacob. How are you feeling right now?" the nurse asks.

"A little out of it. What happened?" I ask him.

"You passed out," he says simply.

"Am I okay?" Panic starts to fill my chest again, fears of my own health moving to take center stage.

"Yes, you're fine. It happens sometimes. The mental trauma of what's happening to your father combined with not enough food, water, or sleep. It's a bad combo."

"But it felt like I was…" I hesitate, not wanting to sound stupid. But then again, I am in a hospital. "I felt like I was dying. Like I couldn't breathe, and my heart was racing."

He studies my face. "Let's get you on the couch. I'll check your vitals, but it sounds like a panic attack. And everything you've experienced in the last twenty-four hours would certainly be enough to trigger one."

He takes his time checking my vitals, reassuring me as he goes. "You're okay, but you've got to rest. Why don't you lay back here for a while? Or I can call someone to come get you?"

I mentally scroll through who I could call. Katie immediately pops into my mind, but even thinking of her is like pushing a bruise. I think about Rhett, but I've already had him cart me up here once today. I suddenly realize that, as many acquaintances as I know, I haven't made many true friends. I'll likely have to swallow my pride and call Rhett. "I have a friend. I'll reach out to him."

"Do that and lay down for a bit. Try not to worry about your dad for now. We're taking good care of him," he says.

Taking his advice, I lie back on the water-resistant hospital couch. Its waxy surface and solid cushions make me feel like I'm lying on a cheap tablecloth, but I don't have much choice at the moment. Scrolling through my phone, I find Rhett's number and hesitate. And then my phone starts ringing. I blink twice to make sure that I'm seeing the screen correctly.

Margie is calling me.

"Hello?" I answer.

"Jacob. You okay, son?"

"Yea, I'm alright," I tell her.

"Liar," she says.

I chuckle roughly. "Nothing gets past you, Margie."

"Look, I'm calling because I got your car all fixed up. I talked to Amelia earlier, and she and Rhett are both working late and asked if I'd collect you from the hospital. What time should I be there?"

I sag into the unforgiving couch. I do have my own sort of family, it seems. At least I do until they learn what an ass I've been to Katie.

"Whenever works best for you, Margie," I sigh into the phone.

"Great. I'll see you in an hour. I'll bring you to my place so you

can get your car. Keep your phone on you. I'll text when I get there."
She hangs up.

I tap to open my messages and pull up my last text exchange with
Katie. I need to reach out to her.

"Hey. I'm sorry. It's been a lot. You okay?" I type out.

I hesitate, re-reading the text three times before finally hitting
send. I don't deserve a response from her, and I wouldn't blame her
if she ghosted me after this. But we still have one more festival
assignment together, and I need to try to make things right before
then. Again.

My phone pings with a text.

Katie: I'm okay. How's your dad?

Relief floods my body at seeing her response.

Jacob: Dad has a long road ahead of him.

Katie: And you?

Jacob: Tired. But I'll be alright.

I pause, hesitating on my next words.

Jacob: Can I see you tonight?

Katie: I'm not in town right now. I'll be back in a couple of days.

Not in town? What?

Jacob: Where are you? Is everything okay?

Katie: Yes. I went to visit Celia in Dallas. Wanted to give us both some space.

An ax sinks into my heart at those words. I told Katie I needed space, though, and she's giving it to me. I have no reason to complain.

Jacob: See you when you get back?

Katie: Sure. We have a meat pie festival to get to.

The ax sinks deeper. So it's going to be all business with Katie. Okay then. I deserve that.

Jacob: Wouldn't miss it. But I miss you.

A minute passes.

Katie: I miss you too, J. See you Friday.

I WALK OUTSIDE THE HOSPITAL and see Margie's truck rumbling near the curb. The nurse offered to get a wheelchair and roll me out, but that's the last thing I need. Margie would never let me hear the end of it. I open the passenger door and slide in.

"You look awful," Margie says.

"No, please, don't hold back. Tell me how you really feel," I deadpan to Margie. I take an odd sort of comfort in her direct approach and the way we've always taken jabs at one another.

"How's your dad?" She asks, pulling out of the hospital parking lot and driving back toward her house.

I shrug. "Honestly, not great. He had a stroke."

"Rhett told me. Is he alert?"

I shrug again. "Sort of. He doesn't seem to be able to move the right side of his body. Sometimes he seems to know who I am, and other times..." I trail off, trying to figure out how to explain what's happening with Dad. "Well, his eyes are open, but he isn't registering what's happening in front of him. It's… fucking *terrifying*."

I feel her calloused hand reach out and pat my shoulder, then retreat back to the steering wheel.

"That's real shitty," she says.

This small truck cab has turned into my confessional, and I feel the need to bear my soul to this woman who I can tell has seen her fair share of difficult things in life.

"I don't know what I'm going to do with him," I choke on a sob that slips through the rock-solid emotional barrier I've attempted to erect. "I can't stay home and take care of him full time. I have to work, but he can't be home alone. I can't afford assisted living…" My vision starts to tunnel again.

Then Margie's strong hand is back on my shoulder, squeezing this time. She's pulling me back into reality like some gritty, Southern guardian angel. "Jacob. You don't have to figure all that out on your own, and you certainly don't have to do it right now. Take a deep breath. There you go. Now let it out, slowly."

She turns her truck onto a street toward my house.

"Where are we going? I thought you said we were headed to your place to get my car?"

"We need to make a pit stop first," she says in her matter-of-fact way.

As we pull up to my driveway, I turn to look at her, confused. "How do you know where I live?"

"Rhett gave me your address. Come on. We'll still go get your car, but I think someone wants to see you first."

I hear the low woof before I see Ollie and immediately feel the tension that's coiled in my shoulders begin to ease.

"I've been keeping an eye on him," Margie says. "He's a good boy. Bring him along for the ride with us. He misses you."

I walk up to the front door and open it. My aging, chubby bulldog wheezes in delight when he sees me. I bend down and wrap my arms around him, not even minding when his giant tongue slaps my cheek.

"Come on, Ollie. Let's go for a ride." I scoop up the heavy guy and haul him onto the bench seat in Margie's truck.

He turns to her and whines in greeting. "That's a good boy. I told you he'd be back soon," she says affectionately and rubs his wrinkled head.

As her truck rumbles out of the driveway, I'm struck again by how much love is in my life—love I didn't even realize. My mind strays to Katie. Her warm smile and infectious laugh fill my heart. I'm suddenly aching to see her. But I can wait. I have to wait. I need to make things right between us, for real, this time. That is if she'll give me a chance. If I haven't ruined things past the point of no return. If she even wants a man who will have to place his dad at the forefront of his attention. I begin to doubt myself again but do my best to push it aside. At least for now. When she gets back in town, we'll talk. We'll figure this out; figure us out. And if she doesn't want me in that way, that will be okay, too. It will have to be. I'll take whatever she's willing to give me.

The crunch of gravel on Margie's driveway pulls me out of my reverie. I spy my car parked near Margie's infamous she-shed, and the sight of that space immediately reminds me of Rhett's bachelor party and Katie's singing entrance. I smile, the first I've managed since kissing Katie at the lake.

"How much do I owe you for fixing the car?" I ask Margie.

"She just needed a couple of new tires. I was able to get them wholesale, so you can just reimburse me for that, and we're even Steven. I'll give you my Venmo."

"Margie, let me pay you for your labor," I try, but she quickly dismisses me.

"It's no trouble. Gave me a project to work on." I step out of the truck and help Ollie get to the ground. He takes his time wandering around the country yard, sticking his wrinkled nose into rabbit burrows and weeds. I notice Margie staring at him affectionately.

"Maybe you should get a dog," I tell her.

Her nose wrinkles. "I don't need another mouth to feed." But then her weathered smile comes back, and I wonder how long it will be before she finally caves and gets a four-legged friend of her own. I walk over to my car, and Ollie trots over to where I stand.

"Jacob?" Margie asks. "Are things between you and Katie okay?"

I freeze. "What do you mean?" I ask a little too casually.

"Just that, well, you two seemed to be getting close. And, take it from me, you don't want to let someone like her get away. She's a catch, and you're not so bad yourself. The two of you work well together."

I'm stunned to hear someone speak so plainly about the two of us as more than just friends that I don't know how to respond at first. "I think I messed up," I finally say.

"Maybe. I don't know what happened between you two. But I know Katie. She likes you, Jacob. And she has a big heart. She feels deeply and is easily hurt. But, I have a feeling the two of you can mend each other's hearts if you make a go of it."

Impulsively, I reach out and wrap my arms around this fortress of a woman. "Thank you. For everything."

She hesitates before sliding her arms up around me and pulling me in tight. "Don't be so hard on yourself, Jacob. You're one of the good ones. Don't forget that."

I pull away and quickly wipe away the tears threatening to spill down my cheeks. I walk to my car and scoop up my boulder of a dog, and put him in my passenger seat. As I flick on the headlights and pull out of Margie's long gravel driveway, my heart swells with gratitude. As soon as we hit the paved road, I notice that the new tires ride like a dream. The whole drive home, I dedicate my thoughts to what I'm going to say when I see Katie in a few days. As if he can read my mind, Ollie gives me a supportive "Woof."

168

Chapter 29

KATIE

My time in Dallas with Brian and Celia passes in a distracted dream. I have a wonderful time with my friends, but whenever I get even a moment alone, my brain locks onto thoughts of Jacob like a heat-seeking missile. I messed up. *He did too,* the defensive part of my brain immediately jumps in to scream, but I try to make defensive Katie stand down and behave. Jacob and I both messed up. But I've committed to the plan Celia and I talked about. I'm going to take some time and think things through.

My whole four hour drive back to Ruston, I'm an indecisive mess. When I get home, I decide to make a pro-con list. In my notebook, I label one page "Ruston" and the other "Dallas."

On my Dallas page, the "pro" list includes things like creative freedom, challenging, making more money, living near (or with) Celia and Brian. Under the cons I've listed: higher cost of living, being away from family, and awful traffic.

I turn to my Ruston page. Under pros, I list: Living near Mom, Dad, Rhett, and Amelia, the band, newspaper work, Margie, affordability, and… Jacob in my life. Under the cons column, I list: limited career growth opportunities, no Trader Joe's nearby, and Jacob in my life (non-romantic).

I stare at both pages of lists and sigh, feeling like I've made zero progress on the decision-making front. Setting aside my notebook, I decide to focus on this week's problems. Namely, I am about to spend a whole two days at the Natchitoches Meat Pie Festival with Jacob, who probably still doesn't want to be around me. If he can even be away from his dad right now. I realize how selfish I'm being and immediately reach for my phone.

Before I can stop myself, I type out, "Hey, how's your dad?" And text it to Jacob.

The three response dots immediately pop up, causing a confusing storm of relief and anxiety to crash through my system.

Jacob: He's about the same.

I wait, but nothing else comes across the screen.

Katie: I'm back in town.

Jacob: Glad to hear you made it back safely. Looking forward to seeing you in a few days when we head down to Natchitoches.

Well, at least that answers my question about whether or not he plans on going. But, even though I told him earlier via text that I'd see him this weekend, I still feel an uneasy sense of rejection. I guess I was hoping he'd ask me to hang out again. I try to slam the breaks on those emotions and step back to look at things more objectively. That's what Cee advised me to do, but my needy little heart can't help but try to crawl into a corner and hide under a blanket.

I pull up my calendar and am relieved to see that I'm scheduled to work at the coffee shop for the next two days. That work has become rote, and there is something calming about getting lost in the motions of brewing espresso and blending frappes. But even as I find relief in the idea of mindless work, I also wonder if this is really what I should be doing with my career at this point in my life. My mind drifts back to the Dallas job again, and the turmoil tornado inside my soul leaps into action like it's ready to play a starring role in *The Wizard of Oz*.

"Katie!" Mom calls from downstairs. "Dinner time!' I wince, mad at myself for still living like an angsty teen with mom and dad. Even the journal in my hand looks like the ones I've been writing in since I was twelve. I tuck the journal under my mattress and mentally prepare myself to be fake happy through dinner with my parents. One thing is for sure, regardless of where I end up, I have got to get out from under their roof soon. I'm too old for this.

IT'S FRIDAY, D-DAY. The day that Jacob and I have to drive to Natchitoches to spend two days and one night at the famous Meat Pie Festival. While there, we plan to scope out the city's popular bed and breakfast scene. I'd like to stop at the house where they filmed *Steel Magnolias*, but we'll see what our time looks like.

I'm a nervous wreck. I have to spend two hours in a car with Jacob, who I haven't had a real conversation with since I had my tongue shoved down his throat, and he got an eyeful of my boobs in a wet shirt. This is going to be more awkward than showing up to church drunk and wearing a see through string bikini.

I mentally start creating a list of conversation topics to keep things from getting painfully awkward, but my heart begins to wilt at the thought. Conversation and trading jabs have always been our thing. Just the thought that Jacob and I may not have that anymore is enough to make me want to join my heart in the corner under a blanket. With a bottle of wine. And emo music.

Time to be brave, Katie. Jacob has every right to cancel going to Natchitoches this weekend with his dad in the hospital, but he didn't. I have no excuses to duck out of this. I just have to make it through the drive. Once we get there, we can go our separate ways for the story and then hole up in our respective bed and breakfast rooms and unwind. Two hours is nothing. Two hours is everything.

My phone vibrates. I look down to see a text from Jacob.

Jacob: I'm here.

He's picking me up since we will be gone overnight, and I don't want to leave my car in the parking lot at the newspaper offices. I grab my camera bag, but before I've even made it down the stairs, I hear his booming voice. Jacob is Rhett's best friend, after all. He's spent many evenings at our house and has known Mom and Dad for years. They love him, and the feeling is absolutely mutual. I pause, eavesdropping on the conversation happening just out of sight.

"Thank you for your prayers, Mrs. H. To be frank, Dad isn't great. But I know how much it would mean to him to know that you both are thinking of and praying for him during this trial."

My heart rate picks up, and my body aches with restraint as I prevent myself from running down the stairs and wrapping Jacob up in my arms, holding him close. I want to ease his pain, but I'm terrified that my presence will only make it worse. I take a deep breath and steady my trembling hands before stepping into the entryway where the three of them are standing. I've got a small overnight bag over one shoulder and my camera bag over the other.

Jacob looks up when I enter the room, and his eyes lock with mine. My heart rate jumps sky-high, and I distantly wonder if I'm going to pass out as my vision starts to tunnel. My mom looks between the two of us, and her brows furrow.

"Is everything okay?" She asks.

I clear my throat. "Yes, fine. Jacob, how is your dad?"

Mom must think that my concern over his dad makes things tense because she relaxes slightly at my question.

Jacob gives me a weak smile. "He's stable for now. You ready to hit the road, Katie?"

How words are so formal. My heart aches for him to call me "Bun," or, hell, I'll even take "Kid" at this point. I nod my head and follow him to the front door. I hug Mom and Dad, and tell them I'll see them late Saturday.

When we walk out to the car, Jacob pops the trunk so I can put my stuff in there. I notice a new spare tire stowed in the back. He sees me staring and says wryly, "Just in case. Our track record isn't the greatest."

I toss my bags in, walk over to the passenger side, and climb in. When Jacob gets in the car, he stays quiet and focuses on his phone, pulling up the GPS to our bed and breakfast. We pull onto the road with only the sound of Siri's voice telling us when to turn to fill the silence between us. My guts churn, and it feels like an angry beaver is trying to chew its way through my intestines. I'm desperate to say something to him, but so scared of messing things up between us even further. I run my hands through my tangled auburn strands, then reach for the radio.

Music is my love language. Say a word, and I immediately sing a song lyric back to you with that word in it. It's a game Rhett and I played as kids and sometimes still do if we're ever in a car together for an extended time. And right now, I need music. The radio comes to life when I turn the dial on the old car's dash.

Steven Tyler immediately croons, "There was a time when I was so broken hearted. Love wasn't much of a friend of mine."

Well, shit. Thanks, Steven.

I pretend to be unbothered by the lyrics and lean back in my seat. Maybe I'll just nap through this whole awkward car ride. But when I close my eyes, I swear I can feel Jacob's presence around me, like some avenging spirit haunting me until he gets what he wants.

"Katie," Jacob says. And my name clangs through the car like an old bronze bell. My eyes snap open, but I'm scared to look at him.

"Yea?" I ask cautiously. I turn my head but only manage to stare at his thigh muscle pressed against his shorts. I swallow. I wish I could wave a magic wand and make all this tension disappear. Then I could slide my hand over his muscled thigh. He'd press his hand over mine, and we'd smile at each other sheepishly.

"We need to talk," he says.

His words instantly douse my fantasy. I wince. I look at him. Jacob is staring straight ahead at the road, jaw clenching and unclenching. I can practically see the words rolling around in his head. I don't want to have a difficult conversation, but it has to happen. So I reach out and turn the radio down.

"Yea," I finally say. "We do."

He turns to me then, finally looking at me. His eyes have the glassy look of someone who has either been crying, not sleeping, or an awful concoction of both.

"I'm sorry about what happened between us," he starts.

Hot and cold flashes race through my body. Is he talking about the hospital, ghosting me the next morning, or the kissing? I suddenly feel like I'm going to puke.

"Which part?" I finally manage to croak out.

"All of it. I shouldn't have pushed you away when Dad was at the hospital or disappeared on you the next morning. I was just..." He lets out a frustrated growl and it takes me by surprise, but I don't say anything. "I was just. I don't know. I was struggling with my emotions, still am. And I don't want to drag you into all that. You're so happy all the time, and you don't deserve to be pulled into my painful mess of a life. My dad, he's always taken care of me. And I wasn't there to take care of him when it mattered. I was being selfish." He glances at me covertly as he says that last sentence, and a swarm of guilt bees take flight in my stomach.

"And then there was my all-consuming sense of fear for Dad. I just didn't know what to do with all those emotions. No one besides Dad has ever tried to care for me like you did, and I didn't know how to react. I know that sounds so stupid, but it's the truth."

"And, the kissing? Are you sorry that happened?" I ask, attempting to keep my voice neutral, but I'm both terrified and desperate for his answer.

He turns from the road to study my face. "No. I'm not sorry for that, not one bit." Then his gaze drifts to my lips before turning back to the road.

I flush at his words. "I'm sorry, too."

"Katie, you have nothing to apologize for," he says.

"Just listen," I demand. I'm intent on saying my piece. "I am sorry. I was pushy because I was scared too. You had just given me the best kiss of my life, and then suddenly, you were pulling away from me. Even though the reason why was obvious, I couldn't help but think I was just another notch on your belt. It hurt. But that was so stupidly selfish of me, and I realize that now. It's just I didn't want you to run from me, so I latched onto you like a damn leach. Probably not all that helpful in hindsight."

"I needed someone to take control that night, Bun." My whole body softens at the nickname. "And you did the right thing. I don't like this distance that's formed between us. Once I finally got my head on straight, I realized the only person I wanted to be around was you."

His words hang in the air between us. My mind drifts to the email I sent the Dallas company, and guilt courses through my veins. But this is not the time for that conversation. We have to sort some things out between us first. So instead, I give into my desire and reach over to slide my hand over his thigh. I feel his body tense, then relax under my touch.

"I missed you," I tell him plainly.

"I missed you, too. And Katie, I want whatever you want, okay? I'll be your friend if that's what you need."

"And what if I want more?" I dare to ask.

"Then… I'd like that, too," he says, swallowing to cover his nerves.

We sit in silence for a while after that, the radio playing like a low lullaby as the sound of the road lulls the lingering tension between us. Finally, I speak up. "Let's focus on getting our work done over the next couple of days. And then, when we get back to Ruston, let's go on a real date and see how it goes."

His mouth quirks a half smile. "I'd like that."

"And, in the meantime, if you need any help with your dad, please ask me. I want to help him, help you."

His hand trails down the steering wheel and finds mine, giving it a squeeze. We stay that way, holding hands for the rest of the drive.

Chapter 30

JACOB

I shouldn't have doubted Katie. And, I guess I didn't. Not really. I doubted myself. But having her hand in mine is a balm to my weary soul. And, while I'm still anxious about dad, I'm grateful to be on this work trip and for the distraction it provides. Miraculously, we make it safely to Natchitoches without any hiccups. I smile as we drive into the charming city.

Natchitoches is one of those small Louisiana towns I always recommend to out-of-towners. Not only does Main Street have an old hardware store and a bricked road, but some of the best food in the state can be found in the small, locally-owned restaurants. And while Christmas is probably the best time to visit, the Natchitoches Meat Pie Festival is definitely a close second.

I've been to the Meat Pie Festival before, but this is, surprisingly, Katie's first time going. I'm excited to experience it through her eyes. Though, in order to do that, I'm going to have to stop staring at *her*. And, quite frankly, I don't want to. Even though we've come close to the topic before, our conversation in the car was the first time Katie and I both admitted we wanted something more between us. I'm already imagining how I will make our first official date perfect. Though, every time my mind starts to wander down that path, images of my dad in the hospital flash into my brain, and I feel an overwhelming sense of guilt.

As we park the car and walk over to the meat pie festival, though, I do my best to harness my reporter energy and get to work. Katie breaks away and starts taking photos. I lose her in the crowd, but this time I'm certain no random cowboy will scoop her up.

Like most of the other festivals we've attended for these features, I immediately spy rows of white pop-up tents that house some of the best-smelling food I've ever encountered. Natchitoches meat pies are so popular that they can even be found in the frozen sections of most local grocery stores. But there is nothing, and I do mean nothing, like eating a fresh fried pie in person.

I follow my nose to one of the stands and turn on my signature charm. I start chatting with the lady at the tent, telling her who I am and the paper I'm with, and she immediately erupts into laughter. Oh, Sugar, I know who you are. I've seen that video of you getting a face full of crawfish. Lawd, I know that hurt. Here, let me get you a pie, baby."

Francine, it turns out, is quite eager to talk to me. She tells me how she got into the pie-making business and all about her family history. Spying Katie, I flag her over to take some photos. Francine "just call me Franny" Johnson invites us both back into her workspace to show us the ins and outs of making the perfect pie. Katie is photographing, and the energy is good. I know, in my bones, that this will be the best article and set of photos we've gotten so far.

By the time we're done chatting with Franny, we're walking out of the tent wearing our own sets of aprons that say "Franny's pies" on them.

"That woman is going to show up at the paper with pies for you next week. Just you wait and see," Katie teases.

Things are easy between us again, and I finally feel like I can breathe.

"So, now that we've mostly covered the festival, I'm dying to see some of the bed and breakfasts around here. I looked at photos online, and the ones in restored Victorian homes look divine," Katie enthuses.

I'm caught up in her excitement and eagerly agree. "Maybe we should check into ours first?" I ask her.

"Nah, we have plenty of time for that. Let's go exploring!" She says it with all the delight of a child going to Disney World for the first time. I grab her hand and pull her to me, sliding my arm around her waist. We've been so cautious around each other for so long that the casual physical affection in public makes me feel vulnerable. But I love it. I love showing the world that Katie is mine. Or almost mine. Or whatever. I honestly don't care. I'm just happy to feel her fingers tapping on my hip as we walk.

We spend the rest of the afternoon wandering in and out of the bed and breakfast houses. When we let the owners know that we're reporting on them for the Ruston paper, we're welcomed with open arms and offers of drinks and dessert samplings. We try everything from freshly made pecan pie and homemade whipped cream to peach parfaits and warm chocolate chip cookies.

"I could get used to this," Katie says.

I glance down at my watch and see that it's nearly six p.m. "We need to go check into our place before they close up for the evening."

We pull into the parking lot of the beautiful Victorian home where we'll be staying tonight. Katie oohs and ahs at the large wrap-around wooden porch and white rocking chairs outside. Roses creep up trellises, and a fountain sits in the garden, water quietly trickling out.

"It's just so sweet," Katie says with delight. "Like something out of *Anne of Green Gables*."

We go inside, and our hostess, Grace, walks in to greet us.

"Hello, how can I help you? Checking in?"

"Yes, we have two rooms, both under *The Ruston Daily Leader*," I tell her.

She disappears through a door. And when Grace comes back, a frown deepens her wrinkled forehead. "I'm not sure what happened," she tells us reluctantly. "But someone called earlier today and canceled both rooms."

"Wait, are you serious?" I ask her, my heart sinking. Already my brain is running through various other options. It's getting late, and I know how much Katie is looking forward to staying in one of these beautiful homes.

"Oh no," Katie says, dejection clinging to every feature on her face. "I've been looking forward to this so much."

Grace eyes both of us, thinking. Then finally, she seems to come to a conclusion. "I tell you what. We just finished renovating our Rose Room and haven't opened it back up for reservations yet. I know you asked for two rooms, but there's an extra couch in there if the two of you want to stay. I feel just awful about this mix-up. No charge. It's up to you."

I turn to look at Katie, and her eyes have turned pleading, a puppy dog at the pound desperate to be adopted.

I turn to Grace, "Well, if you're sure?"

"Of course, let me go get your keys."

When Grace leaves the room, I turn to Katie. "I wonder what that's all about. Why would someone call and cancel our rooms?"

"I know. That's super weird. Did Lauren think you were staying back in Ruston because of your dad?" she asks.

"No, I told her I was still going. It makes me wonder if all these weird things happening to us on these stories are more than just coincidences," I say.

"Yea, but why would someone try to sabotage us? These are just festival stories for a small, local newspaper."

But before I can say more, Grace is back with our room keys. "Here you are. Go up to the second floor, third door on your right. Breakfast is at 8:30 a.m. Just come down to the main dining room and find a seat. You won't want to miss it. I've got something delicious planned for our special guests!"

Thanking her, we climb the stairs and find the room she directed us to. We use the old key to open the door to the space. We walk in and...*I have no words.*

There are roses *everywhere*. The wallpaper is imprinted with them. There are vases filled with clusters of roses in varying shades on every surface. Hell, there's even a rug adorned with roses. But what really catches my eye is the giant four-poster bed with a floral covering and rose-shaped pillows.

"She wasn't joking about this being the rose room," I mutter.

I glance around, looking for the couch where I'll be spending the night, but the only thing I spy is a small chaise lounge that I predict will barely support my weight when I'm sitting on it. There is no way my six-foot, two-inch frame can sleep on that thing.

Katie follows my line of vision and simply says, "Oh."

"Yeah, oh. That *thing* is not a couch. It looks like something small Victorian children were sent to sit on as a form of punishment," I say, horrified.

"Well, I guess that means I'm going to be tonight's small Victorian child," she says, walking over to it. But when she tentatively sits on the crude thing, it makes a loud creak, and a rusty spring shoots up through its rose-patterned cushion. Katie squeaks and hops off of it. "Or not."

"Definitely not. You take the bed. I'll use some of those rose pillows and make a pallet on the floor," I tell her.

"Don't be ridiculous," she says. "I know I had my heart on staying at this place, but I saw a Holiday Inn Express by the interstate. We can go there."

"And dash your dream of staying in an old Victorian home? I would never," I say dramatically.

"Fine then. We're both adults. We'll share the bed," but I don't miss the flush that creeps up her beautiful throat.

I can't help myself from teasing her. "I'm the most adult to ever adult. It won't be a problem, scout's honor," I say and salute her. She gives me a playful shove.

"We'll worry about that later. I'm starved. Let's go find some food."

"Even after all that dessert?" I ask her playfully.

"Like I'd miss out on the chance to have some delicious Cajun food in Natchitoches. Just let me run to the restroom to freshen up."

Katie disappears into the bathroom, and I take my time exploring the space. There are old photographs on the wall of families and children. They look like pale little ghosts. I step away from the photos and turn to study the bed that I'll be sharing with Katie tonight. My mind starts to venture places it probably shouldn't when Katie bursts out of the bathroom wide-eyed.

"Um, Jacob." At first, fear rips through me, but then I notice she's trying to hold back a laugh. "You have got to come see this."

I follow her into the bathroom and freeze. A giant, heart-shaped jacuzzi tub is in the middle of the space. Beside it sits a framed paper. I lean in closer to read it. "Welcome to the Honeymoon Suite," it says. I freeze and turn to Katie. The laughter she's been attempting to hold back rips out of her in a torrent. She begins laughing so hard that tears fall down her cheeks. It's infectious, and before I know it, I'm laughing too. All the tension between us, all the stress of the past week, the mix up over the room, it all spills out of us in fits and starts of gasps and giggles.

"We are in the freaking honeymoon suite," she says. "And look." She holds up a bag of rose petals with a note on them. "They're for the tub," she says, eyebrows wiggling.

My brain is seized by the vision of her in that tub, rose petals drifting across the surface. And suddenly, this isn't so funny anymore. I stare at her lips, fixating on them, desperate to press mine into hers, to remember what it feels like to brush her tongue with mine. I shake my head. I can't go there, not in this confined space, *this damn honeymoon suite*, where *anything* could happen. We are still trying to figure things out between us, and I intend to be a perfect gentleman.

"So, dinner?" I ask abruptly.

"Let's do it. I found a good place not too far from here," she says, nodding to her phone in her hand. "Let's go get some crawfish!"

I wince. "I don't know if I can ever eat crawfish again," I say, thinking back to Mudbug Madness.

"I'll eat yours for you, you big baby," she says with a wink and grabs her purse.

Chapter 31

KATIE

I still can't believe how well the day has gone. Despite all the awkwardness of the past week, Jacob and I have fallen back into our usual banter, but with something a little... *more*. The way he steals glances at me and studies my face, how his hand lingers a little too long on my arm or the small of his back, the way he sits just a little bit closer to me. All of it makes me feel *desired*, like I'm the center of his universe. I bask in the feeling, rolling around in it like an excited dog in a pile of leaves.

My brain flickers to the Dallas job, but I squash those thoughts like overactive bullet ants for now. I'm going to live for tonight. La Vie Boheme and all that. And I think Jacob is doing the same. I sink into his smiles and flirting, wrapping it around me like a snuggie on one of our few cold days.

We find a Cajun restaurant with twinkle lights decorating the outside. It's on the Cane River and so quintessentially "Louisiana" that it makes my heart ache with a nostalgia that I don't fully understand. As we exit the car, Jacob walks next to me, his hand resting on my lower back. It feels so right like we've been in a relationship forever, not like we're trying to figure out what's building between us. And, in a way, I guess we have. We've known each other for years. I just never, even in my wildest dreams, expected that Jacob would come to have romantic feelings for me.

We walk into the restaurant and ask for a table for two. While the hostess steps away, Jacob leans down to me and whispers, "What are you smiling at, Bun?" His warm breath tickles my neck and crawls down my spine, curling my toes.

"Just enjoying the moment," I whisper back to him.

We sit at a small table with a view of the river. That, paired with the candlelight at the table and the twinkle lights hanging on the building's eaves outside, makes this feel almost as if we really are on a honeymoon. *And that bed.* No. I won't think about that. I am a grown-ass woman, and this thing blossoming between us is too new and delicate. Definitely too soon to think about sharing a bed with Jacob beyond just sleeping.

"Can I start you with a drink?" Our server asks.

"Yes," I gasp out, then look to Jacob. His megawatt grin is in place, and I consider crawling across the table and nestling into his arms like some deranged, well, baby bunny. I turn to the server, who's waiting for something more from me. "House white wine, please."

She turns to Jacob. "And you?"

"Abita Amber, please," he says, ordering the popular Louisiana beer.

As we study our menus, quiet falls between us, and I start to feel awkward again. I'm not sure if it's all the naughty thoughts threatening to take control of my brain or the fact that Jacob and I haven't talked much this week. I decide to be brave, to actually make a decision and seize control of the moment.

"So, um, want an appetizer?" I ask. *Real smooth, Katie.*

"Sure. What do you think about crab claws?"

"Oh, definitely!' I say a little too enthusiastically. Jacob raises one eyebrow teasingly. When our waitress returns with our drinks, she takes our appetizer order. We sit across the table and stare at one another. *Crushing it.* I groan inwardly at my sudden awkwardness.

I clear my throat. "So, um. How did the story interviews go today?"

I run the tip of my shoes across the restaurant carpet, enjoying the sensation now that I'm finally out of that leg vice generously called a medical boot.

Jacob settles back in his chair, running his fingers up and down the cold glass of draft beer, painting lines into the condensation. "I think they are some of the best I've gotten so far. This will be a fun article, especially incorporating some of Franny's stories into it."

I nod my head and look around the restaurant. *Why am I suddenly so awkward?*

Our waitress returns with the crab claws and tells us she'll be back in a few minutes to take our order. I reach out for a crab claw at the same time Jacob does. We knock hands, and I jerk mine back like I touched hot coal. In my haste to retreat, I slam my hand into my wine glass, and it tumbles over and spills directly into my lap. I jump up, arms darting across the table like an eager octopus as I try to pick up the glass and grab cloth napkins, all the while whisper yelling, "Shit, shit, shit."

Jacob jumps up, too, and grabs his cloth napkin, eager to help. He reaches out, patting down the spill on my dress… which just happens to be on top of my lady parts. He realizes it the same time I do. I leap back like someone just set fire to me. My foot catches the chair, and I go ass over tea kettle onto the restaurant floor. And because I'm wearing a dress, most of the people in the small restaurant are treated to a front-row seat of my pink polka-dotted underwear.

Jacob rushes to me, leaning down to help me sit up. I pop up, anxious to escape the scene I'm causing, and ready to pretend like this whole incident never happened. But as I move forward, I slam my forehead into Jacob's nose.

He lets out a yelp as he tumbles backward. We are suddenly staring in our very own live action slapstick comedy show. My stomach lurches at the sight of Jacob sprawled out on the floor, and my head pounds where I just clocked him. I crawl to where he now lays, holding his nose, eyes closed.

"Um, Sir, Ma'am? Are you okay?"

I turn and look to see a small crowd of waiters and waitresses gathered around us, obviously struggling with how to handle two injured and possibly deranged people rolling around on their restaurant floor. I look up and notice someone has their phone out, recording this whole fiasco. Great, just freaking great. What ever happened to common decency?

"Yea," I say, refusing to look at them. "We're okay. But I think we're going to place a to-go order." Jacob, hands still holding his nose, nods his head in agreement.

"What do you want?" I whisper.

"You pick," he says through his hands. "Just no crawfish."

I push myself off the ground, attempting to muster my dignity. I hold my head high like I'm the queen of this establishment, turn to the crew of wait staff and tell them we will take two orders of shrimp etouffee to go. They hustle off, and I reach down and grasp Jacob's hand, helping him to his feet.

"Well, that was a disaster," he says under his breath. He grabs his beer and practically chugs it.

"I'll drive. Again." I say, but laugh, letting him know there are no hard feelings. "You and I are constantly on the hot mess express. You know that?"

He chuckles, then finally pulls his hands away from his nose. "How bad is it?" Jacob asks me. I lean and study his nose and his eyes. My breath catches as I inhale his familiar scent. Impulsively, I lean in, kiss his nose softly, then pull away.

"It's fine," I tell him. "Everything is where it's supposed to be." My cheeks flush with a combination of embarrassment and arousal. His gaze lingers on my lips, and the two of us stare at one another, pretending for all the world like nothing and no one else exists.

When our food arrives packaged up and ready to go, Jacob quickly pays the tab, and we walk out of there, heads held high as if we meant to recreate an episode of *The Three Stooges* in the middle of a nice restaurant. As I drive us back to our bed and breakfast, hysteria seizes me. I try to squash the bubbling laugh down, but it's too late. It bursts out of me in gasps and high pitched squeals.

"We are quite the pair, aren't we?" Jacob says.

"You can say that again."

We are starving by the time we park and end up digging into our meals while we sit in Jacob's car. This, at least, feels normal. I feel less shy and awkward as we dig into our etouffee while playing some of my favorite nineties songs through the car speakers.

"I'm sorry for being an awkward mess at the restaurant," I tell him. "I guess I don't know quite how to act now that we aren't pretending to be just friends anymore."

"Katie, you don't have to act. That's the whole point. Just be you. You are who I want, not some formal date version of you that you think you have to be. We're still the same people. We're just Katie and Jacob like we've always been. Except now… maybe we kiss sometimes?" he asks, a hopeful smile flitting across his lips.

"Yes, I think I can manage that."

WHEN WE FINALLY OPEN THE DOOR to the Rose Room, we're confronted again by the giant four-poster bed. The thing has presence, and it's far more intimate and imposing at night than it was in the stark light of day. I inhale deeply, trying to push away the nerves threatening to take over my body at the thought of sharing a bed with the man I've fantasized about for years. Even though we'll just be sleeping in it. Because that's really *all* we'll be doing.

"I'll just go change in the bathroom," Jacob says. While he disappears into the space, I remove roughly eighty rose-shaped pillows from the top of the bed and attempt to stack them somewhat neatly on the torture device formerly known as the chaise lounge. I fail miserably, and the whole lot of them end up spilling on the floor. Giving up on the effort, I fold back the bed covers and plug in my phone, readying myself for bed. *I can do this. Everything will be great and not awkward. Completely platonic. It will be fine. Perfect even.*

When Jacob finally emerges from the bathroom, I can't even look at him. Knowing what he wears to bed feels so intimate that I can already feel the hint of a blush trying to take over my entire face. I stand and dart past him into the bathroom with my entire overnight bag tucked under my arm like a football. "Touchdown, Katie!" I mentally cheer as I slide into the bathroom, quickly closing the door behind me. I press my back against its wooden surface and take four slow deep breaths. *You've got this Katie.*

I pull open my bag and examine its contents. I usually just sleep in a tank top and underwear… so that's all I packed. And no amount of wishing upon an evening star will make pajama bottoms materialize in front of me. It's time to improvise. I quickly change into my tank top and brush my teeth. Grabbing a towel, I wrap it around my waist so Jacob doesn't get an eye full of my underwear. Or I guess I should say another glimpse. He certainly got an eyeful earlier when I somersaulted across the restaurant floor. *Way to take control that situation, Katie.*

When I emerge, I see that Jacob is already in bed. The covers are folded down around his waist, and he's wearing a gray tank top. His rippling biceps are on full display, and I can't help but examine them—in great detail. My eyes follow the curves and movement of muscles that have been honed by time in his garage gym.

"Katie?" He asks cautiously.

"Uh huh," I say.

"Why are you wearing a towel around your waist?" He asks.

"Close your eyes," I tell him.

He looks at me curiously but does as I ask. I drop the towel and jump into bed, pulling the covers up and over my hips in one quick motion. It reminds me of the years as a child that I used to run and jump into bed so the monsters couldn't reach out from beneath it and grab my feet. I smile to myself at the memory, and turn to look at the man I've, quite literally, lept into bed with.

"Okay, you can open them," I tell him. He looks at me with humor and curiosity. It's only then that I notice that he's wearing glasses. Good grief. He is not playing fair. The thick black frames awakened something in my lusty librarian heart that I didn't even know was there. And the way he's studying me in them…. I swallow.

I find my voice. "Well, um, I only sleep in a tank top. I wasn't planning on sharing a room, so I didn't pack any bottoms," I say sheepishly.

He lifts his eyebrows in response. "No bottoms? *At all?*" He swallows and I can practically hear the "gulp" he makes. His gaze heats as his eyes trace the lines of my legs beneath the covers.

"I have underwear on, you perv." I try for light humor, but it comes out more like a husky come hither. Jacob shifts in the bed uncomfortably.

"So, anyway. Mind if I read for a bit?" I ask, my voice coming out in a mousy squeak. I'm anxious to diffuse the building tension between us.

"Actually," he says. "I wanted to talk about something with you."

"Oh?" I say, panic and desire threatening to turn me into some lusty woman of the night intent on stealing his virtue. *Get a grip, Katie.*

"Yea, so I've been thinking about how things seem to keep going awry with these articles we've been working on. The runaway dumpster, the wire tripping you at the pageant, the stage fire, the pot brownies, the flat tire, and now the bed and breakfast. It seems like more than just a series of coincidences."

"Oh, I didn't think about that," I say a bit lamely, disappointment fills chest. He's obviously not as affected by this moment as I am. But, he's right, I realize. I need to cool my lady jets so I can focus on the conversation.

"It's weird, right? I mean, it makes me wonder if someone is doing this to us on purpose," Jacob says.

I turn on my side, propping my head on my hand, and face him. "But why would anyone want to sabotage feature pieces for the newspaper? It's not like we're covering some mob boss trial or something."

"I've been considering it, and I can think of a few people who might want us to fail," he says, rubbing his and along the back of his head.

I'm surprised, but I give him the space to share his thoughts.

"I know this might sound crazy, but just think about it." Jacob holds up a finger. "One. We're in competition with a new magazine that's trying to get off the ground. Any of them could be trying to undermine us and steal advertisers. Two," he says, holding up a second finger. "There was that guy, Brock, who seemed intent on stealing you away to work with him. And that ass stole plenty of my work in college."

"But that seems like a lot of work for either option," I protest.

Jacob shrugs his impressive shoulders. "I know, but it's just too weird. We've sailed past coincidence territory here."

"Okay, those are two possible culprits. Other thoughts? What about that Bianca chick?" I ask.

"Why would she want to undermine us?" He asks.

"Correction, undermine me," I say.

"Oh, is someone jealous?" Jacob asks, mouth curving into a delicious smile. He rolls to his side, arm propping up his head. His bicep bulges in his new position. We face each other in mirrored poses.

"Now, why would I be jealous?" I say with indignation.

"Katie…" he purrs in a low warning tone.

Shivers rocket through my body at those words, his nearness, and this damn honeymoon love nest we're in. I flush and close my eyes, steadying my breath. When I open them again, I study Jacob's face. His breathing is ragged, and he's not looking at me. Well, at least not my eyes. I slowly look down and notice that my tank top has been pulled down, exposing my cleavage. I move to pull my shirt back up but then pause when my hand reaches my shirt's neckline, considering my next move. Decision made, I keep my eyes on Jacob's face as I slowly pull down the tank top, allowing more cleavage to show. I watch as his pupils dilate, and his breath catches in his throat. He momentarily stops breathing. I am energized by the effect I'm having on him. It makes me feel brave and reckless.

"Like what you see?" I whisper our familiar phrase in a voice that can't possibly be mine. It's full of husky desire and want.

His hand darts out as if he's going to touch me then pauses mid-air. He slowly pulls it back, a stern and determined set to his features. This won't do. I know he wants me, and that obnoxious cheerleader inside my head is coaxing me to do more, to *make him* touch me. I tug my shirt down a little more. I'm not wearing a bra, so there is nothing between my shirt and my skin, allowing his eyes to drink in every inch of me.

"Katie, I… I am trying to be a gentleman here." He says, voice pained, but his eyes never leave my breasts.

"Oh, how very noble of you," I say. And then, in a fit of impulsivity, I pull my tank top completely off, baring my breasts to Jacob.

He lets out a noise that's somewhere between a choke and a growl, and then he's on me. He drags himself across the bed and fastens his mouth to mine, kissing me deeply. His tongue licks into my mouth, and his hand comes up and lightly squeezes my breast. I respond immediately, desperately. I chase his tongue with my own and reach behind him to pull up the back of his shirt.

"This needs to come off now," I tell him. He grunts, then pulls back and nearly rips the shirt off his body, knocking his glasses off. He snaps them up, places them on the nightstand, then turns back to me. He reaches for me, cupping my jaw, eyes studying mine, and then his mouth dives back to mine. For the first time, we are skin to skin, my breasts pressed against his hard chest. His hand trails down until his thumb is lightly grazing my nipple. We are a storm of sensation and desperate want—a desire that's been building between us for months or maybe even years. I writhe against Jacob, desperate to touch every part of him to every part of me.

He reaches down and grabs my thigh, hoisting it over his hip. The change in position allows him to press into me, grinding his arousal between my thighs until I dig my fingernails into his back in desperation.

"More," I breathe into his hungry mouth. "More, please."

He pulls back, a magnet ripped from its pair. "Katie, this is not taking it slow," he says, pressing his forehead against mine.

"Jacob, we've been practically dating for months now. I can't take much more of this pent-up desire. I need you," I say, kneading his shoulder muscles with my fist. "That is if you want to. I don't want you to do anything you aren't comfortable with."

My words unleash something in him. Jacob groans as if in pain, then seizes my mouth with his own again. His hand comes up to cup my neck, his thumb tracing along the column of my throat. We kiss as our hands explore each other's bodies with frantic energy. Touching, teasing. His mouth finally breaks from mine, and he makes his way slowly down my neck. He pauses when he gets to my breasts and looks up at me, a question in his eyes. I nod my head in affirmation, and he presses his mouth to my nipple and slowly licks the sensitive bud. I am about to crawl out of my skin with the intensity of the sensation. My whole body is on fire, and I can't take much more of this slow-burning ache. I have to do something to relieve it.

I lean in and leverage a push with my whole body until Jacob is lying on his back, and I'm straddling him. He stares up at me, lost in a haze of lust. Our underwear still creates a thin barrier between us, but I rock my hips, and the delicious friction it creates licks up my spine and settles down low in my pelvis. Jacob's hands settle on my hips, gripping me and guiding me into a rocking motion on top of him. Even through our clothes, the sensation is almost enough to push me over the edge.

"Jacob, please," I whisper, practically whimpering.

He throws his head back and closes his eyes before nodding. "Katie, protection. Hang on." Jacob twists and reaches for his wallet, sliding out what he needs. He looks down at the last pieces of clothing that stand between us. I follow his gaze and slowly slide my hands to the hem of my underwear and begin to ease them off. Jacob freezes. The only thing indicating that he's still alive is his rapid breathing and heaving chest.

Once my panties are off, I stare at him and lift one eyebrow. "Your turn," I say, daring him to join me. He swallows, and his hands start to drift down to the hem of his boxer briefs, but he's moving too slowly. So I reach to help him, yanking them down and off of him. Now it's my turn to be transfixed by what I see. I freeze and take him in, letting my eyes feast on every inch of his beautiful, exceptional body.

"Are you okay?" Jacob asks tentatively. I reach forward, wrap my hand around his length, and stroke him, and he lets out a gasp. "Katie, fuck."

"I guess that's a yes?" I whisper as I continue.

I chuckle deeply because, even at this moment, we're still us. He reaches for me, sliding his hand between my thighs and rubbing me where I ache the most as I touch him in turn. I inhale at the sensation, knowing that if this continues much longer, everything will be over before it begins.

"You're so beautiful, Katie," he says, and Jacob's voice is filled with some emotion I've never heard from him before. I lean forward and press my mouth to his, kissing him deeply.

Our bodies are a hair's breadth from joining, and I know he needs to put on protection before things go any further. I reach out and tap his hand, indicating what I want. He laughs into my mouth and complies. When he's ready, he reaches up, grabs my hips, and rolls me to my back, pressing his weight down into my body. Jacob loops his hands around my wrists and pulls them up over my head, studying my expression. I bite my lip as his eyes linger, stretching out this final moment before everything irrevocably changes between us.

"Yes, Jacob. I want this," I say, answering his unspoken question. His eyelids flutter at my words. He wraps his left arm around my leg and pulls it up and over his hip. Then he angles his hips and presses into me. He goes slowly, easing in, letting me adjust to him. But my body is ready and aching for him, so I angle up, allowing him to enter me fully.

"You feel…" he starts.

"So good," I say, our words synching, and we both laugh.

This isn't my first time, but I would not consider myself an expert in the bedroom. This, however, is over and beyond anything I've experienced before. As Jacob moves inside of me, we seem to connect beyond just the physical. Yes, it feels amazing as waves of pleasure course through my veins, but it's also strangely emotional.

Our hands move across each other's bodies, exploring, touching. As our desire continues to build, our pace picks up. I drop my hands down from where he placed them above my head and slide them around his back. I luxuriate in the feel of his muscles contracting with movement and exertion. His hips shift slightly, and he finds the magical spot inside of me that takes my breath away. And suddenly, I'm there, crashing over the edge, orgasm rippling through my body like a sound echoing around a cavern. And just as I cry out, Jacob follows me, gasping out his own pleasure. Jacob sinks down on his elbows and pants into my neck. I tilt my face to his and press a kiss into his stubbled jaw.

"You okay?" I ask. Indecisive Katie is suddenly making me wonder if this was a mistake. But when Jacob lifts his head from my neck, a huge grin spreads across his face, and it's not the fake kind he plasters on to win people over. It's full of joy, elation, and some other emotions I can't quite pinpoint.

"I am… abso-fucking-lutely amazing," he says. He reaches up and brushes my hair back from my face, pressing a kiss to my forehead.

"You?" He asks.

"Yes. Good. I'm more than good. I'm… wow." I stumble.

He chuckles in a deep rumble. "So Bun, how about a bath?" He asks and lifts one eyebrow.

My face breaks out into a grin. "With rose petals?" I ask, lifting one eyebrow to mirror him.

"Well, we are in the Rose Room, after all. We need to embrace the full experience," he says. Jacob rolls over and pulls me with him until I'm draped over him like a weighted blanket. I lay my head down on his chest and listen to his heartbeat. Its thrumming comforts me in a way I've never known before. His hands trace up and down my back, sliding over my ass to give it a squeeze.

"I like this side of you," Jacob says. "Less bunny, more wild hare."

I give him a playful slap. "Oh, you have no idea." Jacob lifts an eyebrow at my challenge. "But you'll have to wait and find out because I'm going to go fill up that giant heart-shaped tub."

I slide off of him and saunter into the bathroom, moving my hips a little more than necessary, knowing he's enjoying the show.

Chapter 32

JACOB

I am in so much trouble. That's all I can think as I watch Katie's bare hips swing side-to-side on her way to the bathroom. I blink, still not quite believing all of this is real. The guilty part of my brain tries to hijack my thoughts. It ranges from "I just had sex with Rhett's little sister" to "my dad is in the hospital, and I'm out getting laid." But I try to put a damper on all of that. I already planned to be away from home tonight and arranged for Mary to check on Dad and keep me in the loop. I tear my eyes away from watching Katie moving around through the slit in the bathroom door and grab my phone. I look but have no missed calls. I fire off a text to Mary, asking her how Dad is doing. She replies almost instantly, telling me that nothing has changed and to try not to worry.

I put my phone back down and stare again through the cracked bathroom door. The sound of running water fills the room as Katie starts to fill that ridiculous tub. Katie left the door open just enough for me to catch glimpses of her freckled skin and auburn hair as she moves around the space. Even though my desire should be sated, I can't get enough of her. My eyes devour her and before I even realize what I'm doing, I'm out of bed and moving toward the bathroom. I open the door a bit more and poke my head in. Katie is leaning over the tub, checking the water temperature.

I stand back and take her in, visually feasting on her curves. She turns her head and smiles at me through her now-tangled hair. "Well, don't be shy *now*," she teases. "Come on in."

I open the door further and stride over to her. Moving to stand behind her, I wrap my arms around her waist and lean my chin down on her shoulder. Her hands rise and wrap around my arms. She leans her head into mine. We fit perfectly, two puzzle pieces cut and destined to snap together.

"Are we okay?" She asks again. I answer by pressing a kiss into her neck, followed by a nip. She turns to me and snaps her teeth playfully. "Two can play at that game." She turns and presses her lips to mine. We're both still so hungry for each other that the light kiss quickly goes deeper until we're lost in each other. Katie pulls away suddenly and squeaks as she notices the almost too-full bathtub. She hustles to turn the water off and sighs. "Well, that was almost a disaster. Let me grab those rosebuds and…"

But she freezes, and I notice that she's staring at me again. We're both completely bare with no covers to hide behind this time. She notices that I'm turned on again and lifts an eyebrow. "So soon, Mr. Edwards?"

"It's hard not to be affected with a beautiful woman sauntering around me naked," I tell her, lips quirking.

"Hmmm," she purrs. "Let me just get those rose petals. There are also some fake candles over here. Hang on. She turns the switches on the bottom of the candles, and they begin to flicker with faux flames. She reaches for the light switch and turns it off, letting the warm glow of the fake candles fill the space. Katie dumps the rose petals in the tub, then climbs in behind them.

"Oh," she groans as her body sinks into the warm water. "Oh, this is goooooddddd."

Her voice sounds so sexual that I nearly yank her back out of that tub, toss her over my shoulder, and carry her back to the bed. But I have to get things under control, so instead I climb into the tub with her. Each of us takes a section of the heart to lean our backs into. Our feet stretch forward to touch, and it is the closest thing to paradise this side of heaven.

"Damn. This does feel good," I say. I lean my head back and close my eyes, doing my best to clear my thoughts as the warmth of the water sinks into my bones. For the first time in, God, who knows how long, I feel stress seeping away from my body. The low light, the warm water, the sex… At the thought, I roll my head to see that Katie is watching me.

"Feels good, doesn't it?" She asks, a hint of a smile playing at the corners of her lips. I'm mesmerized by the flush in her cheeks and her swollen lips.

I slide my hand over to her thigh beneath the water, gently squeezing it. "Feels real good," I say with mischief.

"Keep doing that," she throws back. "I could use a full body massage."

"Oh, full body, huh?" I say and lean over to her. My eyes snag on her breasts floating in the water, but I will myself to look up. She's staring at me, laughter dancing behind her emerald eyes. "You're doing this on purpose, you naughty little bunny."

She shrugs and tries for all the world to look innocent.

"Lean up. I want to do something if you'll let me." Katie tilts her head at my request but obeys. I reach for a pitcher sitting nearby. "I want to wash your hair," I tell her.

She turns around and looks at me like I have caterpillars crawling out of my nostrils.

"Okay. Why?" She asks, but doesn't say no. I dip the pitcher into the water. "Is this some ploy to dump water in my face?" she teases.

"Can't a guy just do something nice for his girl? Now, quit being obstinate and lean your head back," I tell her. She does as I ask, and I pour the water over her auburn waves, marveling at how her lighter red highlights stand out against her darkening hair as the water soaks in. She lets out a soft sigh.

"I've wanted to run my hands through your gorgeous hair for years," I say before I can think better of it. She stiffens, but I bite my tongue, refusing to take the words back. We agreed that we need to be better communicators with one another, so here we go.

"Oh? I'm not sure I believe that. No need to exaggerate with me, Jacob. We both know you've seen me as Rhett's little sister since we've known each other. Well, at least until recently." She dips her head. *Is she embarrassed?*

"Please don't bring your brother's name into this room right now," I laugh and pour another pitcher full of water over her hair. "You know that's always what it was, though, right? I didn't want to mess things up with my friend. But more importantly, I didn't want you to hate me or think I was a weirdo. Or, even worse, make things bad between you and Rhett."

I reach for the shampoo, giving her space to respond. Just when I think she isn't going to say anything, Katie says, "I liked you, too. For a long time, I mean." I suck in a sharp breath but don't say anything. "It's just, you were always with other gorgeous women, like Bianca, and I thought you saw me as a kid. Hell, you even called me 'Kid.' You never gave me any kind of indication that you were interested..." she trails off.

"And you never gave me any sign that you were interested either." I tell her.

"Because I didn't want to look like a fool with a ridiculous crush on her older brother's friend. Having secret feelings for you and you not knowing seemed much better than you finding out and rejecting me. I had visions of you, I don't know, overhearing a conversation I was having with Celia and laughing at me. You have no idea the kind of insane rejection fantasies I cooked up in my head," she says.

"Were there other fantasies too?" I ask too casually as I begin to massage the rose-scented shampoo into her hair.

She barks out a laugh. "Of course," she says.

"Do go on," I tease, working my fingers through her scalp.

She sighs. "That feels so good."

"Tell me about your fantasies, Bun, or I'm going to stop rubbing your scalp," I tell her, pulling my hands away to emphasize my point.

Her cheeks and neck flush, and she fidgets uncomfortably. "You really want to know this?" She asks.

"I wouldn't ask if I didn't. Besides, how am I supposed to make your fantasies come true if I don't know them," I say?

"Okay, fine. I'll talk. You rub my scalp."

I chuckle deeply and move my hands back to her head.

"This is so embarrassing," she grumbles. "You have to promise not to make fun of me."

"Now, where's the fun in that?"

"Ugh. Fine, but you have to tell me one of yours in return. Deal?" She asks, looking over her shoulder to catch my gaze. As if I could deny this woman anything.

"Deal," I say.

Katie inhales deeply and lets it out. "Okay, so, I used to have this fantasy where I would walk into the bar, and you and Rhett would be sitting there, laughing and telling jokes. Whatever dumb stuff the two of you talk about. Just like you used to do all the time in college. But when I walk in, you turn and look at me like I'm the only woman in the room. You walk over to the jukebox and pick out a song that's meant just for me. It's something cool but kind of cheesy. Like, I don't know, "As Long As You Love Me." And then when the song starts playing, you walk over to me and sweep me up in your arms and dance with me through the bar to the envy of every woman in the room."

"And I'd be the envy of every man," I interject.

She smiles at that. "So we dance, and then, at the end, you bend me down in a dip and kiss me. Then you tell me you've wanted me for as long as you can remember."

"And then?" I ask, fingernails lightly scratching her scalp now.

"And then that's it." She says.

"Wait, what?" I ask incredulously.

"Well, that was my first fantasy about you when I was a teenager. You weren't specific about the kind of fantasy I had to tell you about."

"Naughty Bun," I say with a rumbling laugh.

"Now, your turn. Spill. And please don't stop that scalp massage."

"Hmmmm. Let me see," I say, dragging my hands down the back of her neck and pushing my thumbs into the muscles there. She hums with pleasure.

"Remember Rhett's bachelor party? How you came bursting into that room singing and swishing these sexy hips?"

"I may have been a little overly enthusiastic that evening," she laughs.

"Well, I wanted nothing more than to walk over to you, toss you over my shoulder, and carry you into one of those shed closets. I'd push you up against the wall and kiss you until we both couldn't breathe. Then, I wanted to strip you out of those clothes and have my way with you. Against the wall." My voice has dipped, and I'm trying to behave, despite where my thoughts have wandered. I pour another pitcher of water over her hair, washing the shampoo out. As the water cascades down her shoulders, I lean in and lick a drop of water, tracing it across her shoulder and up her neck with my tongue.

"Oh," she gasps, then turns her face into me and finds my mouth with hers. My words stirred our mutual desire back to life. She twists her whole body around and straddles my hips.

"You are very naughty," she whispers, nipping my bottom lip.

"Trust me, Katie, that's only the beginning of where my naughty thoughts start. I'd love to tell you more… and show them to you." She leans in and nips my lip again. In the tub, with all the shampoo and soap, our bodies slide against one another. The sensation is maddening. I wrap my hands behind her, grabbing her ass and pulling her in close.

"Would you like to hear another fantasy?" She whispers into my ear.

"Hell yes," I growl out as my hands make their way from her ass and trace down her thighs. I'm slowly seeking her center. She presses her lips to my ear. "I have this fantasy where we stay in a bed and breakfast together, and there's only one bed and one cheesy heart-shaped bathtub. But we get in it together, and you let me ride you until we're both drunk on pleasure."

Her dirty words surprise a groan out of me. "I don't have any more protection, and I am very, very close to making that fantasy a reality for you, Bun. We have to stop."

"It's okay," she whispers into my ear. "I'm covered and clean."

This woman is going to kill me. "Are you sure, though? Don't rush into anything you might regret."

"I'm sure," she says, then moves her hips to mine and presses down. The sensation is a lightning bolt through my entire body.

"Katie," is all I manage to get out before giving into her body, to our love making. And that's what this is. I've had plenty of one-night stands and relationships that didn't mean anything. But when our bodies join, it feels as if my soul is connecting with hers. I've never felt this level of desire, of connection, with anyone, and it scares me. "Yes, Bun, take what you need from me," I whisper into her shoulder as she moves.

I don't want this to end. *Ever.* "Hang on," I say, then stand, lifting us both. She laughs at the sudden change in temperature. I carefully step out of the tub, drying my feet just enough not to slip, then carry her to the bed. I toss her onto the covers, and she lets out a delighted laugh. I go back to the bathroom and, grab a towel, then lay it across the bed. "Come here, Bun," I say in a low, guttural voice. She stares at me, her body flushed from the heat of the bathtub and our love making.

She does as I ask, crawling toward me slowly. It almost undoes me, but I force myself to stay calm. "Roll onto your back and put that sexy behind on this towel." Her quick compliance makes my desire surge. I like seeing my bunny eager to please me. I lift one eyebrow, then sink to my knees in front of her.

"Oh shit," she gasps out.

"See something you like?" I ask her what's quickly become our favorite question. She swallows and nods her head emphatically. "Good," I say slowly, intentionally. Then I grab her thighs and pull her to where I kneel. "Hang on, Bun. We're about to have some fun." With those words, I dive my head between her thighs. At my first taste of her, she cries out and reaches to place her hand on top of my head. I don't have much hair, but that doesn't deter her. She pushes her hand into the back of my head as I press into her. I've dreamed of this moment for years, and I take my time giving her the pleasure she deserves. As her body begins to tense, I know she's close, but she surprises me. Pushing me back, she drops down to where I kneel on the floor and shoves me back, reclaiming her earlier position. That's always been the way with us, the two of us battling for the upper hand. This time though, I don't mind. Especially as she settles on top of me and begins to ride me in earnest.

And just like she does with everything else, Katie takes my body by storm. We lose ourselves in each other on the floor like a couple of lusty teens.

"Katie, what are you doing to me?" I ask her.

"You told me to take what I want," she banters back.

And then I can feel her begin to reach her peak. Our bodies are in perfect sync as we climb together. I feel her tense around me, and my body responds instinctively. Together we crash over the edge, the both of us shouting loud enough to disturb other guests. But I don't care. We're in the damn honeymoon suite after all.

Katie collapses on top of me with a happy sigh of pleasure. Both of us are still damp with bath water and sweat, smelling of roses. Her damp hair falls over me, a cold press to my warm skin.

I trace my fingers over her back, savoring every dip and curve. She leans her head down to press a kiss on the ribbon tattooed over my heart. The sweet gesture makes tears suddenly well in my eyes. I press my eyes shut to keep them from falling. I don't know where this is coming from, but I don't want to scare Katie away. We're perfect together, and that terrifies me.

What am I going to do if she decides to leave me one day? I won't think about that, not tonight. I get this moment just for me, just for us.

"Come on, Bun, let's get you to bed." I rise and scoop her up in my arms. I carry her like this really is our honeymoon. My heart lurches with hope at the thought, my ultimate fantasy, but I refuse to entertain it—at least not tonight. I drop her into the bed so she bounces a little on the mattress, but Katie only laughs. She's so fucking perfect for me.

I grab the covers and pull them over her, tucking her in. I walk around to the other side of the bed and climb in. Before I turn out the lamp, I lean over and press a soft kiss to her lips. "Good night, Bun."

"Good night, Jay," she murmurs, already half asleep.

Chapter 33

KATIE

When I wake up the next morning, the first thing I feel is the warmth wrapped around my body. The scent of roses permeates the room. I hear a quiet snore and tilt my head slightly to see Jacob asleep behind me. A smile creeps over my face remembering everything we did last night. Even with the proof physically behind me, all of this still seems like one of my many fantasies.

Someone raps loudly at our room door, and I startle to a sitting position, knocking Jacob to the side. He moans in displeasure as a cheerful older woman–likely Grace–calls out, "Morning! Breakfast time." I sink back into the bed and groan. Jacob slides his arm back around me, and as I feel his body shake, I realize he's laughing. I grab one of the rose-shaped pillows and bop him with it.

"Hey!" he cries, good-humoredly. And before I realize what's happening, he grabs another rose-shaped pillow and whacks me back. And then we're in a full-fledged pillow fight, smacking each other, our soundtrack of laughter and "ow's" filling the room. This activity is made all the more dangerous because we're both still naked.

I scramble to the floor, grab two pillows, and lift them above my head, ready to go in like some sort of Mortal Kombat warrior intent on completing an epic kamikaze. But Jacob catches me halfway through my attack, knocks me down to the bed, and pins me down with his body.

We're both breathing hard; happiness sketched on every inch of our faces. I reach up and press a kiss to his mouth. He responds immediately, kissing me back with enthusiasm. Slowly my senses come back to me. I don't want this perfect snow globe moment to disappear, but if we don't show up for the breakfast Grace prepared especially for us, I have a feeling the woman will use her extra key to barge in. That's all we need.

Mustering all my willpower, I pull back from Jacob, but he doesn't let me go that easily. He moves to my neck, continuing to press kisses along my jaw and neck. "Jacob," I gasp out. "We have to go to breakfast."

"I have everything I want to eat right here," he says wickedly.

I reach out and grab a rose pillow and bop him with it again. He bursts into laughter and pulls back to stare at me.

"Down, boy. You know Grace will bust up in this room and drag our naked asses down to that breakfast table if we don't show up at 8:30 a.m. sharp."

Jacob groans, conceding the point. "Fine, but when do we have to leave? Think she'll give us a late checkout for the inconvenience of being forced to share a room?"

"Hmm, maybe," I say with a smile, then press a quick kiss to his lips. I roll out from underneath Jacob and land on the floor. "This no-shower thing really is inconvenient," I say absently.

"Don't worry, Bun. I'll make sure you're nice and clean after breakfast," he purrs.

WE WANDER DOWN TO BREAKFAST and join the other guests already seated around the elegantly set glossy, wooden dining room table. There is a couple in their late sixties, some lovebirds who might be newlyweds, and two men who could pass as brothers, but upon closer look, I notice they are holding hands. Yep, this bed and breakfast is definitely a love nest.

We sit down at the table, and the older woman greets us. "Well, aren't you two just the cutest couple? I'm Cara, and this is my husband, Hank. We're from Houma and just love checking out bed and breakfasts. This one has one of the best ratings on Trip Advisor," she says proudly. She pauses expectantly, waiting for us to respond. Jacob steps into the space, always a charmer, especially with older women.

"Well, it's so nice to meet you, Cara, Hank. I'm Jacob, and this is my..." he turns to look at me, not sure of the right word to use. I decide to play dirty.

I plaster on an overbright smile and give them a little wave. "Don't be shy, darling. I'm Katie, Jacob's wife. He's still getting used to saying it. We just got married."

Cara clasps her hands together in delight. "Oh, I love young love! And it looks like you two aren't the only ones. What about you two?" she nods to the other young couple who can't keep their hands off each other.

"Ashley," the young woman demures. "Josh," the guy says, but doesn't look up from the woman he's next to. That's weird, I think distantly. Maybe he's just shy or really in love.

"Well, that's nice, dears," Cara says. "And you two fellas?" she asks, unsure of how to address them.

"I'm Gavin, and this is my husband, Jared." I turn my gaze to the old woman, curious to see how she'll react to this revelation. Society has become far more accepting of same-sex couples, but the deep South is a different animal, and it still has a lot of barriers to overcome.

"Well, it's so nice to meet you both," Cara says cheerily, not missing a beat. I relax.

Our cheerful hostess, Grace, struts into the room looking like she just stepped out of a Hallmark movie. She's wearing a frilled apron with—no surprise—roses patterned on it and carrying a pot of coffee. "Who wants coffee?" she asks, all smiles. Everyone at the table nods in encouragement.

As Grace walks around the table filling coffee mugs, Jacob slides his arm around my back and pulls me in close. He leans in and presses his mouth to my ear. "Well, good morning, wife." The rumble of laughter that follows those words sends electric shivers down my spine. "I had no idea one night in a honeymoon suite would be all it takes to make you mine forever."

He says it with humor, but his words fill an aching place in my heart, hell, in my very soul. I shouldn't desire anything like that. Jacob and I just moved out of the friend zone, and I've already staked my claim on him like some sort of alpha grizzly bear. I swallow and smile, then whisper back. "Thought it would head off any judgment from the old couple," I whisper to him. But I know better. I wanted to publicly claim Jacob as mine, and this was the perfect opportunity to do it and make light of the situation.

After Grace leaves, Cara chirps back up. "So, how long have you two been married?" She's grinning, and I can practically see the hearts in her eyes.

I start to answer, but Jacob cuts me off. "We just got married last weekend. This is our honeymoon," he says, an ooey-gooey look plastered across his face.

At his words, Cara nearly falls out of her chair. "Oh my goodness! Honeymooners, Hank! Do you remember our honeymoon? Lawd, it's been nearly fifty years ago now, but it seems like yesterday. How did you meet? I just adore hearing other people's love stories."

I turn to look at Jacob with expectation. He just smiles at me and says, "Go on, Bun. You tell them the story. I know how much joy it gives you." Wicked delight is all over his face, but I refuse to back down.

I turn to Cara. "Well, it's kind of a funny story, actually. Jacob and my brother are best friends, and have been for ages. One night they were at this party, and Jacob had had a little too much to drink. He didn't know I was there, but he was so handsome that I couldn't keep my eyes off of him." I turn to look at him, admiring the way his eyes crinkle as he waits to see what I will say.

"I wasn't *that drunk*, honey," he says.

"Don't let him fool you. He was three sheets to the wind," I tell Cara confidentially.

She lets out a chuckle. "Happens to the best of us," she tells Jacob comfortingly.

"So there he was, drunk as a skunk. And I was there with a few of my girlfriends. I had a crush on him forever, but I don't think he even knew I existed." I hear the truth in my own words, struggling to keep it light. "So I took a shot of liquid courage, and my girlfriends and I hatched a plan to get his attention. I figured that he was drunk, so if it was a bust, then at least he probably wouldn't remember. I decided to lose my sweater, sauce up my look a little like Sandy in Grease." Cara is now nodding in encouragement. "I linked my arm with my bestie's, and I decided that I would 'stumble' into him. So there I was, feeling all sexy and confident. I strutted over to him, only to find him *kissing another woman!*"

"No!" Cara cries out, hand fluttering at her chest. I refuse to look at Jacob because I didn't plan on telling a real story, but here we are. No backing out now.

"I was devastated, but my friend, Celia, encouraged me to carry on with the plan. He had been drinking, obviously, and it was a college party. That girl probably meant nothing. I tried to channel my inner Rizzo and kept walking toward him, losing confidence the whole time. When I finally got close, I couldn't do it. I was too chicken. But when I tried to turn away at the last minute, Celia bumped her shoulder into mine hard. And I was wearing heels! So over I toppled and slammed right into the girl he was kissing. We both hit the ground. It was horribly embarrassing."

"What did you do?" Cara asks Jacob, eyes wide.

I turn to look at him hesitantly. I'm pretty sure Jacob doesn't remember that night, so we can switch our story to fiction now. He can tell them some fabulous tale of being captivated by me and never looking back. But what he actually says takes me by surprise.

"I looked at these two women on the ground in front of me. One, the one I had been kissing, I really didn't know at all. And the other,

Katie here, was the most beautiful woman I've ever seen in my life. I actually feel kinda bad for that other girl because I instantly forgot about her. I reached down and pulled Katie up to her feet, and she swayed into me a little. I had a thing for her for a long time, but she was always my best friend's little sister, and I didn't think it was a good idea. But I had a couple of drinks, so after I helped her to her feet, I leaned in, kissed her cheek, and told her how beautiful she looked."

Oh, holy shit. He does remember that night. I have replayed that memory at least five hundred times in the years that followed. I always wrote that night off as Jacob being caught up in the confused haze of alcohol. But now? Well, now Jacob is staring at me with wonder and confusion.

"Who wants Belgium waffles?" Grace calls out as she glides back into the dining room, her voice like tinkling bells. Thank you, Grace.

For the rest of the meal, Cara and Gavin take turns telling stories about their dates and long-standing relationships. The other couple stays strangely silent, so we do our best to participate in the conversation. All the while, this new tension burns between Jacob and me. I simultaneously want to ask him if he really meant what he said and never bring up that night again. What was I thinking sharing that story?

As breakfast comes to a close, we start to get up, but my foot catches the chair, and I stumble into the guy half of the quiet couple sitting next to us.

"Oh, I am so sorry," I start to say, but when I turn, I realize why the man was keeping his back to us the entire time. It's fucking Cowboy Josh, my earnest savior and dance partner at the Farmerville Watermelon Festival.

"What the?" I start to ask, but he shakes his head no desperately, face turning a dark shade of red.

"Aren't you…" Jacob starts.

"Um, must be someone else you're mixing me up for. I have no idea who you are," he says, then grabs his new wife by the hand and darts out of the room.

"Okay, that was weird," I say.

"Very," Jacob agrees. "I guess he was trying to get some on the side with you, Bun. No wonder he hauled it out of here."

It seems almost too coincidental that I'd run into him here, nearly three hours away from Farmerville, but now isn't the time to discuss it. We'll talk about it later on our drive back to Ruston—along with that little story he just told at the table.

Chapter 34

JACOB

Katie and I need to talk. Not only about our relationship and what happened between us last night but also about what's been going on with all our weird work disruptions. As I ease on to I-20, I can tell there is a storm brewing inside Katie's head too.

"So that was weird, seeing that Josh guy there," she says.

While I agree, that's not what I expected her to say. "I mean, yea. The dude has his own issues, obviously. Not our problem."

"But Jacob... Hear me out. It's really strange that he was at the Farmerville Watermelon Festival when we were... and now in Natchitoches, of all places, at the same time we were. What if, I know this sounds crazy, but what if he is behind the story sabotaging?" she asks.

Her theory takes me aback. "Katie, we don't even know that guy. Why would he be out to mess up our work?"

"What if he's working for someone else?" she asks.

She could be on to something here. "Okay, so say that's true. Who? And, more importantly, *why?*"

She throws up her hands in frustration. "I don't know. But maybe we should start asking some questions. I could talk to Kylie at the new magazine. Offer to take her to lunch, feel her out. She and I met at the Peach pageant, and I don't think that would be out of the bounds of normalcy."

I nod my head. "And Brock? Could you talk to him, too? I mean, that guy has a history of stealing other people's work. I don't think it's too far of a stretch."

"Seriously?"

"Just play it off like you're interested in that job he offered you. I'll put myself on mute and listen in if you want me to."

Katie's eyebrows furrow. "Okay, I guess I can do that. But you have to talk to Bianca."

"Katie, I'm telling you, it's not like that with her," I say. She lifts an eyebrow at me, and I sink down into the seat. "Fine, I'll talk to her. What else can we do? Maybe go back and look at that video you took at Mudbug Madness? See if there is anyone there who might have shoved that dumpster at me?"

Katie nods thoughtfully. "Yes, and I can go back through all my event photos. And I know Margie was recording some the night we had the show at the Peach Festival."

"Sounds like a plan," I agree.

"I could call Brock now," she says, reaching for her phone. But I reach out and place my hand over hers, halting her.

"Let's enjoy this drive, just the two of us, before we have to go back to the real world," I say, pleading in my voice.

Her shoulders drop, and she nods her head. "Yeah, okay. So... about that date?"

I smile. This is more like it. "You leave that to me, Bun. What are you doing tomorrow night?"

Katie grins. "Hopefully you."

I cough a laugh. "Sounds like a plan," I tell her, reaching out to snatch her hand and press my lips to her knuckles.

AS WE DRIVE BACK INTO RUSTON, all the joy of last night starts to fade into anxious turmoil. Back in the real world, I know I have to face the reality of caring for Dad. I still don't have a plan for him and don't know where to begin. I'll talk to his doctors, I decide. Maybe see if we can get a social worker advocate. But I know, in my heart, that we don't have the kind of money to put him somewhere nice. And just the thought of him being in some low-budget, state-run facility is enough to make me nauseous.

"Hey," Katie says, cutting into my thoughts. "Where did you go?"

"Dad," I murmur.

"You don't have to face this alone, you know. Just let me know what you need," she says. I swear my heart does a weird little thump in my chest at her words.

"Thank you," I tell her. "I'm going to head to the hospital for a bit and talk to my neighbor, Mary, who has been keeping an eye on him for me. I need some time to get my head on straight about all this; start working on a care plan for Dad."

Katie nods her head. I can tell that she wants to say more but is trying to give me space.

I pull into her driveway and park my car. I turn to look at Katie, noticing that she's worrying her lip with her teeth.

"Hey," I say, capturing her hand in mine. "Don't worry. I'm going to take care of Dad today and spend some time with him. I need to see if he is 'waking up' more. But thinking about our date tomorrow night is going to get me through the next twenty-four hours."

She turns to look at me, a weak smile darting across her lips. I lean in and press my mouth to hers. She answers my kiss with her own. I allow myself these last few precious seconds with her before the spell of the last twenty-four hours bursts. I want to live inside of it forever, this happy space with just Katie and me. I want to bask her kisses and banter until we're both doubled over laughing. I want to kiss her and make love to her until we pass out from satisfied exhaustion. It's almost enough to drive to my place now and pull her into bed with me.

But thoughts of Dad surface in my mind, and I pull back, pressing my forehead to hers. We're both breathing heavily after that kiss. Katie pulls away and presses her lips to my forehead.

"Call me for anything, okay?" she asks, eyes searching mine.

"I will. I promise. In fact, I'll call you tonight and give you an update on Dad if that's okay?"

She gives me a genuine smile. "I'm looking forward to it."

"And I'll pick you up at six tomorrow evening? For our crawfish-free date?"

She laughs. "Sounds like a plan."

I'M STANDING OUTSIDE THE DOOR to Dad's hospital room, mentally preparing myself for what I'll see when I enter the room. I want to cling to the hope that Dad will be sitting up, smiling, and talking to me like he used to. But he's probably asleep. Honestly, that might be a blessing. My heart thumps in fear that I'm going to be greeted with that distant, lost stare.

"Can I help you, sir?" I turn to see the nurse who has been there nearly every day since Dad has been in the hospital. "Oh, Mr. Edwards. Good to see you. Is everything okay?"

"I… " I swallow, feeling lost. "I guess I'm just nervous about seeing him."

He nods in understanding. I look down at his name tag. Ted. I should have noticed that earlier.

"I'll go in with you if you like. But he's been alert today," Ted says.

I nod. He opens the door, and we walk in together. Sunlight filters through the hospital windows, bathing Dad in its warm glow. Dust particles dance in the sunbeams, and the whole sight makes him appear ethereal, almost angelic.

"Hey there, Mr. Edwards," Ted says with enthusiasm. "Your son is here to see you."

I walk over to him, preparing for that hollow look. But when Dad turns to look at me, awareness fills his eyes, and half of his mouth lifts in a smile. I nearly collapse at the sight, all my anxiety exiting my body through my wobbly legs.

"Dad. How you doing?" I ask, trying to keep the tears out of my voice.

"Jacob," he slurs. "Come give your dad a hug." I lean in and wrap him in my embrace, lingering there to soak up his familiar presence.

"I'll give you two some space. Hit the nurse's button if you need anything," Ted says as he leaves the room.

I slide into a chair next to the bed and reach out to grab Dad's hand. "How are you Dad?" I ask.

He shrugs one shoulder. "I've been better," he manages to say. I can't help it, I laugh, overwhelmed with joy at seeing my Dad acting like himself.

"You look good, Dad."

He makes an attempt to roll his eyes. It takes him a while to get the words out, but he asks me how work is going.

I tell him all about my latest festival assignments and how much I'm enjoying them. And then I take a deep breath. I don't know how much time I have left with my dad, and I want him to know about Katie.

"Also, there's this girl…" I say. Dad's mouth quirks up in a smile, and I swear his eyes light up.

"'Bout time," he says. "Tell me."

And so I do. I tell him all about Katie–how brilliant she is, how gorgeous she is, how much she likes to sing and brings sunshine into every room she enters. By the time I'm done, I can see contentment settle over his body.

"I… want to… meet her," he says, closing his eyes. I freeze at the words, looking down to think about the implications of that, of meeting the parents. But when I look back up, Dad is asleep.

Chapter 35

KATIE

"So, um, I have something to tell y'all."

I'm sitting at the dinner table with my parents, pushing my mashed potatoes around my plate. Mom and Dad both turn and stare at me.

"Katie, is everything okay?" Mom asks.

Maybe I should have kept my mouth shut. Too late now, I guess. I force myself to sit up taller. "I'm going on a date tomorrow," I say.

Mom beams. "Oh, wonderful, honey. Who's the lucky man? Do we know him?"

My insides feel like a dog rolling in the mud. "Yea, actually. It's, I mean, he's, um. Well, he's Jacob." I look down at my plate, I'm not sure I can face any kind of shock or lecture my parents are going to level at me.

"Well," Dad says, pausing a moment. "It's about time."

I snap my head up and look at him in shock.

"Oh, don't look at me like that," he says. "The two of you have been acting like a couple since we started the band nearly two years ago. Everyone knows it."

My mouth hangs open in shock. "But what about Rhett?"

"Honey," Mom says, trying to stifle a laugh. "Rhett definitely knows. He's just been trying to get out of your way so he doesn't make things awkward for you both."

Well, shit on a stick.

"Are you really that surprised?" Mom asks. "Jacob has been looking at you like you hung the moon for years. We all knew it was a matter of time."

"It would have been nice if one of you would have clued me into this apparently obvious fact," I say, a bit defiantly.

"You had to come to it in your own time," Dad says with affection. "Not that it really matters, I suppose, but I approve. He's a good man, and you two make each other happy. The boy is practically a member of our family already."

"But what if it doesn't work out between us?" I ask, suddenly fearful. All the repercussions of what that will mean for Jacob's relationship with my entire family slam into me. "It would be like a family-wide break-up."

"Katie, you can't live in fear. It's okay, good even, to take some risks, to choose something that's scary. All the big, wonderful things in life are achieved through bravery. And, if for some reason it doesn't work out, well, then we'll cross that bridge when we get there," he says.

I'm stunned. I honestly thought this building attraction between Jacob and me was a great big secret I had cleverly hidden away from everyone. But I should have known better. These people, my parents, my family, know me better than anyone. And then it hits me that if they know, other people have probably realized it too. Maybe choosing Jacob won't be so hard after all.

JACOB: ARE YOU STILL AWAKE? Can you talk?

It's ten p.m. and I've been waiting to talk to Jacob all day. We've chatted via text on and off throughout the day, but I've been worried about bothering him when he has to focus on his dad.

Katie: Yes.

My phone rings immediately. I answer on the first ring.

"Hey, how are you?" I ask him.

"I'm okay, Bun. Good even. How are you?"

The sound of his voice over the phone is a warm blanket around my heart.

"I'm good. Better now. I missed you today." I tell him.

"I've missed you, too."

"How's your dad?"

Jacob lets out an exhale. "He's good, surprisingly good. He was sitting up and alert today. We actually got to talk for a while."

"Oh, that's great news, Jay. How are you feeling about everything?"

"Better, I guess. I still don't know what to do about his care. He'll be headed to rehab next, but the options in Ruston aren't great. I need to do some more research and figure out where he can go, and what we can afford. I'm going to be honest with you, Bun. It's all a lot to process, and it's overwhelming. I'm trying to take it day by day, hell, even moment by moment sometimes."

"He's lucky to have you as a son," I tell him.

"I'm lucky to have him as my dad," Jacob says. "And Katie?"

"Yea?"

The phone goes silent for a moment. "I told Dad about you. I hope that was okay. I just… I don't know. All of this has made me realize how short life is, and I wanted him to know about you. I told him how happy you make me."

My inner Katie dons a pink, glittery tutu and leaps across a stage. "Oh?"

"Yea, and he wants to meet you, Katie. That is if you're okay with it."

"I'd be honored to meet your dad, Jacob," I tell him truthfully.

He lets out a sigh of relief. "Okay, good, good. I'll figure out a good time to bring you by the hospital."

"Jay, I have something to tell you too. I, um, told my parents that you are taking me out on a date tomorrow. I thought that might be awkward if you show up to pick me up and we aren't going to a work thing," I hurry to tell him.

"Oh, okay. So is Mr. Ben ready to beat me up now?" he asks, half joking.

"No, actually. They told me that it was about time," I say.

"Well, no shit?" he asks. And I'm relieved to hear that he seems as surprised as I was.

"Yea, apparently, everyone already saw the chemistry building between us. I think they were taking bets on how long it would take us to get together," I tell him.

"And they're really okay with it?" he asks.

"I sort of think my parents are ready to push us down the aisle and make you part of our family already," I tell him.

He laughs into the phone in relief. "Okay, so meeting the parents is happening. Or, erm, as your date anyway."

"Just my date?" I ask innocently. A pause hangs between us for a moment, and I'm scared that I overstepped. "Sorry, I didn't mean.." but he interrupts me.

"I'd love to introduce myself as your boyfriend if that's okay with you?" he asks, tentative.

"Yea, I'd like that," I tell him.

"Okay, good. I thought you were going to insist on me calling you my wife again," he says.

"Now, that would surprise them," I say. We both laugh, and a sense of rightness fills my chest.

"WEAR THE GREEN ONE," Celia says to me from the FaceTime screen. I'm holding up dresses for her to examine. She's always had a stellar sense of fashion, and I want this date tonight to be absolutely perfect.

I hold up the emerald dress, the one that hugs all my curves, then turn to look at Cee and raise an eyebrow. "I still live with my parents, Cee. I don't know."

"And they want you to marry Jacob, so I don't see what the problem is," she says. "And grab those gold strappy heels."

"Cee, I've only been out of the boot for a week. I'm not sure heels are a good idea. Hang on."

I rummage through my closet and find a pair of flat, gold sandals. I hold them up for her inspection.

"I guess those are fine," she huffs. "Hair down and wavy. Gold hoop earrings."

I follow her instructions. As I put my makeup on, I fill her in on the rose room. All of it, or nearly all of it. Some things a girl has to keep to herself, after all. By the time I'm done, Cee's mouth is hanging open, and she is utterly, disgustingly delighted.

"Katie! You sexy little minx. I am so proud of you. And you're practically glowing. Damn girl. Well, I guess that means Dallas is off," she says.

My heart sinks at her words. "I don't know what to do about that," I confide.

"What does Jacob think?"

" I haven't exactly told him about it yet."

"Katie Elizabeth Hebert. You talk to that man of yours about that job if you are still considering it. You can't do that to him," Celia says.

I know she's right, but just the thought of telling Jacob about a potential job in another city after everything we shared together the past two days makes my insides want to crawl under a bed and shrivel up like a dead spider.

"But I haven't made any decision on it," I plead with her.

"You will have to, though, and soon. Talk to him, Katie. Trust me on this one. You don't want to undermine trust in a relationship. That's a death sentence to anything that might happen between you two. And I want to see you happy. Plus, maybe he'll surprise you. You won't know until you talk."

"Yeah, okay. You're right," I admit, my nerves ratcheting up to a tier-three emergency.

"Katie!" Mom calls from downstairs. "Your DATE is here!"

"Oh shit," I say and look at the clock. "I gotta go, Cee."

"Bitch, you better call me later and tell me all about it. Oh, wait, you know what? You better not call me tonight. Enjoy that fine man.

Call me tomorrow. I want all the details." She blows me a kiss and disconnects the call.

I slide my feet into my sandals, grab my purse and make my way down the stairs. This feels a lot like prom night with my parents waiting to see me off. Shame washes through me at the thought of Jacob having to make small talk with my parents while he waits for me, like I'm a teenager going on her first date.

It's compounded knowing my parents want me to figure out a way to get out of their house and finally be a real adult like everyone else my age. They've never said that out loud, of course, at least not in those exact words. But I sense that their enthusiasm over my date with Jacob has many layers, like the perfect cake baked with ingredients of motivation, encouragement, independence, and happiness. And the icing on top? Meeting someone who makes me happy and, preferably, gives them adorable grandchildren one day.

When I walk down the stairs, I see Jacob talking to my parents. He is dressed in a navy polo shirt tucked into dark slacks. His beautiful grin is on display, and my heart lurches at the sight. I can't believe I'm going on a real date with this beautiful, kind, amazing man. He turns to look at me, and his eyes shift from friendly to sultry in a blink. *Oh, I am in so much trouble tonight.*

"There she is," Mom says. "You look beautiful, honey." I wince a little, feeling all the world like a child playing dress up at her words.

I walk over to Jacob and begin to feel even more awkward. I know I told my parents about us going on a date, but the two of us together in front of them makes it all very real. I don't know what to do with my hands, so I start to fidget.

"Okay, well, um, I'll see you later," I say and turn toward the door. Jacob slides his arm around my waist and halts me.

"It's okay," he says quietly. Then he turns to my parents. "I'll take good care of her tonight." My shoulders tighten. Jacob means well, but it only makes me feel more like the kid he referred to me as for so long.

"Oh, we know, honey," Mom says. Then she reaches up and presses a kiss to Jacob's cheek. That small gesture releases the stopper on all my shame, allowing it to drain out of me. Seeing the way my mom is with Jacob, who hasn't had a mother most of his life, makes tears well in my eyes. *Get a grip, Katie.*

"And Katie," Dad says. "We know you're an adult. Don't feel like you have to rush home. We're going to bed when we usually do, and we are not staying up to wait on you."

"Dad!" I cry out, cheeks flushing. And hello shame, there you are again. He just shrugs his shoulders.

"Like I said, my girlfriend is safe with me," Jacob says. My heart starts jumping rope inside my body at those words. *Girlfriend.*

I look at my mom and swear I can see hearts circling around her head like deranged tweeting birds.

"Okay, time to go," I say, taking Jacob's arm. "Otherwise, these two are going to make us play board games with them all night, and I am ready for my date."

JACOB WANTS TO SURPRISE ME tonight but told me to dress nicely. I'm a little anxious about the evening, though. Up to this point, all our time together has been the two of us pretending not to be into each other. I'm not sure what to do now that we're "official."

"You look beautiful, Katie," Jacob says as he drives us out of my parent's neighborhood.

I fidget, pushing my cuticles back. Why do I suddenly feel so awkward again?

"This is where you say, 'You look hot too, Jacob,'" he mock whispers.

I turn to him, laughter bubbling. I relax. This I know. This is us.

"Someone thinks awfully highly of himself," I say. He grins, then reaches over and holds my hand. "So, where are we headed, hot stuff?" I ask, my familiar confidence filling my voice again.

"Food first, then I have a couple of options for us. Lady's choice," he tells me. His words warm my body as my eyes trail down his body and my thoughts roam to what I'd choose if I were truly given the choice. Jacob raises one eyebrow knowingly.

"For dinner, I thought Portico might be nice. I know it's not super fancy, but…"

I cut him off. "But it's perfect." I say.

We park at the restaurant, and Jacob runs around to my side of the car to open the door like some kind of old-world gentleman. Part of me wants to tease him, but… I like how special he makes me feel. So when I climb out of the car, I lean up on my tiptoes and press a kiss onto his cheek instead. Or at least that's what I intend to do, but Jacob turns his head right before my lips connect. Just like that, our lips are pressed together. It's only a light brush of our lips together, but the sensation manages to take my breath away.

"I've been thinking about doing that all day," Jacob whispers into the space between us. Then he snags my hand and we walk into the restaurant for all the world to see.

Portico is nice, but not overly fancy. The American bistro has curved alcoves for booths, and the waitress ushers us to one. We slide in across from one another. Between the alcove and the low lighting, it feels like we are in our own intimate little bubble.

We steal heated glances at each other across the table, like two infatuated teens drunk on first love. I can't get enough of him, in public, with me. After we look at the menu and place our orders, we're left to stare at one another without the protection of the large menus to hide behind.

"How was your day?" I ask him.

He shrugs. "I went to see Dad again. He's doing well, surprisingly well. I'm still trying to figure out the next steps, though. It looks like rehab will be up next, but then? Well. I'm not sure. I'm researching some options. Ruston, great as it is, doesn't have much in the way of the long-term care Dad will likely need. It's… a lot."

I nod with empathy. A huge part of me wants to jump in and figure out the answer for him. I love helping others with their problems, though I'm terrible at figuring out my own. But, in this, at least, I don't think I can figure it out for Jacob. Instead, I say, "I'm here for you. If you want to talk about it, I'll listen. Or bounce ideas off of me, or whatever." I finish lamely.

Jacob reaches his hand across the table and places it over mine. "Thank you, Bun. That means a lot to me. Right now, it's just nice to have someone to talk to about it. Makes me feel less lonely."

It feels like Jacob just wrapped my heart up in ribbons and gave them a firm tug.

"Anyway," he continues. "Tell me about your day. Anything fun and exciting happen today?"

I think about the Dallas job but see how much Jacob is struggling to keep his sad emotions at bay. Now isn't the time, I decide. Later, when things are less… tense.

"Well, I put in a few hours at the coffee shop this morning. Thought picking up the extra hours might be nice. I don't want you to have to keep picking me up from my parents' house like we're both still wearing braces and watching the time for curfew."

"Don't overdo it, though, Bun. I'm sure if you're tired of coffee shop work, Lauren would give you more work," he says, hopefully. "Then I'd get to see even more of you." His eyes turn sultry at his words. Guilt twists those ribbons around my heart, and I slip my hand from his. Jacob frowns, but doesn't say anything. I start tangling my hands together under the table.

"I didn't mean to tell you what to do or upset you," he starts. But the waitress interrupts with our food. Jacob's pot roast smells amazing, and the French onion soup and crostini in front of me are making my mouth water.

I dip my spoon into the soup and blow on it. "You didn't upset me. I just…I'm terrible at making decisions about everything. Work, dinner, men."

"Well, you did alright choosing me," he says playfully.

Dinner continues with easy conversation. And before we know it, dinner is done. Jacob insists on paying, though I can't stop thinking about what this hospital stay for his dad is going to cost him, and I feel my old friend shame rearing her ugly head. But I think I'd make Jacob feel worse by denying him this, so I try to shove the feeling back down inside the cage in my chest.

When we get back in the car, Jacob turns and looks at me. "Okay, now it's time for lady's choice. Option one: we go see a movie at the Dixie Theatre. They have some kitschy, old horror movies playing tonight. Or, option two, we go get Eskimoes custard and star gaze. There is also an option three, but we aren't really dressed for it."

"And that is?"

"Well, I've been dying to try out the new rock climbing wall at Louisiana Tech. But that means going home and changing clothes. And, well, I'm not really sure what you would wear. I guess we could run by Walmart and grab gym clothes if you don't want to bump into your parents." I wince.

I consider my options. While rock climbing sounds like a blast, there is no way in hell I'm going to pause my date to go back to my parents' house. The horror movie does sound like fun, especially the thought of snuggling deep into his arms. But, ultimately, my romantic side wins out.

"Custard and star-gazing. With music. On your back porch," I tell him confidently.

"I thought we might drive somewhere…"

"You said lady's choice," I remind him. He pauses, considers, then nods.

"So I did. At least Ollie will be happy for the company tonight," he says, referencing his dog.

"I miss having a dog," I tell him. "I really want to get one, but I feel weird about getting a pet while still living with Mom and Dad. I can't wait for some Ollie snuggles."

"Hey now, you and Ollie are going to make me jealous," Jacob says.

I stick my tongue out at him. "Don't worry. You'll get snuggles, too."

Chapter 36

JACOB

We drive through Eskimoes for custard. I select peanut butter chocolate chip, while Katie, oddly enough, goes for the key lime pie option, complete with graham cracker crumbs on top. She's delighted with her unconventional choice, moaning in pleasure with every bite—and I am having to mentally talk myself down from tossing her in the backseat and covering her with my body. I was excited about all my date options, but, I have to admit, I love the one Katie proposed the best. I still feel weird about bringing her to my worn house, but now that I really know Katie, I know I have nothing to fear.

By the time we park in my driveway, Katie has nearly finished her custard. She holds up the empty cardboard cup and jiggles the plastic spoon inside it. "So good," she says. "Round one of Lady's Choice was a complete success. Now, on to round two."

We walk to the front door. I can hear Ollie shnarfling behind the door, ready to attack Katie with his giant, lolling tongue.

"Look out. Ollie will try to lick you as soon as we get in the house. I'll try to keep him back and let him get to know you," I tell her.

I open the door, flip on the light switch, and maneuver myself between Ollie and Katie. He whimpers, anxious to meet this new friend I've brought home. But Katie doesn't miss a beat, leaning around me to ooh and ahh at him.

"Who's a good baby?" She asks in her doggy-talk voice. "Yes, Ollie, you're a good boy."

His high-pitched whines grow in intensity.

"Come on. Let's go sit on the back porch and let him out for a bit. I have wine and beer. Want some?"

"What kind?"

"Um, I've got some 318 Commotion on the beer front, and I think Pinot Noir is our wine option. It's nothing fancy, but at least it's not in a box or off the bottom shelf."

"Red wine makes me all flushed and itchy," Katie says, crinkling her nose. "I'll take a beer."

I tuck away that piece of knowledge, another thing that makes Katie so very *Katie*. Then I grab a beer for both of us. We walk out on the back patio, following in Ollie's waddling wake. Even though the sun has set, the heat clings to the cement. Louisiana's ever-present humidity is thick in the air tonight, and I light a citronella candle to help keep the mosquitos at bay. We make our way over to my outdoor couch and sit. Katie kicks off her sandals and tucks her feet under her before leaning into me. I'm her own personal cushion, and I love every second of it.

This feels natural somehow. I had fun at dinner, but I love the comfort, the *rightness*, of having Katie at my home. Ollie slowly shuffles out into the yard, sniffing at bugs and frogs.

I slide my arm behind Katie's back, pulling her in close to my side. She sinks into me easily, the two of us a pair of interlocking magnets, one always seeking the other. I slide my thumb up and down her arm, admiring the perfect feel of her smooth skin, and trying to convince myself that this moment is real. She hums with contentment. I lean down and press a kiss to her auburn hair. Her frizzies tickle my nose.

"This is nice," she says, staring out at the night sky. "I don't know the names of many constellations, but that there," she says, pointing out to the dark expanse above us. "That's Orion's Belt. See the three stars?" I turn and look to where she points, leaning down so my face is next to hers.

"I see it," I tell her. I turn from the stars to stare at her, taking in the delight and wonder on her face. I press a kiss to her cheek. She swiftly turns her head, and her lips find mind immediately, pressing a gentle kiss to them. I lean in to deepen it, but she pulls away.

"Playing hard-to-get tonight, Bun? No matter, I'm a patient man," I say as I trail fast kisses down the side of her neck. She gasps and giggles.

"Jacob, we need to talk," Katie says. I halt, fear branding my gut like a hot poker. My hackles raise, instinctively knowing that whatever she's about to say is going to tear something inside of me. I slowly pull back and stare at her, watching for some sign that she is about to dump my ass.

"Not this again," I say, aiming for levity.

"It's just," she says, her hands twisting in her lap. "It's just, well, um." Her words and hesitation are killing me. I want to reach into her brain and extract whatever she's about to say. Either that or grab her words and throw them in the fireplace and set them on fire. Fear digs its roots in my gut. *Is Katie going to… leave me?*

She takes a deep breath and tries again. "So here's the thing. Before things between you and me turned into, well, this," she says, gesturing between us. "I, well, uh, actually, um, well, Cee, um."

I reach out and cup her face, thumb lightly stroking her cheek. "Breathe, Bun. Just breathe. It's okay. Whatever it is, you can tell me." My eyes find hers, and we gaze at each other for a heartbeat. Finally, she nods.

"I'm interviewing for a job in Dallas," she says. Her words are like a strip of wax being ripped off my body. The sting her words leave behind causes me physical pain. I blink, start to speak, stop, and look down. She's leaving me. I think I'm going to be sick. I pull away from her and prop my elbows on my knees, tucking my head down to keep it from spinning.

"It's just an interview," she sputters in a hurry. "And I didn't even apply for the job. Cee sent in my resume and talked to them. Before we were together," she says.

But I knew that what we had was too good to be true. I've always known that Katie deserved better–better than Ruston, better than a small-town newspaper, certainly better than me. But the thought of another person I love leaving me causes my vision to tunnel. Yes, love. Because that's what this is, it's what it's been for years. And now, just as I have love, have Katie in my grasp, she's *leaving me*. Leaving me like Mom. Leaving me like Dad. I push up and turn away from her, struggling to get my emotions under control.

"When?" I push the words out. They come out more harshly than I intend, but I don't want her to hear the tears in my voice.

"Nothing is set in stone. I mean, it's just an interview and…" she's saying as she starts to stand.

"When?" I cut her off, hurt ripping my body to shreds like vultures on roadkill. I'm crumbling inside. And where the hurt festers, another emotion starts to rise: anger. I'm furious that we kissed, that we made love, that she let me take her on a fucking date when she knows, she knew the whole time, that *she's leaving me*.

I hear Katie step up behind me. When she places her hand tentatively on my shoulder, it hits me like an electric fence. My body goes rigid. She quickly pulls her hand away. "The interview is over the phone next Friday," she says. "But Jay, you know I'm terrible at making decisions. This doesn't mean anything yet."

I turn to her. Hurt, anger, and fear course through my veins. "Well, it sounds like you already made a pretty big decision to me."

I watch as my words hit her like a physical blow, and she stumbles back a step. I hear a whimper as Ollie wanders up to us, whole bottom shaking. He makes his way to Katie and presses his body to her in support.

"Jacob, I'm trying to tell you about this because I want to make the right decision. And you are a huge part of that decision now," she says defensively.

I clench my jaw, wrestling down my emotions and attempting to compartmentalize them in the same place I've stored the agony over Mom, the fear about Dad, all the reasons I've refused to truly date someone. It's all inside a long buried treasure chest of pain, but it's finally too full. I can't push anything else into it. It ruptures, and everything comes spilling out at once. Mom's death, Dad's progressing dementia, and his uncertain future. And *Katie. Katie. Katie.* My body begins to tremble, I can feel the shakes start, and suddenly I know that if I don't get to the ground, I'm going to pass out just like I did in the hospital.

Without thinking, I sit down on the patio concrete, place my head between my legs and start taking deep breaths. And then Katie is there, her arms sliding around me in a tight embrace, squeezing me, pulling me to her. She strokes circles along my back, whispering words in my ear. "It's okay, Jay. Shhh. It's okay. Take a breath. I'm not going anywhere. I'm here. I'll stay…"

And that's when I realize what an ass I'm being. I can't keep her here, chained to me out of some misguided fear of abandonment. I look up at her and feel a tear slide down my cheek.

"No, Katie, no. I'm sorry. I shouldn't have said that. I'm just, shit. I'm scared of losing you. But you can't stay here. Not for me. I'm not worth it," I tell her, urging sincerity into my voice. "You have to do that interview."

She stills. "No, this is the sign I needed. It's not worth it, not when you and I are just starting to grow close, to l…"

I press a finger to her lips, silencing her. "Listen to me, Katie. I'll figure out my shit, okay? You can't put your life on hold forever." Then before she has a chance to fight me on it, I replace my finger with my lips, kissing her passionately, deeply. I think she's going to resist for a minute, then I feel her melt into me, giving our shared emotions over to lust and attraction. I know, deep down, that this passion is just a band-aid to the conversation. But my heart is beginning to bleed out and I need to put a tourniquet on it before there's nothing left. So I give myself over wholly to the kiss, to my hands as they fly wildly over Katie's back and shoulders.

I feel a cold nose bump into my arm and turn to see Ollie's bug-eyes staring at me. I let out a small laugh, then stand, bending to scoop

Katie up into my arms. I kiss her again, and she clings to me, digging her nails into my shirt and my skin, desperately kissing me back. I fumble my way back into the house, kicking the back door closed behind me.

When Ollie steps in front of me, I stumble to avoid kicking him. I'm still holding Katie as we topple to the floor. We land roughly, our hands breaking our fall. I'm doing my best to hold my weight off of Katie as lays back on the yellow linoleum floors. "You okay?" I ask, but then notice that she's laughing. God, her laugh. I grab her hand, pulling her up to stand in front of me.

"Jacob, maybe we should talk," she says, a rainbow of emotions painting her face.

"Not tonight," I say, pushing her hair back from her face gently, soaking in the feel of her skin against my fingertips. "Tomorrow, I promise. But I want tonight for us. No pain, no fear, no uncertainty."

Katie slides her hands up and over mine, clasping them gently as they cup her face. Finally, she nods. I lean in and kiss her deeply, searching her mouth with my tongue. I'm desperate to taste her, feel her, and push away every inch of pain away. "Bedroom?" I ask through heavy breaths.

In response, she jumps into my arms, wrapping her legs around my waist. "Calgon, take me away," she cries delightedly. Chuckling, I slide my hands under her ass and carry her to my room, bumping into walls and entryways as I continue to explore her mouth with my own.

When we finally find our way to my bedroom, I don't even bother with the lights. I fall onto the bed with Katie beneath me. I land on my elbows, ensuring she doesn't take the brunt of my weight. My hips settle between her thighs. We're both still fully clothed, but I think Katie might rip my shirt off like a raging werewolf if I let her. We're a whirlwind of hands, touches, and tongues. I'm dizzy with longing and need and know that this is about to be over before it even truly begins if I don't dial it back a little. I start kissing my way down her neck, moving to her chest. Her dress is low-cut, but not enough for me to reach where I want to go.

"Katie," I whisper between kisses. "I don't want to destroy this dress. Help me out?"

She sits up suddenly, clonking her head into mine. "Ow!" We both cry at the same time and then we burst into laughter. My gosh, I love this woman, but I can never tell her. She can't know, she can't… Katie reaches down and, in one swift motion, pulls her entire dress off her body. She sits before me in nothing but a bra and very tiny, very silky panties. It's dark in the room, but I can see enough. I freeze at the sight, my brain scrambling at the sight of her perfect curves and her flushed skin dotted with freckles.

"Well?" she declares. "Quit staring at me and get naked."

"Yes, ma'am," I purr, snapping out of it. I start unbuttoning my shirt slowly, teasingly. But Katie is impatient and reaches down to help me finish the job. As soon as my shirt is off, she is at my belt buckle, and I'm straining to get to her, get inside of her. When she finally gets my buckle undone, she shoves my pants down past my hips, and I nearly come undone. I love how she's not scared to go for what she wants in the bedroom. I pull my clothes off the rest of the way.

Feeling my way forward in the dark, I seek out the straps of those tiny little underwear. When I finally find them, I start pulling, but I can't quite get them off. "Oh, come on!" Katie cries out, then grabs her underwear, thrusts up her hips, and yanks them to mid-thigh. I have them from there. I pull the dainty little things off and toss them to the floor, then bring my face back up to the space between her thighs. I inhale deeply, losing myself in the scent of her. I grab her left leg and place it over my shoulder, then her right.

"Jacob," she moans out. "You don't have to if you don't…"

But there is no way I'm letting her stop this. I dive into her and lose myself.

Chapter 37

KATIE

I am an inferno. A volcano. My body is on fire. I am losing myself to sensation as Jacob dives between my legs and devours me whole. The pain of this evening, of watching Jacob collapse in fear and despair still lurks at the back of my mind, but he is quickly chasing it away as he explores me with his mouth. The pleasure rippling through my body at every touch of his tongue, his hands, and his fingers is sending me up and up, a rocket soaring into space. But I'm not ready for it to be over, not yet.

"Jacob, wait," I gasp out. He looks up at me from where he kneels before me, face covered in the shadows of the dark room.

"I need you now," I tell him.

"You already have me," he says, kissing me in the sensitive space between my thighs. I whimper, wanting to pull him closer, to hold him there. But I pull away slightly.

"No, I need you."

"Tell me what you want," he growls.

He knows what I want, and I feel momentarily embarrassed at the thought of saying it aloud. "I need you inside me," I finally say. I can feel the embarrassment coloring my cheeks. But the words light a fire inside of him.

"Good girl," he says. My brain scrambles at the words, on the verge of short-circuiting.

Then he stands and crawls over my body, dragging himself up inch by delicious inch until he's perfectly aligned over my entrance. He sinks down softly but doesn't enter me, not yet. The torture is heaven and hell, pleasure and pain. I writhe beneath him, desperate to unite my body with his.

"Use your words," he says. He knows what he's doing to me, and I know he loves this kind of physical banter just as much as he enjoys our verbal sparring.

"Let me ride you," I say. I am grateful for the darkness because, even though I love to be mouthy, dirty talk has never been something I'm comfortable with. But for him? For him, I'll say whatever he wants me to.

"Mmmm," he purrs out. "What's the magic word?"

"Are you kidding me?" I squeak.

He pulls away and off of me. "Wait! Please. Please let me ride you," I say.

His laugh comes out low and husky. "Good girl." He grasps me by the hips and rolls me on top of him. I settle onto him, gasping as he fills me.

"Yes," he drawls out. "Just like that."

We move together in a perfectly coordinated symphony of desire. I love being in control and the full source of his focus and attention. Jacob runs his hands up and down my hips, and the soft sensation contrasts the friction between my thighs. It is nearly my undoing. I stop moving, then lean down, hovering my face over his. We're both breathing hard, barely able to see one another in the moonlit room. Still, though, I want to see his face, to look at him as I fall over the edge. I start to move again.

"Katie," he groans out, his hand drifting from my hip to cup the back of my neck. He pulls my face to his and as we kiss, we move together. We find our release together, both of us gasping in pleasure, tongues tangling, bodies shaking.

I collapse on him, tucking my nose into the space between his chin and shoulder. He smells like cedar body wash and sweat. Like Jacob. Like… home. We lay there in comfortable silence as our breathing begins to regulate, moving from raging storm to soothing ripples.

Jacob's arms move up and around me, enveloping me. He's a cocoon, and I'm his willing, squishy caterpillar. I can feel his heart pound beneath my ear. My eyes slide closed as I'm hypnotized by its soothing rhythm. *We should talk*, I think distantly, before the post-orgasmic serotonin pulls me into a blissful sleep.

I WAKE UP TO THE SOUND of my phone buzzing. Daylight filters through the window, and I squint to avoid its assault against my eyeballs. I roll over to my nightstand. Or at least I try to, but there is something very heavy laying on top of my right side. My brain fumbles in confusion, trying to make sense of what it is. I crack open my eyes and realize I'm not in my room. Panic starts to seize my lungs as I begin to wonder if I've been kidnapped. In my sleep. From a second-story window. But then the heavy thing next to me takes a deep sigh. I smile and turn and see… a heavily-jowled dog staring me in the face, his drool making a slow descent to the bed.

I startle and pull back, squawking like an angry parakeet. My covers drop, and I realize that I'm naked. Still naked… from the night before. With Jacob. Right.

Ollie's mouth breaks into a wide grin as he lumbers toward me for some snuggles. "Where's your daddy, huh boy?" I ask, noticing the Jacob-less space next to me on the bed. I rub Ollie's wrinkled forehead. His ears make a valiant effort to lift at my question before sliding back down.

I grab Jacob's covers, converting them into a makeshift toga as I shuffle to the bedroom door and peer out. I spy him in the kitchen wearing nothing but gray sweatpants and his glasses. Well, hot damn. I gently close the door, deciding to go in search of my clothes. I finally find my green dress crumpled on the floor. I pick it up, hold it out in front of me and examine it like I might magically transform into a t-shirt and shorts. Resigned, I drop the sheet toga and get ready to pull the crumpled dress over my body. But then I spot Jacob's dresser and act impulsively.

I slide open a drawer and spy a stack of t-shirts. Much better. I laugh when I see the Crawfish Hero one he got for the crawfish-eating contest back in May. Grabbing it, I slide it over my head. It fits me like a dress, the hemline barely covering my ass. My panties are a lost cause, so I don't even bother with them.

I suddenly remember my buzzing phone and reach for it. Opening the screen, I see a text from Kylie, the new magazine owner. She's agreed to meet me for coffee. There's also a reply back from Brock. Even through the text screen, I can read his smug attitude. He's agreed to a call later this afternoon. It's time to dig into what was happening with the festival stories more deeply. Maybe it doesn't really matter now that it's all wrapped up, but curiosity has sunk her claws in deep, and is refusing to let go. A couple of conversations can't hurt anything, right?

I carry my phone with me as I stroll into the kitchen. Jacob is humming to himself–a Backstreet Boys song, if I'm not mistaken. I chime in, belting, "You are… my FIRE!"

Without missing a beat, he spins around, spatula in hand as a makeshift microphone. "My one… DESIRE."

"Believe it when I say," I croon as I saunter toward him.

He joins me, "That I want it that way!"

I pump my fist in victory. "Epic!" I declare and wrap my arms around him from behind and clasping my hands over his taut stomach.

"Whatcha cookin'?" I ask, peering around him.

"Peach pancakes," he says. "I have some whipped cream in the fridge. I thought that sounded good."

"You'll make a girl get attached treating her like this," I say. His shoulders wilt, and I immediately realize what I said. "Jacob, I…" but before I can finish, I see his finger fly toward my face–and it's covered in whipped cream. He drops a whole glob of it on my nose. "Hey!" I cry out.

His shoulders shake with laughter, so I swipe the fluffy stuff off my nose and smear it across his cheek. "Two can play at that game," I say proudly, placing my hands on my hips in triumph. He lifts one eyebrow, then leans in as if he's going to kiss me. Just as my eyelids flutter close, I feel him rub his whip cream-covered cheek over mine, smearing my face.

"How dare you—" I start to say, but then I feel his tongue lick across the cream topping, and all of my protests stop.

"Good morning to you too, Bun," he says, then turns his back to me to flip pancakes. I stare at the flexing muscles of his bare back, contemplating my revenge when Jacob says, "By the way. I like you in my shirt."

I grin wickedly. I walk to stand next to him, turning to face him as he cooks. "Do you now?"

"Hmmm," he says appreciatively.

"Well, let me get some plates for us to eat on." I spin around and bend over, knowing full well he can see my naked ass as the shirt rises up. "Are they down here, in this cabinet?" I call, then look at him over my shoulder.

He's staring at me like he's going to bend down and take a bite of my behind.

"Jacob," I say calmly. "The pancakes are smoking."

He snaps back to the fumes now flowing from the griddle and frantically scrapes them up and drops them on a plate before turning the burners off.

"You're wicked, Bun," he says as he carries the burned pancakes to the trash and tosses them. He walks back over, reaches around me, and squeezes my naked behind.

"Now, now," I tisk. "We wouldn't want the pancakes you worked so hard on to get cold."

He grins, then slaps my ass playfully. "No, we wouldn't want that."

I sit down at the table across from him, and he serves us each a stack. I take a bite and nearly melt out of my chair and onto the floor. "Oh my gosh," I murmur while stuffing my face. My eyes roll back in my head momentarily. "These are heaven."

"I'm glad you think so," he says, digging into his own stack. "I made some extras to bring by the hospital today for Dad. Want to come with me?" he asks.

I wither a little inside, indecision ripping at me. This is big for him to ask, but my meeting with Kylie…

"You don't have to. It's no big deal," Jacob says a little too quickly.

"No, it's not that I don't want to. It's just that I set up a lunch with Kylie today. I was going to try to feel her out on the weird stuff. But I can totally reschedule. No worries," I say. I reach for my phone to text her, but I feel Jacob's hand press down on top of mine.

"No, meet with Kylie. That lunch is important. We don't need a saboteur in our midst," he says, shifting his eyes and moving his shoulders like he's on the lookout for some film noir criminal.

"I do want to meet your dad, though, Jacob," I say.

He nods his head. "You will. Besides. I need to swing by the office afterward and put the final touches on our Natchitoches story. Lauren wants it to run this week," he says.

"Maybe we can meet up later? I'm supposed to chat with Brock tonight. And then, maybe we can talk about the whole… Dallas thing?" I try to say it lightly, but Jacob's shoulders tense, and I know that no matter what happens with that, it's going to drive a wedge between us. Part of me wants to just call and cancel it. I'm so happy with Jacob right now, but as I think about my work, my career, my heart wilts a little. I loved all these summer assignments, but I knew going in that it was only temporary. I can't keep working at coffee shops and living with my parents…

"Yea," Jacob says, cutting into my thoughts. "Tonight. I'll call you after work, okay?"

I nod as a chasm of indecision yawns open in my stomach. "Yea, tonight works great."

Chapter 38

JACOB

I am at war with my panic. I want *everything* for Katie, would give anything to Katie. But I also want to grab her, hold her in my arms, and marry the shit out of her to keep her by my side.

Who even am I? A man in fucking love. This is the worst.

When I brought the plate of peach pancakes to the hospital earlier, Dad was alert but confused. One moment he was telling me how proud he was of my reporting work. The next, he was calling me "Dad" and sharing stories about his own childhood. Add that to all the tumult of this Katie-Dallas thing, and my whole body felt like it had been thrown into the spin cycle of a washing machine. My stomach churned until I thought I was going to throw up, pass out, or both.

I talked to his care team, and they let me know Dad will move to rehab tomorrow. But then? I don't know. The "what ifs" writhe in my head like a pit of vipers as I drive to the office. I'm on autopilot, and as I park, I'm vaguely horrified that I don't even remember the drive.

Walking into work, I rub my hand back and forth over the top of my head, contemplating what to do next. I'm completely lost in my own thoughts when I hear someone calling my name. Turning, I see Rhett. Right. He must be finishing up a story too. Guilt slices through my insides, and I feel like he can see straight into my brain and knows that I slept with his sister. More than once.

"Jacob, you okay?" he asks, his brows furrow and I see the worry written across his features.

"Um, yea," I try to say casually. "Just thinking about my dad."

Rhett's shoulders soften as he nods his head solemnly. "How is he?"

I shrug. "They are moving him to rehab tomorrow. He should be there for a couple of weeks. But then? I don't know, man. He's not well. He can't stay home alone, and I have to work."

He places his hand on my shoulder, "What can I do to help?" he asks solemnly. I turn to look at my best friend and see the same green eyes as Katie's staring back at me. It jolts me, yanking all my worries about Katie back to the surface to spin and tumble with worries about Dad. I pull back from Rhett, not knowing what to think about everything right now.

"Nothing, I'll figure it out," I say more gruffly than I intend. I tuck my hands inside my pockets and shrug. "Anyway, I've got a story to finish up, so I'll catch up with you later."

Rhett looks hurt but nods. "No problem. But Jay? Ask me if you need anything, okay man?"

Nodding, I turn to walk to my cube. I decide I need coffee if I'm going to power through the rest of this day and have enough energy to still talk to Katie about her–*our*–future later tonight. I veer toward the break room, seeking the Community Coffee I know I'll find warming in a pot there. I go to the cabinet and dig out an old mug with *The Ruston Daily Leader* printed on its faded white side.

"Hey Jacob," a voice behind me says. Carl holds his mug up in greeting.

"Hey man," I say back. I'm not in the mood to visit, but I can't find it in me to dismiss my longtime coworker and friend. The guy's been clinging to his job with a desperation that I understand now more than ever.

"How's your dad?" he asks.

"About the same," I mumble, not wanting to talk about it.

"I hear you got into a bit of trouble with your bed and breakfast in Natchitoches," he says easily.

I shrug. "Yea, the whole thing was really weird," I say. "You wouldn't think they'd just cancel rooms like that, especially knowing they were going to get some free publicity on their place."

"Shit happens, I guess," Carl says. "Sorry to hear the story fell through."

My brow creases in a frown. "What do you mean?"

"With the place canceled and all. I know that was going to be a big part of what you were covering. That sucks, man," he says, placing his hand on my shoulder. "I guess that means it's the end of the line for this festival series. Don't be sad, though. You had a good run with the articles... and I'm sure with that photographer girl. What was her name again?"

"Katie," I say, as a buzzing sound fills my head like a tornado of bees beginning to swarm and look for a place to attack. Or maybe murder hornets.

"Ah, that's right. Rhett's kid sister. Pretty, that one," he says. "Anyway, tough luck on the story."

Numbly, I move out of the way of the coffee pot, my eyes finding a stain on the break room table and fixating on it. Pieces are starting to click into place inside my mind.

"Carl?"

"Yea?" he asks, filling his mug.

"How did you know about the rooms getting canceled at the bed and breakfast?" I ask, willing my voice to stay calm.

"Hmm, oh, um, Lauren mentioned it in the staff meeting," he says.

And while that makes sense, I know that Lauren would have also mentioned that our story is still running and on the front page, no less. Which means that Carl knew our rooms were canceled... without talking to Lauren. The cogs of my brain are beginning to whirl faster, trying to place Carl at the scene of each festival.

"Well, see you later, man," he says as he strolls out of the break room, freshly-filled coffee in hand. I stare at his retreating form as he walks away.

I stride quickly to my desk and grab a notepad and pen. Thoughts, hypotheses, and suspicions are coursing through my brain, leaping out like salmon climbing a waterfall. I start writing.

"Is Carl a suspect?" I write, underlining the words twice. My hackles raise, just like they do every time I find the trail of a good story.

I keep writing:

Evidence:

He knew about the B&B but thinks the story is dead. Possibly lied about Lauren telling him the rooms were canceled?

1. Mudbug Madness - I didn't see him there, so that doesn't work. But what if he was there and I didn't see him? Is he working with someone?

2. Dugdemona festival - I accidentally got high, but that was kind of my own fault. (Don't take food from strangers. Always a bad idea). But! I don't think Carl knew we were going to that one. And that old couple seemed totally into making pot brownies, so maybe this is a moot point.

3. Peach festival - I saw Carl at the event. But we are in Ruston, so not that surprising since we live here, and everyone goes to the Peach Festival.

4. Watermelon festival - I was parked at work, so Carl could have done something to my tire. Note 1: Ask Margie if she still has the flat tire to see if it was tampered with. Note 2: Ask Lauren and maintenance about surveillance videos.

5. Meat pie festival - Carl knew we were going. Did he call and cancel our rooms?

Other things:

1. That cowboy dude was at the watermelon festival and Natchitoches Bed and Breakfast. Weird, but inconclusive. A coincidence?

Note: investigate Carl's family. Maybe there is a connection there.

2. What about Kylie and Brock?

I stare at the hastily scrawled list in front of me. Am I crazy? I feel a little crazy. But the prickling sensation of intuition crawls up my spine and sinks its claws deep into my psyche. I can't shake the haunting sense that I'm on to something. And so far, in my reporting work, going with my gut has never led me astray.

I grab my phone and text Katie.

JACOB: Can you talk?

KATIE: I'm at lunch with Kylie. What's up? Is your dad ok?

Right, I forgot. She's doing her own investigations today.

JACOB: Yea, Dad is ok. Just call me when you're done with lunch.

KATIE: Ok. You sure? I can step out and call you if you need me.

JACOB: All good. Just call when you can.

I put my phone down and stare at my notepad again. Why would Carl go to such extremes to stop stories that support his job? It doesn't make sense. Maybe all of this is the stress getting to me, boring into my brain like angry, tired, brain-eating worms.

First things first. Since I'm already at work, I can put in a surveillance review request. I wander down to Lauren's office but can see through the window that she's talking to someone on the phone. Her door is closed. And for a boss with a liberal open-door policy, this means it's not the time to talk to her. Instead, I head back to my desk and send her an email.

"Hey Lauren, I need to request a look at some surveillance footage. And I have a question about the festival story. Call me when you get a minute?" I hit send and stare at my inbox.

I don't know how I'm going to manage to finish this story with the locust storm of thoughts in my mind right now, but I take a deep breath and exhale. I try to bring the Natchitoches meat pie festival into focus, remembering the details and setting the stage for my story. The memories are full of flashes of red hair and bright smiles. There's just so much Katieness to all of it. I can work with that, though. I start channeling her joy, her curiosity, and her zest for life into the story. I let it shape my sentences, form my adjectives, and define my adverbs. I'm wholly lost in the art of storytelling, letting it pour out of me. My fingers struggle to keep pace with my thoughts as they dance across the keyboard.

"Jacob, you wanted to see me?" Lauren's voice punches into my writing hypnosis. I blink twice and look up at her. My editor stands above me, arms folded and resting on the side of my cubicle. She's staring at me, waiting for me to say something.

"Oh, um, yea. Can I talk to you in private for a minute?" I ask.

She nods and turns to walk back to her office. I follow her, closing the door behind me, and take a chair across from her desk. "What's this about?" Lauren asks. "You mentioned surveillance footage. Did someone break into your car?"

"Not exactly," I say on an exhale. "I suspect something weird is going on," I tell her. "But I need to ask you about something else first. And it may sound unrelated, but just bear with me." Lauren gives me a curt nod. "Did you tell anyone about the bed and breakfast rooms getting canceled when Katie and I were in Natchitoches?"

She pauses, taking the time to think through her answer. It's one of the things I love most about Lauren. She never dismisses me or anyone who works for her. She takes our concerns and questions seriously.

"I talked to Chandler in finance to let her know that we wouldn't need to include the room expenses in the budget. But that's it. I can't promise that she didn't tell anyone, though."

I nod. "Did you tell anyone that the story was canceled?"

She responds immediately. No need to contemplate her answer this time. "Why would I do that? It's running front page, top headline on Sunday, assuming all the editorial goes through without problem. But you've never had any trouble with turning in a good story, so I'm not planning on it being a problem. Unless?"

The question hangs between us.

"No, the story is solid. That's not why I'm asking," I say. She lifts one eyebrow. "I'm actually asking because of Carl."

"What does Carl have to do with any of this?" She asks.

"This might sound crazy. I know that, but I just have this feeling. It's like someone is tapping me on the shoulder and telling me to pay attention."

"Out with it, Jacob," she demands.

I sigh. "Today, Carl mentioned to me that he was sorry the Natchitoches story wasn't happening because of the rooms getting canceled. He said you mentioned it in a staff meeting. I thought it was odd, of course, because as far as I knew, the story was still running."

Both of Lauren's eyebrows lift at this revelation, but she remains silent.

"And weird things have been happening with these stories. You know about the Mudbug Madness fiasco, of course. But other things too. Katie tripping at the Peach Festival, the rooms getting canceled in Natchitoches. And, I didn't tell you because I never even realized that it might be important, but I got a flat tire on the way to the Farmerville Watermelon Festival. It all seems a little too…. coincidental. And I think the tire had a puncture. I'm going to find out more on that, but thought it couldn't hurt to check surveillance and make sure no one tampered with my car while it was parked here."

I look to Lauren for a reaction. She's deep in thought, fingers pinching her bottom lip.

"I know it might sound crazy, but…" I start again.

"No, I don't think it's crazy," she says. "Email me some possible dates and times that this could have happened. I'll talk to IT, and we will pull security footage. At the very least, it's easy to look through and rule things out."

"Thank you," I say simply.

She nods. "And the story?"

"Will be on your desk in ten minutes."

Lauren nods. That, at least, is expected. "Looking forward to it. Have a good weekend, Jacob."

I stand and walk out of her office, mind reeling. Checking the time, I realize that it's already 5:00. I hurry to finish the article and send it to Lauren. It's time to talk to Katie.

Chapter 39

KATIE

It's been an interesting day. I pride myself on being able to talk to just about anyone—from a tired, senior woman emoting about her gout at the coffee shop to a small, sticky-handed child begging mom for a cookie. But today's lunch with Kylie was unexpected. We have chemistry, like potential adult new friendship chemistry, and I've discovered just how rare that is once you start pushing thirty.

I expected to awkwardly dance around the subject of story tampering with her while she eyed me defensively and threatened to call her lawyer. Instead, we fell into easy conversation. She told me all about her plans for her new magazine, which isn't launching until January. She envisions a lifestyle periodical that will appeal to everyone, from moms to seniors, and include things like medical advice, recipes, and book reviews. Basically, everything the newspaper is not.

When I casually brought up our festival coverage, she gushed about how much she loved what we are doing. In fact, she disclosed, she's been a newspaper reader since she stole it off her parents' kitchen table as a little girl. She was thrilled to see a younger writer and photographer putting together articles relevant to a broader audience. She even offered to write a guest feature for the newspaper if Lauren wanted her to.

Was she playing me? I guess it's always possible. But it didn't feel like it. She emanated authenticity. From how Kylie described her battles with rabbits sneaking into her backyard garden to our shared laughter over my tumble at the Peach Pageant, it felt real, and a lot like things feel between Celia and me.

No, I don't think Kylie is our saboteur, and I'm honestly relieved. I *want* to be her friend.

I'm aching to tell Jacob all about my lunch with Kylie, but my stomach practically does an award-winning triple axel at the thought of all we still need to talk about tonight. And then there's that vague text he sent me earlier. I check my watch. It's nearly 5:00. I hop in my car and drive over to his house.

I PULL INTO JACOB'S DRIVEWAY right behind him, his tail lights flashing red as he shifts his truck into park. The air is thick with humidity, and I can smell the rain in the air. Charcoal-dusted clouds form a line to the west of us. And as the world takes on a darker cast, I can hear the whirring of cicadas rise. It all feels ominous.

I climb out of my car and stride over to Jacob as he exits his truck. Without pausing, I walk straight into his arms and press my body tightly into his. I wrap my arms around his waist, clasp my hands behind his back, and squeeze. I feel him press his nose into my hair, inhale, and sigh. The cicadas whine louder, and I step back to look at him.

"Let's go in?" he asks, gesturing to his house. I nod. Jacob leans in and presses a brief kiss to my lips. I taste the minty hint of gum. He holds my hand and walks to the front door. I can hear Ollie's cacophony of snorts, half barks, and toenails clacking on the linoleum as he waits to greet us inside.

When Jacob opens the door, Ollie grins widely in the way only a bulldog can. I lean down to pet his wrinkled head, and he shakes his entire bottom back and forth in response. Thunder rumbles, and the sun seems to virtually disappear as the stormy sky draws the blinds on the outside world.

Jacob steps up next to me and pulls me into another hug. "I missed you," he whispers, his lips brushing the shell of my ear.

"I missed you too," I say as I turn my head and lightly nip his neck. His laugh rumbles beneath us.

"I've got a lot to tell you, and you're distracting me," he says, pulling back. "Let's go sit on the couch and talk."

"I don't know if the couch will be any less distracting," I say, eyeing the plush cushions.

Jacob groans. "I'll put a pillow between us."

"Better make it a pillow wall. With a drooling bulldog on top," I say.

"I don't have the energy to lift Ollie. He's been overdoing it on the dog food while I'm at work," Jacob says, eying his pup critically.

The thunder rumbles again, and I hear the wind pick up outside. The wind chimes come to life, and their soothing tones starkly contrast the rumbling thunder.

"I guess we'll just have to be responsible adults then," I say with an affected sigh. "Plus, I have to tell you about my lunch with Kylie."

We both fall onto the couch, but despite our noble intentions to stay apart and talk, I sit next to Jacob, grab his arms, and wrap them around me like my own personal seatbelt. "There, that's better," I say, snuggling deeper into him.

The thunder rumbles again, and I can hear the rain begin to pelt the windows outside. It's strangely comforting. Summer storms always remind me of a childhood spent grabbing our bikes and running with them to our garage while the wind ripped at my hair and the drops pelted my face. It helps me relax.

"Why don't you go first," he says. So I tell him about my lunch with Kylie—the easy conversation, the way she seemed to want to help the newspaper, not make it go under. She even called The Leader a Ruston institution, for goodness sake.

"And Brock?" Jacob asks. "Are you still planning to call him?"

"I mean, I guess? But Jacob, does it really matter at this point? The festival series is done," I say, looking for any reason to get out of calling the douchebag.

"I do think it matters still, Bun. If whoever did this was willing to try and stop our stories, who's to say they won't continue doing that with other stories? After all, they've gotten away with it so far. What if they grow bolder?"

Jacob is passionate about this, as he should be. I've only been freelancing at the paper for a few months, but Jacob has worked there for years. He's invested in his career, and in his success as a reporter.

"You're right, I'm sorry. I guess I just don't want to talk to Brock. That guy makes my skin feel like it's covered in tree sap and dead mosquitos," I tell Jacob.

"Well, you may not need to," he says. I turn in his arms to look at him. His brows knit in thought.

"I have a hunch," he says. "And I think that as strange as it might sound, it's plausible."

"Go on," I tell him.

"So you know Carl at *The Leader*?"

"The photographer?"

"Yea, well, today he mentioned our room cancellations in Natchitoches to me. Which may not sound like a big deal, but then he also told me he was sorry the story wasn't going to run," he says.

"Wait, what?" I say. "I had to send Lauren all the photos for that story earlier today."

"Right? He said Lauren mentioned it at a staff meeting. News to me since I was at the office writing that very story," he says. "I thought it was odd. So I asked Lauren about it, and she denied Carl's claim. I started thinking about ways he could be connected to the weird things that happened with the festivals, and it's plausible. Lauren is working to pull security footage from the parking lot cameras to see if anyone tampered with my tire while my car was parked there."

"But what's his motive?" I ask. "I mean, he works for the paper. It doesn't make sense that he'd want to see it fail."

"I thought about that," Jacob says. "And I know he was irritated that Lauren didn't give him the festival photo assignments. But that still seems like a thin motivation to hurt us and mess with my car. But I guess we'll see if the footage turns anything up. We can wait and call Brock if we still need to after that."

Jacob's fingers move to my shoulder and start tracing circles there. Even with everything hanging between us—this mystery, his dad, Dallas—we still seek comfort in one another. I close my eyes and focus on the movement, basking in how much he wants me. When I open my eyes, he's staring at me, affection and lust lighting his gaze.

"Dallas," I say on an exhale, and he pauses. I've effectively thrown an ice bucket over the two of us.

"Dallas," he echoes back and looks down. A mix of emotions dart across his face, and I watch as he seems to force them all back down and assert cool control. When he turns to look at me, his poker face is firmly in place.

"Jacob. I don't know what to do about this. I want to be with you, but I feel stuck in my non-existent career. I'm twenty-seven, work at a coffee shop, and still live with my parents. It's never what I envisioned for myself. What am I even doing with my life?"

I feel his fingers start tracing circles on my shoulder again. "Katie, I want you. You know I do. More than anything. But I couldn't live with myself if I caged you here. You are a bright light, and it can't be contained in Ruston, Louisiana. You should go for the Dallas job."

Tension fills my body at his words. Objectively, they're perfect. I know he means all of them, but I can also tell it's not what he wants to say. And, selfishly, I want him to fight for me and make the decision for me.

"You could come with me," I say desperately, hopefully.

"Katie, I want that. More than anything. You have no idea. I want to grow in my career and find something more challenging that will push me. I'm tired of living every day the same way. Before this festival assignment, I barely even paid attention to the passing of time. It's all begun to blur together. And in another life, I'd follow you, follow my dreams, to the ends of the earth. But Dad needs me here. He gave his entire life to raise me as a single dad. I can't abandon him when he needs me now more than ever." His voice catches on those last words, and my heart stutters, echoing his pain.

"You're right. Of course, you're right. I won't do the interview," I say immediately. *I don't want him to be upset. I don't want to fight for something I'm not even sure I want. It's easier to stay here. I'll figure something out. I'll..*

"Katie, no. You have to do the interview," Jacob says firmly. I look into his dark brown eyes, studying the traces of gold that weave through his irises.

"I don't want to lose you now that I finally have you," I say, voice wobbling.

He pulls me in tighter. "You'll always have me. I swear you're imprinted on my soul, always have been. There's no one else for me."

I feel a tear trickle down my cheek and reach to hastily wipe it away, but Jacob gets there first. He cups my cheek and swipes the tear with his thumb. "Don't cry, Bun. We'll figure this out. Nothing is set in stone yet. Do the interview. I'm going to work on a plan for Dad," he says.

"And in the meantime?" I ask.

"In the meantime," he says. "We soak up our time together. If there's anything I've learned from losing Mom and going through this hellscape with Dad, it's that life goes by a lot quicker than we realize. And Katie, I don't want to lose a single moment with you."

My body trembles with emotion, with *love*, I realize, as I reach for him. I kiss him tenderly, affectionately, telling Jacob with my body what I'm too afraid to say out loud. *I love you. I love you. I love you.* He brushes his lips against mine, then moves his lips to my forehead, cheek, and neck. I feel his words in each point of contact, the way his body instinctively knows how to touch my own. We are made for each other, and I'm furious that it took us so long to move past our fears and claim what has always been between us.

We kiss and touch, taking our time exploring one another. It's not heated like every other time before. Instead, each brush of a tongue, a lip, a thumb is a raindrop falling into a vast puddle. Each fills up my well of emotions until it threatens to flood over. I climb into his lap and wrap my arms around Jacob's neck, drinking in his mouth with mine. It's heady, and I feel tears begin to slip down my cheeks again. I wonder if Jacob will think I'm unhinged for crying while making out with him, but instead, he brushes the tears away with his fingers, pulling back to press a kiss to each of my eyelids.

"Katie, I..." but the sound of his cell phone ringing cuts him off.

He glances to where it sits on the table, and we both register that the incoming call says "Lauren" at the same time. He reaches for the phone and answers.

"Hey, Lauren. Everything okay?" He stares at me as he listens to what Lauren says on the other end.

"Wait, what?" Pause. "That is odd. Okay. Yea, I will. Okay. Yea. See you in a few."

Jacob hangs up the phone, staring at it in his hand for a moment, then looks back up to me.

"I need to go into the office. They found some surveillance footage of someone messing with my car, but it wasn't Carl. They want me to see if I can identify the guy. Come with me?"

"That's a given. Didn't we just agree to spend every moment possible together?" I ask.

He smiles at my response. "I'll get my keys."

Chapter 40

JACOB

The rain pounds against the windshield as I drive us to the office. Summer storms are fierce and loud; although I'm used to driving in them, I don't like to. While we make our way there, I fill Katie in on the few details Lauren told me. A white man was seen bending down next to my car the day before we left for Farmerville. He appeared to be young, though, where Carl is somewhere in his mid-sixties.

Katie runs her hands through her hair as she thinks it over. "And Lauren didn't recognize him? It's a small town. Doesn't seem like there would be many people she doesn't know."

"No, she didn't recognize him, and neither did any of the facilities guys," I say.

By the time we park, the storm has finally rolled past us, leaving behind steaming asphalt and thick puddles in the parking lot. The rain came down so heavy and fast that it hasn't had time to drain away. As soon as I step out of the car, a mosquito lands on me. I slap it and stare at the smear of blood on my hand. Damn, bloodsuckers.

We walk up to the office, and I use my keys to let us in. It's nearly empty this evening. I text Lauren to let her know we're here. She replies and tells me she's in the IT office. Katie and I navigate through the rows of cubicles until we get to the IT room. The servers whir loudly, making it difficult to hear, and the air conditioning blasts to keep everything from overheating. I spy Lauren bent over a screen. Charlie, our head of IT sitting in front of her. They are scanning through video footage, pausing to zoom in on a section.

"Oh good, you're here," Lauren shouts over the hum of the servers. "Come see."

We stride over to look at the screen. I squint, leaning closer to look at the man who walks over to my car, looks around, then leans down. He's tall, wearing a t-shirt, shorts, and a baseball cap. It's hard to see the details of his face. But this guy obviously isn't Carl. He's tall, seems to have an athletic build, and is definitely on the younger side. Something about him seems familiar though.

"Rewind it thirty seconds," Katie says intently. I turn and study her as her eyes dart across the computer screen, intent on the footage. She senses it too—the familiar. I see the moment her eyebrows move from furrowed confusion to cautious recognition. "Oh shit," she whispers.

"Rewind it again. Can you zoom in anymore?" she asks. Charlie obliges, and Katie leans in, nose nearly tapping the screen. Her finger snaps up and she points. "There. See that?" she asks. "His tattoo?"

I squint, trying to make out the lines on the man's bicep.

"It's a bear claw," she whispers. We are all staring at Katie now, waiting for her to tell us more. Finally realizing that we're staring, she turns to us. Her eyes focus on me.

"Jacob, remember that guy I danced with at the Watermelon Festival?"

I wince. "I try not to," I tell her.

"He had a bear claw tattoo in the same spot. What are the chances we would see a guy in Farmerville, Natchitoches, and now in Ruston with the same tattoo?"

"Not fucking likely."

"Exactly," she says. "He said his name was Josh… But shit. I don't know his last name."

"I wonder if I can sweet talk Grace at the Bed and Breakfast to give us the last name of the man who stayed there when we did. So we could… reconnect."

She grins up at me. "If anyone can sweet talk an old lady, it's you, Jacob Edwards."

TEN MINUTES LATER, I'm on the phone with Grace. I call under the pretense of letting her know the story will run on the front page this weekend. I ask her if she'd like a copy once it prints and she is utterly delighted with the whole thing. She tells me she'll frame the story and hang it in her bed and breakfast.

"How are things going with the photographer you were with?" she asks, mischief lingering in her voice.

We have the phone on speaker, and Katie is listening to every word of our conversation. When I look at Katie, she winks at me and bites her bottom lip.

"Things are good. Thank you for asking Grace," I tell her.

"I thought you two were the cutest together. I'm glad to hear it's going well," Grace says.

"One more favor to ask you, if you don't mind," I say, coating my voice with Southern charm.

"Anything, darlin'."

"There was another couple who stayed there the same time we did. Newlyweds. We met them at the breakfast table. We hit it off, and I just wrote down the guy's first name, but now I can't find his number. I was wondering if you could give me his last name. Maybe his number?"

The phone goes quiet between us for a moment. "Now, darlin', you know I'm not supposed to do that," she says, pleading.

"I know it, Miss Grace, but I was hoping you could bend the rules a little. I had his number before, so he'll never know I misplaced it and where I got it from," I tell her. The lie burns at my conscience, but this is too weird not to pursue.

"Well, alright, I guess. Which one was it?" she asks.

"First name is Josh," I tell her.

"Hang on, Darlin'." After a minute, she returns. "I have it right here. Joshua Richter." I freeze, recognizing the last name immediately. I jot down the number she gives me, then thank her profusely. I promise that Katie and I will visit her bed and breakfast again before hanging up.

"Well, holy shit," I say, looking at the name I wrote down in front of me.

"What is it?" Katie asks.

"Come on, let's go talk to Lauren."

WE SIT ACROSS FROM our editor.

"Joshua Richter," I say, sliding my hastily scrawled note across to Lauren. Her eyebrows lift in recognition.

"Carl's stepson? That Richter?"

I nod, satisfaction at an intuition itch scratched.

"I guess this means it's time to have a conversation with Carl," she sighs heavily. "But he's out today and won't return until Monday."

"Should you call him in?" I ask urgently.

"No… no, I don't think so," Lauren says. "I don't want to tip him off, make him run, or do something crazy. I'll talk to him when he comes into the office on Monday. You two will be here?"

We nod. "Monday. 1:30. My office."

Chapter 41

KATIE

Breathe, Katie, breathe. I inhale, hold my breath until my chest burns, then exhale in a slow whoosh. I check the clock. It's 1:55 p.m., and my stomach is threatening to grow legs and run straight up through my chest, sprint through my throat and exit my mouth.

I open my email and click on the link for the Zoom call with the hiring director at Grinding My Gears, the Dallas tech company I'm interviewing with. As the app opens on my Macbook, my phone buzzes. I look down and see a text from Celia.

CELIA: You got this, babe. Channel your inner badass bitch and slay that interview.

CELIA: Also, I tried to convince Brian to listen outside the door at work and give me the scoop on what he hears.

CELIA: But I don't think even my attempts to woo him with homemade apple pie were enough to get him to break the rules.

Another text pops up on my screen.

JACOB: Good luck, Bun. You've got this.

As I stare at his words, my stomach turns over like a pair of wrestling border collie puppies.

The app opens on my laptop. I hurriedly place my phone on the side table next to me. I quickly check my hair, which is down around my shoulders and tamed into submission for once. It looks good. My dark suit jacket makes me feel more mature like I might actually be a professional who deserves this job. Imposter syndrome be damned.

A feed pops up on the video call. Jeremy, the hiring manager I've been emailing with, comes into focus. He looks to be in his fifties, white, slightly balding. He's smiling, so that's a good sign.

"Hello, Katie. Thank you for joining us. Hold on for just a minute. We're waiting for Theresa, our head of marketing, to join the call."

I nod and smile. "No problem." The contents of my stomach are having a sack race. I thought this call was just going to be with Jeremy. Breathe, Katie. Breathe. The other video feed flickers to life and a woman appears in the small square. She looks to be in her late thirties or early forties, of Asian descent, and smiling.

"Hi Katie, I'm Theresa. It's so nice to virtually meet you," she says, smile never wavering.

"Nice to meet you too," I tell her, my voice trembling slightly.

Theresa launches into a description of what the job entails. It's primarily a marketing position–taking photos of their products for their catalog, website, and social media. But the person hired will also collaborate with their social media coordinator to help humanize the company. They will photograph the company's employees, visit job sites to take photos of their products in action, and photograph customers to share success stories.

Before the interview, I was a little worried–and maybe even hopeful–that this job would be utterly boring and make this decision easy for me. But the work actually sounds like something I would adore. I'd get to talk to people, take action shots, learn from others in the marketing department. I realize that I want this job, to work with Theresa. She's self-assured, charmingly self-deprecating, and she seems very interested in me.

"Brian speaks so highly of you," Jeremy says.

"And we've seen your photography portfolio. Really impressive," Theresa adds. "In fact, we're hoping to find someone with photojournalism experience. Our brand is moving towards lifestyle photography and natural lighting. Your portfolio captures that movement, that 'slice of life' look we're hoping to achieve. And, although our rebranding process is nearly finalized, you'd be able to have a voice in the finalized assets."

I want this. My heart is practically a Gospel chorus belting out "Yes, Lord!" at the prospect. And in any other time of my life, the decision to pursue this job for all I'm worth would be one I'd actually be able to make. *But Jacob.* His name thrums in my veins like pulses of electric shocks. I think I'm going to barf, or pass out, or…

"Katie, you okay?" Theresa asks. I realize I've been staring blankly at them, lost in my thoughts.

"Um, yea. Good. Just taking it all in," I say, trying–and likely failing–to sound confident. Theresa's happy expression slides easily back into place. She's used to smiling, I think distantly.

"So why don't you walk us through your portfolio," Theresa says. "Tell us about your process, what you look for when you're photographing."

And so I do. With each photo I pull up on the screen, I talk about what I was looking for when I took the shot, or what about the particular moment urged me to pause and capture it. There are photos from all the festivals we attended this summer. With each click of the mouse, I share a close-up of seasoning-covered fingers cracking and peeling crawfish; the afterglow of a sparkler painting a design in the air at the Dugdemona Festival; a grandmother leaning down next to a tear-stained, sequined toddler at the Peach Festival; watermelon-covered faces lined up and down a red-checkered tablecloth at the

Farmerville Watermelon Festival. I click and talk, smiling as each moment reflects the most challenging and best summer of my life.

I click the mouse again, and a photo of Jacob slides onto the screen. Even though I placed the photo in my portfolio and knew it was coming, my heart still lurches at the sight. It's a photo I took of him on stage at the Peach Festival. But unlike the other candids in my portfolio, Jacob is looking directly at the camera, at me. He holds his drumsticks in his hands, mid-play. His arms are at canted angles as they move from snare to cymbal. But his eyes? His eyes manage to cross the divide between photo and viewer. They're piercing and communicate so much emotion that it makes my breath hitch. I know the photo is technically good—the framing, the motion, the lighting—but the way Jacob stares, the way he was looking at me through the lens, makes it absolutely breathtaking.

"Wow," Theresa whispers.

I swallow. "Wow," I echo, a bit dazed. I forget where I am for a moment, thinking about how blind I was to how much Jacob cared for me then, how much he loved me. Still loves me. Enough to push me to do this interview, even though I know it's likely ripping his heart to shreds.

"Those photos are stunning, Katie," Theresa says.

They ask me a few more questions about my best photography moments—seeing my work in print—and my worst. Unplanned, I tell them about the great Mudbug Madness fiasco and catching Jacob's face-first plunge into crawfish juice on video. Jeremy and Theresa both chuckle, and I realize their reaction to that story means I would likely work well with them. I'm ecstatic. I'm depressed. I'm a chaos machine of indecision.

"Thank you for your time today, Katie. Before we sign off, do you have any questions for us?"

I study the screen as Jeremy and Theresa wait patiently for my response.

"Just one," I say.

Chapter 42

JACOB

I'm starting to draw attention from the nurses. I've been pacing the hallway outside of Dad's room at the rehabilitation center for five minutes. I want to go in, to see him. But seeing Dad in this setting while knowing that Katie is interviewing with a company in Dallas is enough to make the edges of my vision darken with anxiety again. So, instead, I'm pacing and trying to hype myself up.

"Sir," a nurse says, touching my elbow lightly. I turn and face the woman in her mid-fifties with a false smile plastered across her face. I can tell she's wondering if I escaped the mental health ward. "Can I help you with something?"

"I'm just, um, here to visit my dad," I say lamely.

"His name?"

"George Edwards."

Her shoulders relax. "This is the right room," she says, nodding at the door I've been pacing in front of like I'm not sure if I'm in the right place.

"Ah, thanks," I say. And with no other choice, I turn to the door and let myself in. This room has a slightly more homey feel than the hospital. The walls are dusky pink, and I can make out the shapes of roses on the wallpaper. The sight of them shoves me back into that night with Katie in Natchitoches. The warm feeling of happiness that courses through my body at the memory gives me the boost I need to approach Dad.

He's up and sitting in a recliner, food tray in front of him. He's staring out the window, seeming to admire the robins that hop around on the ground devouring the worms that have climbed to the surface after the rain earlier today. Dad's always had a thing for birds. After Mom died, we used to sit outside with two pairs of binoculars and a worn copy of *Birds of Louisiana* between us. We took turns making notes on the pages–where we spied a certain kind of bird, the time of year, and its activity. He told me different birds had meanings. It comforts me to see him watching them now. Dad's still in there.

"Hey, Dad," I say easily, walking up behind him and sliding a hand over his shoulder. His only acknowledgment is a blink. He doesn't move his eyes away from the birds hopping outside the window. "It's Jacob, your son," I try again. Nothing.

Sighing, I grab a folding chair leaning against the wall, and drag it over to sit next to him. My heart aches like it's been run over by a truck, but I have to stay calm. Have to breathe. Sitting next to him, I reach over and hold his hand. I give it a small squeeze, and he returns the gesture. I turn to watch where he stares out the window. This, at least, is familiar.

"Dad, I miss you," I finally say into the silence that hangs thick between us. No response. "I miss you so much, and I'm in love. I wanted to tell you, wanted you to know. You'd like Katie. She's way out of my league, but you'd never know it. She treats everyone with love and respect, kindness and compassion. She's the only woman who's ever made me feel this sense of rightness. Of home. Did you feel that way about Mom?"

I turn and look at him, studying his face. Nothing. I turn to stare back out the window.

"I wonder that sometimes. I remember Mom as this bright light, all sunshine and chocolate chip cookies, watering cans, and pansies in the yard. I wish I remembered more. I should remember more. But I think she would like Katie, too. They'd probably get a kick out of singing together and snuggling with Ollie. God, I wish that were possible," I say, a sob threatening to slide into my voice.

Dad doesn't utter a word as I clutch his hand.

"But Dad, I think she might be moving to Dallas, and I don't know what to do. I can't lose her, but I can't lose you."

A flash of red grabs my attention outside the window, and I watch as a cardinal lands on the bird feeder perched on a pole outside the window. *A deceased loved one is thinking about you.* My mind recites the words Dad told me every time we'd see a cardinal together. Mom, I think. I see you, I love you. I watch as the little red bird pecks at the seed, wishing that it could carry a message to Mom for me. But as I continue to stare at it, I hear a loud caw. A dark shape swoops down to land on the grass near the bird feeder. The cardinal startles and flies away, giving up its domain to the ebony raven. I shiver. Again I turn to look at Dad, but he hasn't moved. He's still sitting and staring at the bird.

ON MY DRIVE BACK HOME, my cell phone rings. I look down to see "Bun" on the screen. My stomach lurches with joy and fear, anticipation and regret. I take a steadying breath, then answer the phone.

"Hey, you. How did the interview go?"

"It went… really well, I think," Katie says, a bit reluctantly. The battle between joy and despair rages in my heart at her words.

"That's really wonderful, Bun. I knew you'd slay it." But even I can hear the false happiness in my voice.

"Can I come by? I want to tell you all about it. And I want to hear how things went with your dad today," she says. Her false hope echoes my own.

"Yea, of course. I'm almost home. I don't have much in the way of dinner at the house, but I'll swing by the grocery store and grab a couple of things."

"Why don't you let me cook for you tonight?" Katie asks.

"You don't have to…"

"I want to. I'll see you in an hour," she says.

"Alright, I l… look forward to it. See you then." As I end the call, I realize that I almost told Katie I love her. I can't do that to her, can't make her think she has to stay here. *Get a grip, Jacob.* Maybe I'd have better luck with placing duct tape over my mouth.

I SEE KATIE'S CAR pull into the driveway and jump up to greet her. *I'm as bad as Ollie*, I think, looking at the grinning dog next to me. I walk to her car door and hurry to help her with the grocery bags she's pulling out of the back seat.

"Hey there, handsome," she says before standing on tiptoe to press a kiss to my lips. Her smell of coffee and lavender engulfs me, making me feel as high as those infamous Dugdemona brownies.

"Hi gorgeous," I say, pulling back and brushing a kiss to her cheek. I can already hear Ollie whining from the other side of the door. That damn dog has it as bad for Katie as I do.

"I guess you better come on in. I think Ollie missed you," I say wryly.

"Well, let's not keep him waiting," Katie says, lifting a brow. Good grief, this woman is sexy. I know we need to go inside and discuss all of it–Dad, Dallas, whatever the hell this cowboy guy did to my car. But all I want to do is take her inside and kiss her senseless, get lost in her body, and pretend like everything is normal.

Pushing those thoughts aside, I unlock the front door, and we step inside. I go through my usual routine of pushing Ollie back with one foot while he grunts and attempts to shuffle to Katie.

"Hey, boy," she coos. "Just let me put these groceries down, and I'll give you all the snuggles."

"Hey now, I'm going to get jealous. I want some of those snuggles."

"Well, then I guess you better be a good boy."

Yep, I'm gone for this woman. I raise an eyebrow at her challenge. "But what if I *want* to be bad?"

"Well then, I guess I'll have to punish you," she quips back. "But first, dinner."

She steps to the sink and washes her hands before turning to the paper bags full of groceries.

"What can I do to help?" I ask, eying the produce she sets out on the table.

"How do you feel about peeling carrots and potatoes?"

"I think I can manage that." I walk around to the kitchen drawer and dig through its contents for the peeler. This is nice. It's been a while since I cooked a meal. These days, with only me at the house, I'm doing good to heat up a can of soup before crawling into bed and obsessing over everything going wrong in my life.

I carry the veggies over to the trash can and get to work. The sensation of picking them up and sliding the peeler along their skins reminds me of Mom. I used to sit with her as a kid while she stood behind me and moved the tool in my hand. "Don't press too hard," she'd say. "You don't want to take chunks out of it. Nice and easy." I'm lost in the memory and the movement when I hear music blaring to life. I look up to see Katie's grin slide into place as she toys with a Bluetooth speaker she brought with her.

The Spice Girls, of all things, blares through the speaker, and Katie starts moving her body to the music and singing as she rinses off my freshly peeled carrots in the sink. "If you wanna be my lover, you have got to give. Taking is too easy, but that's the way it is."

The music is upbeat, and Katie's movements are full of life. But the lyrics, despite Scary Spice shouting them at me, hit a little too close to home. I keep my head down, peeling potatoes, sneaking glances to study Katie's body in her shorts and tank top, her auburn ponytail swinging with her movements.

"Okay, start dicing these onions," she tells me. I've got to get a roux going, and I need these to be ready as soon as it's done."

"Yes, ma'am," I say. She winks and then turns to dig through my kitchen drawers and cabinets, pulling out measuring cups and spoons. *Katie fits here, dancing in the kitchen, sharing cooking duties with me. I* blink. *No, no, she doesn't.*

The music switches, and Hanson starts singing "Mmm Bop." I love her taste for music from the 1990s. I can't help but sing along to this one, and soon the two of us are belting the nonsensical lyrics as we work in tandem. Our movements around the kitchen, anticipating where the other will be, adjusting to get out of the way, dropping veggies into the pot on the stove–it's all like a coordinated dance.

Once the soup–a concoction she calls "yellow soup" that her mom made her as a child in an effort to sneak veggies into her children's diets–starts to simmer, we can take a break for half an hour while it cooks.

When the Goo Goo Dolls' "Iris" blares through the speaker, I'm seized by a sudden memory of Katie's fantasy that she confided in me when we were in Natchitoches together. One of me spying her in a bar, walking up to her and pulling her into a dance. I reach out and grab Katie's hand, twirling her into me. I slide my arm around her lower back and extend our clutched hands out in a mock waltz.

"Hmmm," she purrs, laying her head on my chest.

"I know it's not a bar, but maybe this dance will do until we can go out to one… maybe in Dallas?"

Katie tenses in my arms but doesn't stop swaying with me. I whisper to her, "Tell me about the interview, Bun. I want to know all about it."

I feel her inhale deeply, then let it all out. She starts talking, her head never leaving my chest. She tells me about the interview, about the position, and what will be required. Katie talks me through her portfolio and their responses, telling me how wowed they were by a photo she took of me. My heart clenches. It's too much.

"And Jacob, I asked them about flexibility," she says, finally pulling back to look me in the eyes. She bites her lower lip in contemplation, then continues. "About working remotely and flexible hours. They seem really open to the idea. I was thinking that, well, maybe I could work some from Ruston when I'm doing photo editing and stuff. That way, we could spend more time together, and you can be here for your dad."

There's a question in her eyes like she wants me to tell her this is the decision she needs to make. And I want to. I want to tell her anything and everything that will make her happy.

"Katie, that's. Wow. That's amazing. It sounds like they really want you working for them."

She bows her head in humility. "Yeah, I mean, I don't have a formal offer or anything yet, but I think they do." She peers back up at me, a tentative smile on her face.

"But Katie, you can't worry about me back here. It sounds like you need to be on-site most of the time, and I'm only going to hold you back."

"Jacob. Seriously?" she demands. "Did you hear what I just said? I *want* to be with *you*. And I found a job where I can make that happen. If not all the time, then a lot more than I originally thought. I know this stuff with your dad feels too big to carry right now. But I'm here for you because I want to be, not because I feel like I'm martyring myself in the name of love."

The word hangs between us. Love.

"I um," she stammers, color climbing up her face. "I just mean that…"

"I love you too, Bun." The words practically rip out of my mouth before I can stop them. I didn't want to tell her. Well, *I did*, but I didn't want it to influence her decision. But, hell, this is all I've wanted for years now, and to have her in my arms saying these words is my undoing.

I lean into her, kissing Katie desperately, allowing the love in our hearts to drive our passion. She kisses me back just as furiously, desperately, our bodies communicating all the love and desire that our words can't. Just as I reach for the hem of her shirt, the timer goes off.

"Dammit," I whisper into her lips, wet and swollen from our frantic kissing.

"Let's eat," she says, pulling away. I growl in desperation. "Don't worry, bad boy. You'll still get your punishment later." Then she turns and walks to the stove. "Grab the bowls, will you? And some spoons."

I do as she bids, setting my small kitchen table for the two of us. Ollie doesn't get the memo, though, because he saddles up to the side of the table and sits down expectantly, ready to consume anything that even pretends to be food falling his way.

"We have an audience, I see," Katie says, raising an arched eyebrow at my needy mutt. He clacks his teeth in agreement.

"So, tell me about how things went with your dad," she says, digging into the soup.

I shift uncomfortably in my seat. "It's not great, Bun. Today he was up and awake but didn't acknowledge me at all. He just stared out the window at the birds the whole time. I wish I could, I don't know, shake him, wake him up somehow."

Katie looks at me with empathy in her eyes. "Any luck on finding a place for him after he's done in rehab?"

"Not really. I think skilled nursing at home during the day would be a better option for him. He seems to be so confused all the time. At least having a place he recognizes might help. I don't know, though, because sometimes he knows exactly who I am and where he is. But today, he seemed like an empty shell. It's hard to know the best course. And that doesn't even factor in what we can afford. Dad has a lawyer, someone who helped him manage Mom's small life insurance money after she died. I don't know what he did with those funds, but we've always lived modestly. I have to hope that there's something out there I don't know about yet."

Katie reaches across the table and squeezes my hand. "What can I do to help?"

I sigh deeply, wishing I had an easy answer for her, for me, for Dad. "Stay with me tonight?" I ask. "I, well, I'm struggling at night time. Having someone here with me to help keep the thought demons away would be nice. Especially if that someone is you."

"I'm definitely a bigger and badder demon than any of the ones living in your head," she teases. My heart lightens just a bit at her words. "Yes, of course, I'll stay." Relief washes over me in a cool wave. "Besides, how else am I going to be able to mete out your punishment?"

Chapter 43

KATIE

As we finish dinner, I stand up and pick up our dishes, carrying them to the sink. I hear Jacob walk up behind me. He slides his large hands slide around my waist, their warmth and weight a balm to my soul. I lean my head back, resting it against his chest, resting in him. I wish I could scoop him up, put him in my pocket, and take him with me to Dallas. I wish I could put his dad in my other pocket and take him, too. And then I'll miraculously heal Jacob's dad while I'm dreaming of the impossible.

As if the universe hears my plea, the next song comes on my 90s playlist: "The Boy is Mine" by Monica. *Do not allow the 90s R&B to make you cry, Katie. I mentally chastise myself.*

Sensing that my tear ducts are about to overflow, Jacob leans down and, in a gravelly whisper, says, "I'm ready for my punishment now."

That does the trick. I pull back from him and lift an eyebrow. "Are you sure about that?"

"Oh yes, I'm sure."

I take his hand and lead him back to his bedroom. Ollie trots along behind us, but as we get to the bedroom door, I look down at him. "Sorry buddy, not this time." And I close the door behind us, leaving our four-legged friend to find another bed for the night.

JACOB AND I SPEND the entire weekend in each others' arms, soaking up this time together like it might be our last. My parents now know about the job interview and while they fully support me, they have been a bit weepy at the prospect of me moving away... even though it's only a four-hour drive.

I try not to think about any of that, though, instead giving my mind and body wholly over to Jacob. We explore every inch of one another, figuring out what makes the other tick. We laugh over coffee, spoon in bed, and make an utter mess of his bedroom. The sheets and comforter are in twisted piles on the floor. There are underwear and t-shirts draped over dressers and lamp stands. I only leave briefly to run home to get some fresh clothes when I know Mom and Dad are over at Rhett and Amelia's house. I know they support my relationship with Jacob, but I'm not ready for knowing glances and smirks from my parents yet. *Shudder.*

I don't want this weekend to ever end. But all too soon, it's Monday morning, and the alarm is going off. Anxiousness snags my stomach, and it takes a minute for my brain to catch up with what my body is telling me. *Today's the day that Lauren confronts Carl. Right. Okay.*

I turn in Jacob's arms and attempt to make my way out of our love nest. But he holds on tightly to my waist. "Mine," he says, eyes still closed.

"Yes, and you're mine. But we have to get ready for work. It's C-Day."

This is what we've taken to calling the day that Lauren will confront Carl with his stepson's presence in our parking lot. Lauren has prepared for all potential outcomes. She's already sent the surveillance footage to the police, and there will be an officer there for the whole thing. But it makes me nervous. I don't know how Carl will react. Will he seek retribution on Jacob? On me? The longer I think about it, the more jittery I get. It feels like I drank two shots of espresso, then chased it with a monster energy drink. If I lay here any longer, I might spontaneously transform into a spitting, hissing cat. Though if last night was any indication, Jacob might like to see my claws. Feel them too. I attempt to get out of bed again, and this time Jacob lets me slide out of his embrace, even though he groans in protest.

"Come on, lazy bones. Aren't you curious to see what's going to happen with Carl today?" I ask as I pull on my shorts.

I turn and look over my shoulder at Jacob, ready to prod him to get out of bed. But when I turn, I notice that he's staring at me. No, not staring, not exactly. But watching me, enjoying me. I return the favor, studying his broad chest, eyes drifting to the ribbon tattooed over his heart. The ribbon I now know is for the mother he lost too young to breast cancer. My eyes trail back up, admiring the stubble on his square jaw, and I'm consumed with the urge to press into him like an attention-starved cat, claws and all. Maybe even bite him. Just a little.

His mouth quirks in a half grin. "God, I love it when you look at me like that, Bun. But if you keep doing that, we're never going to make it to the office in time." His last few words come out in a low rumble. It sends shivers racing through my body.

"Later," I force out.

Jacob pushes up until he's sitting and reaches for his glasses. Once they're on he leaps across the bed like a panther, full of power and grace. He scoops me up and twirls me around before planting a kiss on my lips. "Alright. Let's do this, Bun."

RHETT, JACOB, AND I are huddled around Jacob's laptop in his cubicle. We chose the workspace where we could conveniently peer over the cubicle wall to see Lauren's office. It's nearly 1:30 p.m., and Carl is due to meet with her at any moment. We have no idea what Lauren told him they are meeting about, but my nerves are currently sitting somewhere between "just got pulled over by a cop with pot brownies in the car" and "high voltage Jurassic Park velociraptor fence."

"Katie, take a breath. It's going to be okay," Rhett says, cool and collected like always.

"But what if he loses his mind and, I don't know, grabs a fire extinguisher and.."

"And extinguishes Lauren?" Jacob quips.

"Ha ha, very funny," I say dryly.

We hear the footsteps as they approach. I hold my breath, listening for voices.

"Don't be weird," Rhett whispers. And then, more loudly, he starts talking about a story he's working on, attempting to normalize our situation.

When the footsteps pass, I peer over the wall of the cubicle just in time to see Carl walk into Lauren's office and close the door. We sit and wait, all three of us now unable to manage anything close to a normal conversation. We're all nerves. I feel Jacob place his hand on mine, rubbing small, comforting circles over the back of my hand.

I look at Rhett, but when he catches my gaze, he smiles and shrugs. "What, like it's a surprise?" he asks incredulously. "You two have been flirting relentlessly for nearly two years. Honestly, it's a relief to every one of us who has had to suffer through the sexual tension that fills the room anytime the two of you are there at the same time."

"Don't be gross," I tell my brother. But he just snickers.

The tension of waiting to see what is going to happen with Carl is thick around us, and we finally shed all pretenses of playing it cool. The three of us stare over the edge of the cubicle wall like a set of spying neighbors intent on getting the tea. The shades are halfway up in Lauren's office, allowing us a partial view of what's happening inside.

Inside, Lauren stands with a security officer next to her. She's leaning forward, hands pressed into the smooth, large mahogany desk, a barrier between the two of them and Carl. And Carl is standing too. It all seems very… calm. Like they are having a normal conversation.

"Well, this is sort of anti-climatic," I whisper.

"See, nothing to be worried about," Rhett says.

Just as he says that, their voices starts to rise. Carl has gone from standing stock still to gesticulating wildly. Others have stopped to stare.

"Shit's getting real," Jacob murmurs.

Lindsey, who was making copies near Lauren's office, has a look of utter horror on her face. She can obviously hear more than we can. "Let's go," I say and leave Jacob's cubicle, walking to stand next to Lindsey.

"What's he saying?" I ask her.

"A lot of profanity, honey. Something about 'no respect.' I wonder what's got his undies in a bunch?" she muses.

Carl turns toward the door, fury written all over his face. He turns the handle, opening the door just enough for the sound to escape.

"You wait right there, Carl Richter," Lauren says, starting toward him, but she halts as Carl seems to hit peak eruption. He spins and stares at her, a feral look in his eyes. He takes one step toward her, but the security officer steps into the space between them, raising his hands in a "let's calm down" gesture.

"This is an outrage!" Carl is yelling, his color changing from tomato to plum. "I have been at this newspaper for thirty years. THIRTY! And the first time a new opportunity comes along that pays better than anything in years, you give it to some no-talent slut who has never even professionally photographed anything in her life."

The words are like a physical blow, and I step back in half retreat. His words drag up all the feelings of shame, fear, imposter syndrome, and indecision that I've been battling with for years. But Carl's not done.

"Is that what it takes to get ahead around here? She just had to sleep with Edwards to get an assignment a long-term photographer should have gotten? Is that what you had to do, Lauren? Who did you have to fuck to get this editor position?"

I'm so focused on Carl's vitriol, so taken aback by the words spewing from his mouth, that I didn't even notice Jacob leave my side. One moment I'm having tunnel vision and questioning every decision I've ever made in my life that brought me here. The next, I'm staring in stunned horror as Jacob tackles Carl. The two slam to the ground, Carl the unfortunate piece of salami slammed in a sandwich between the floor and Jacob. *Oh shit. I should probably do something.*

But no one does, at least not immediately. Jacob sits up, his body still on top of Carl's. He pulls one fist back and slams it into Carl's jaw. I wince. That had to hurt. Jacob pulls back his fist to land another blow, but the security officer grabs his arm and attempts to pull Jacob off of the now sobbing man beneath him. But Jacob isn't stopping. Hell he hasn't even acknowledged the security officer. I need to do something before Jacob gets arrested.

I hurry over to the pair of them, unsure of what to do. Carl is laying on the floor, hands covering his face in an attempt at protection. Jacob is laser-focused on his face and trying to pull away from the officer attempting to constrain him. The cop is yelling at him to stand down, but Jacob probably has a good thirty pounds of muscle on the guy. Lauren is yelling for everyone to chill the fuck out.

I step in front of Jacob and bend down to his eye level, dipping my head until it's just above Carl's to meet his gaze. "Jacob, hey, it's okay. It's okay. Calm down, baby." I reach out and slide a hand over his chest, feeling his racing heart beneath my palm. It takes a moment, like bullet time in *The Matrix*, where everyone seems to freeze in place, waiting, hoping. Finally, Jacob's body relaxes. He inhales deeply, closes his eyes, and exhales. When he opens them again, the madness has faded.

"I'm okay, man. You can let go," Jacob tells the officer.

"You promise not to hit him again?" he asks firmly. Jacob nods. The cop lets go, and Jacob takes a deep breath, rising to a stand.

Carl, however, seems intent on going out with a bang. Because just as Jacob turns his back to him, Carl snarls out, "What is it about this little whore that makes everyone jump to do her bidding?"

Jacob whirls around and slams a hard kick into Carl's ribs. I'm pretty sure I heard bones crunch, and it makes me feel nauseous. Jacob eyes the cop, who stares at him incredulously. "Seriously?" he asks.

"What? I didn't *hit* him," Jacob says with a shrug. Then he turns and storms out of the office, not looking at any of us. I turn to race after him, distantly noticing the cop placing handcuffs around Carl's wrists.

By the time I catch up to Jacob, he's nearly out the front door. "Wait up, Jay!" I call out to him, but he doesn't stop. He marches out the front door, past his car, and just keeps going.

"What the actual fuck, Jacob?" I yell. That seems to knock him out of whatever lava-monster rage trance he's in. He spins, and I see tears streaming down his cheeks. It jolts me, shaking me to my core. I've never seen him like this, livid and… I don't know exactly. But nothing he could do or say will stop me from trying to comfort him. I stride up to Jacob, then slide my hand up his chest and over his thrumming heart.

"Hey, take a breath, babe. It's okay."

"It's not," he says.

"It is. I saw the cop putting Carl in cuffs before I followed you. They obviously found something damning. I think it's safe to say he'll never work at the paper again."

"Is that what you think I'm upset about?" he says, looking at me like I just told him I like maple syrup on my cheese toast. "Katie. Did you *hear* what that asshole said about you? About Lauren? He deserved much worse than a punch to the face."

"Well, I think you probably broke a rib or two," I say, trying for levity. He cracks a half smile that doesn't reach his eyes.

"Katie, no one deserves to be spoken about like that. I always knew the jackass strayed a little into sexist asshat territory, but that… he should be arrested and thrown in jail with a bunch of armed female guards who have permission to beat him at will."

"Is that a sexual fantasy?" I try again. He finally looks at me, really looks at me, with a hint of humor sparkling behind his eyes.

"It does always come back to punishment with you, doesn't it, Bun?" I smile at that.

"Come on you. Let's go back and talk to Lauren and find out what happened."

Chapter 44

JACOB

That mother fucker.

The words are on repeat in my brain as we walk back to the office. Once we're inside, I search for signs that Carl is still there, but the cop car is gone and I assume, Carl with it. The tension in my shoulders lessens slightly. But I'm still spoiling for a fight, desperate to release the pressure valve on my emotions. Katie squeezes my hand like she knows what I'm thinking, telling me she's there, she has me. All of it is just so much–Dad, Dallas, all of it–and Carl was the tipping point. And he was the perfect, deserving target of my rage. I want to follow him to the police station and finish what I started, turn him into a lump of blood and bruises. I've never been inclined to physical violence, but… I turn to look at Katie, the woman I love. I would do anything for her. She's done so much work to build herself up, figure out her career, and that asshole made her sound like some kind of slutty ladder climber.

"It's okay," she whispers again.

When we finally make it to Lauren's office, she's there talking to a different police officer. I start to turn away, but when Lauren spots us, she beckons us inside. We step in, and I close the door behind us.

"Are you okay?" I'm not sure which of us she's directing the question to, so I turn and look at Katie.

"Yea, um. Okay, I guess," Katie says.

"And you?"

I shrug, "I've been better."

"What you did was stupid," Lauren says to me. "You could have been arrested for assault, Jacob. Probably should have been."

"The bastard deserved it," I say, refusing to let her make me feel guilty. Not about this.

Lauren's lip quirks. "I suppose he did."

"What did Carl say about the video footage?" Katie jumps in. She's been worried about this ever since we first connected the dots.

Lauren looks at the officer next to her. "Actually, I think we need a statement from the two of you first." The cop nods, and she steps forward, pen in hand, recorder at the ready.

WE SIT IN LAUREN'S OFFICE for over an hour, giving testimony of every time we've seen Carl over the past six months. We're asked to detail what our interactions with him have been like if he's displayed any strange behavior, and when and where we've seen him and his stepson. The longer the questions go on, the more I feel the adrenaline ebb from my body, a wicked headache taking its place. I suddenly, desperately, want nothing more than to crawl into bed and tug Katie in with me, forming a perfect bubble of protection against the chaos of this day.

Once the officer is done taking our statements and finally leaves, Lauren turns to us.

"Carl confessed to all of it," she says. "At first, he denied any knowledge of interfering with you two, but once we pulled up the footage of his stepson on the security cameras and he realized precisely why I had an officer with me, a light switch seemed to flip in his brain."

"He went from quietly cursing about his worthless, idiot stepson to giving a speech that even the most diabolical evil villain overlord would be proud of. It's like he wanted us to know that all the times he got away with it were because of his genius planning. He told us about following you to Mudbug Madness. At first, he said that he wanted to watch Katie fail so he could step in and save the day, prove to me what a mistake I made in hiring you. But once he realized that wasn't happening, he decided to take matters into his own hands and shoved that dumpster at you, Jacob."

"But it backfired," I say, remembering how Katie's video went viral.

Lauren nods. "And so he decided he needed to do something to take Katie out of the picture. I don't think he ever had intentions of doing you severe harm, for what it's worth. But that little stunt when he tried to set fire to the band stage and then pulled the cable taut at the Peach Pageant seemed to get him the results he wanted. When he learned you were in a medical boot, Carl came to me and asked if he would be filling in for the rest of the festival photography assignments. Maybe I should have guessed something was up then," she says, pressing her fingers to her temples and massaging.

"But that didn't work either," Katie said, staring at the previously injured foot in question and flexing it.

"No, no, it didn't," she sighs.

"The car tire?" I ask.

"His stepson. You were right. Apparently, the guy owed Carl some money, and he agreed to forgive his debts if he stepped in as an accomplice. He slashed your tire, Jacob."

"And then, what? Followed us to Farmerville?" Katie asks.

Lauren shrugs. "Apparently. He told Carl he'd try to seduce you, win you over, and blackmail that way."

Katie looks like she might throw up at the thought. "Gross," she says.

"And Natchitoches? He canceled the bed and breakfast rooms, didn't he?" I ask.

"And then sent his stepson to claim the last available room so you two wouldn't have a space to stay," Lauren says. "The thing is, most of the stuff Carl did was petty, small enough so that he couldn't actually get charged with anything for his actions. The tire stuff was property damage, but he didn't do the crime. And the speaker tampering might stick, but there needs to be some tangible evidence, I think."

"So why was he arrested then?" Katie asks.

"Disturbing the peace. Threatening people today. But you two could press charges, and file a restraining order. He did kind of stalk you both with intent to do you harm," she says.

We sit with her words hanging in the air between us. I don't know what to say.

"Thank you for telling us, Lauren," Katie says. "I think, if it's okay with you, we'll take the rest of the day off?"

She nods, and I feel relief rush through my body, desperate for the comfort of Katie's body, Ollie's happy greeting, and sleep. We both stand to leave.

"Oh, one more thing," Lauren says. "Katie. We unexpectedly have a lead photographer position open at the paper. I'd like to extend you a formal invitation to take the job."

I thought all of the adrenaline in my body was gone, but it surges back to life at Lauren's words. Hope thrums through my veins. I turn to look at Katie, but her features are a mix of emotion and confusion.

"You don't have to make a decision now, of course. It's been a long, emotional day. Take a few days and think it over. Call me tomorrow, and we can discuss the offer in detail, pay, that sort of thing. But we'd be lucky to have you. The paper could certainly use another young female voice to bring us into the current climate."

"Thank you, Lauren. I don't know what to say. But, thank you."

We turn and leave. I lift my hand and place it lightly on the small of Katie's back, tracing letters there. Telling her I love her without words. Telling her it will be okay, that she doesn't have to take this newspaper job if she doesn't want to. Whatever she decides, I'm right there with her.

Chapter 45

KATIE

My brain is the freaking fireworks spectacular over Cinderella's castle. It's glitching and shaking as I struggle to process everything that's happened today. Carl stalking us. Jacob going all WWE on Carl's ass in Lauren's office. The job offer. As if trying to make this impossible Dallas job decision wasn't hard enough, the universe had to go and up its ante. Ruston vs. Dallas. Ding ding ding. Fight! I think I'm going to puke.

"Pull over."

Jacob does so immediately. "Katie, are you okay?"

But I'm already scrambling out of the passenger side door and heaving the contents of my stomach into the sulfurous ditch along the side of the road. I feel Jacob's hand rubbing smooth circles over my lower back. I hear him murmuring words of comfort, asking me if I need anything. But I'm trembling, overcome with the overwhelming muchness of all this. Decision-making has always been a personal struggle, but something of this caliber is enough to make me want to lock myself in Margie's she-shed, live off her stockpiles of beer and bar nuts, and never emerge again.

"Breathe, Bun. Breathe," Jacob says. And it's almost too much, his kindness and empathy. I don't deserve it, especially when I'm seriously contemplating moving four hours away from him, probably more than that when you factor in Dallas traffic. And his dad, God. I am a terrible, selfish person.

"Whatever you're thinking right now, say it out loud," he commands gently. "Otherwise, it's going to keep eating you up from the inside out."

I look up at him, my face red from hurling my guts up and then baking in the summer sun on the side of the interstate. He braces me, steadying me as I stand.

"Let's get in the a/c, and I'll talk," I tell him.

We return to the car, and Jacob turns the air conditioning up as high as the fan will go, then tilts the tiny vents, so they hit me square in the face. It feels good, kind of like a cold shower. It steadies me.

"Talk, Bun. I'll drive and listen."

I'm trembling and scared, but I love this man. I owe it to him to share what's happening inside of my brain right now. "Jay, I'm so selfish." He turns to look from the road briefly, confusion highlighting every feature of his face.

"Well, I didn't expect that," he mumbles. "Okay, I have thoughts, but I'm going to try not to interrupt you. You need to vent, and get all of this out in the open. But for the record, I disagree with your opening gambit."

"I am selfish, though," I insist. "All of this happening around us—work, your dad's health, the trauma of all of it on you, and I'm struggling with moving away when you need me the most. That is horribly, miserably, unapologetically selfish."

I see him press his lips into a firm line, struggling to keep his mouth closed.

"What is wrong with me? How can I even consider it? And I'm even *more terrible*, more than you know. Because when Lauren offered me that job today? I should have been shouting 'Yes!' and jumping for joy. It's a job I'd probably love. It would keep me here, close to you, close to my family. But my gut reaction was panic. I didn't really understand why at first, but I think I know now. Jacob, I want the

Dallas job. It sounds amazing, and the chance to grow with other photography professionals, paired with opportunities for promotion... well, it tugs at a desire that's been asleep deep down inside of me. And making decisions, especially one this big terrifies me. But, in my gut, I *want* to go to Dallas. But I know I am a selfish, terrible human being if I don't take the opportunity that just magically appeared to me at the Ruston paper."

I take a deep breath, hold it until my lungs ache, then blow it out and keep going.

"But Jacob, God, I love you so much. It's a whole body, whole soul kind of love. And I'm sorry if that was oversharing or too much too soon, but it's true. And if I go to Dallas, it's going to feel like splitting my soul in half. Half of me will be pursuing the career of my dreams, and the other half wasting away, desperate to be reunited with you."

And then I let out a powerful, guttural yell and punch the car dash. It carries all my frustrations, my sadness, my self-loathing, and disappointment. It hurts my fingers, but I relish in the pain.

"That's okay," Jacob says plainly.

I turn to look at him, eyebrows raised in disbelief.

"It is," he insists. "That's a lot to process. And you didn't even get to how mad you probably are at me for losing my shit and attacking Carl," he says, partially joking. "Katie, it's not selfish to go for your dream job, even if it takes you away from those you love. Even if it takes you from me."

My heart is breaking into a million pieces, melting into a puddle like the Wicked Witch of the West.

"But there's something we haven't considered. Or, at least, something we haven't considered together. A third option," he continues. "I'm stuck here too, Katie. I've had the same job for nearly a decade. Hell, before Lauren gave me this festival assignment, I was on autopilot. Not really happy, not really sad, not really caring about *anything*. Well, besides indulging in the occasional fantasy about you," Jacob says with a smirk. "I have dreamed of moving somewhere else for years. I want to grow, want to learn, to find some excitement. But

I didn't want to leave Dad."

I swallow my guilt down and shove my words firmly back into my mouth. It's Jacob's turn to talk, and I need to give him the same space he allowed me.

"But now… Dad doesn't even know where he is most of the time. We have no family left here. Yes, I have Rhett and your family—and I care deeply for all of them. But Katie, none of them hold a candle to what I feel for you. You *are* my other half. So don't think you can scare me off with talk of soul mates." His damn smirk is back.

"But your dad," I say, unable to keep my words in any longer.

"Can come with me," he finishes. "I've been researching care options for him. There are no good options for him here. Best case scenario, I can find something manageable for him in Monroe or Shreveport, but that's going to mean sending him somewhere between thirty minutes and an hour away. He won't be here anyway. But there are a lot more options in Dallas. I've looked."

My heart begins to pick itself up off the floor of my soul. It peeks out, tentatively hopeful. But no, I won't make him do that. I won't.

"And Katie, don't you dare feel guilty about any of this. I've been desperate for a solution for Dad, and this just might be it."

When we pull up to his house, I realize that Jacob didn't even think to drive me back to my parents' home. Already we've become this conjoined thing that doesn't want to be separated. I have a feeling that if I tried to move away without him, I'd be right back here in a few months.

We walk into his house, shuffling Ollie out of the way. He lets the dog out back, then returns to me, wrapping me up in his long, comforting arms. I allow myself to drown in them, be pulled under by his cedar soap and laundry detergent smell. I cry, finally. I sob, making ugly gasps and gurgling sounds. I should probably be embarrassed, but I'm not. Never with him. It's a minute before I realize that he's crying, too, his body convulsing in small shudders.

I finally pull back and look at him. I know my face must mirror his: puffy, tear-stained eyes, damp cheeks, and rumpled hair.

"We are a hot mess, you know it?" I tell him.

"The messiest… and the *hottest*," he replies.

I start to laugh at that, then keep laughing, hysteria taking over. The fact that he can still find a pinpoint of humor in all this is one of the many reasons I'm hopelessly, desperately in love with Jacob.

"Wow, talk about a blow to my ego," he says. It only makes me laugh more.

Jacob reaches down and scoops me up in a bridal carry, then leans in and presses a kiss to my lips. "Now, if you and I can figure out who a mystery story saboteur is and give testimony that leads to his arrest, then surely we can plot a future life for the two of us together in Dallas?"

"Well, it did also involve you punching the problem in the face. So maybe we should give that a try?"

"Hmmm. Okay. But first, I need to kiss you until you feel better."

"How can you even think about kissing me when my face is covered in snot and probably tastes worse than a mouthful of ocean water?"

"Bun, the better question is, how can I not?" And then he leans in and kisses me earnestly, desperately. His tongue presses against mine, and his arms clutch me tighter, pressing me into his body. My hands are free to roam, and they do, cupping his face and reaching behind his neck to pull him closer.

We have a lot to unpack, a path to forge, and a plan to make. But right now, we just need to get lost in each other.

Chapter 46

JACOB

I started researching Operation Move to Dallas a couple of days ago, but I didn't want to get Katie's hopes up, so I kept it to myself. But the more I dug into care options for Dad there, the more encouraged I became. I have an appointment today with his financial advisor. It's time to figure out what we're working with money-wise and figure out how much assistance we can get with Medicare.

The next few days pass in a blur of list-making, apartment shopping, and excited conversation about what we will need to do to move to Dallas. We agree to keep our plans just between us, at least until we have a firm path forward. Well, with two important exceptions: Katie's Dallas-dwelling besties, Celia and Brian. They are our people on the inside and are helping us both look at apartment options and offering advice on which neighborhoods to consider since Katie refused to move into their apartment and kick Brian out of his room. Though I think Celia is still stewing over it.

I've started looking for jobs in Dallas, browsing through listings for various newspapers, magazines, and even news websites. There are several local publications and even a few national ones based out of the metropolitan city. That's something that would never be an option in Ruston.

I'm warring between excitement and a crushing case of imposter syndrome. I never let myself truly believe that it was possible to leave Ruston, and here I am, actively forming a plan to do so. And I'm doing this with a woman I never imagined could be mine.

Katie received her official offer letter, and the salary is good. It's definitely enough for her to live comfortably in a Dallas apartment. We haven't talked about moving in together, though. Soulmate talk aside, I still wonder if it's too soon to broach the topic. Instead, I focus on updating my ten-year-old resume and researching options for Dad… all while keeping my regular job up at the newspaper and visiting Dad at least once a day.

And Dad doesn't seem to be improving. Outside of one glimpse of awareness in the past week, he's been nothing but an empty shell, a doll allowing his medical team to move his limbs. He doesn't protest at being touched and doesn't seem to be in pain. He mumbles incoherent words from time to time, often referencing the birds outside his windows or talking to me like I'm his father. Every so often, he talks about Mom, or really, to Mom, like she's in the room with him. Those are the days he seems the happiest, but they give me the shivers. It's almost as if the ghost of Mom is in the room with us.

His medical and care team confirm that he exists most days in a passive state. It makes me uneasy. So I fixate on researching the hell out of where I can move him to in Dallas. Maybe if he changes locations, he'll snap out of whatever hypnosis he's fallen into and come back to me.

I'm exhausted. I'm exhilarated. Some days I get home from work and collapse on the couch while Ollie licks my fingers in a plea to fill his food bowl. Sometimes Katie is already there, prepping something for dinner. Other times she shows up late, using the extra key I gave her to let herself into my house and then curl up beside me in bed.

Katie is my anchor in the storm. It may have taken us a long time to finally figure out our feelings for each other, but it couldn't come at a better time. She's officially submitted her acceptance letter to the Dallas job and plans on telling Lauren her decision tomorrow. I don't tell Katie this, but it feels like she's still moving forward while I'm dead in the water, a lifeless corpse she's trying to drag along behind her. I love her more than anything, but Dad is now all-consuming.

We lay in bed together, Katie's head on my chest, my arm tucked around her. Two birds in a nest. This feeling of all the people in my life I love leaving me is weighing on me heavier with each passing day, and I'm beginning to realize something I'm scared to say out loud. But I have to.

"Katie, I say, running my fingers down her arm. "We need to talk."

She stiffens in my arms. "About?"

"I don't think I can go to Dallas." The words are out of my mouth before I can stop them or attempt to soften them.

She pulls back to look at me. "Wait, what? I've already accepted the job. We are making plans. What…" she inhales, holds, exhales. In a more controlled tone, she starts again. "Jacob, what's this about?"

"I've been thinking about it the past couple of days. Dad isn't well. I've been doing research on dementia, and I'm scared that if I move him out of town to somewhere new, it will be his ending. So many patients never recover after something like that. And I won't be that son who leaves his only parent to wither away alone. And then there's the job hunt. I've had zero responses to my applications. None. I can't live without a job."

My chest is in agony, my heart beating rapidly. I sit up and look at Katie, studying her broken expression. "Bun, no, don't. Don't look at me like that. We always knew it was a possibility that you would go on without me. And that's okay…"

"It's not!" she yells in frustration. "But what am I supposed to say? I can't tell you to leave your sick father. And I've already lined up a start date for my new job. Jay… can't we keep looking? For a job? For care? Maybe we could set something up so your dad could live with you? But don't give up. Not yet. Promise me."

I study her features, her broken expression, and it tugs at my heart. I can't deny her anything. I'll have to deny her something. But not now. Not yet. I nod my head. "Okay, I promise."

Katie immediately wraps her arms around me, squeezing me like I'll evaporate if she lets go. We sink to the bed like that together, the two of us clutching to one another, desperate to stay afloat.

I WAKE TO THE SOUND of my cell phone ringing. It takes me a minute to realize that it's not part of a dream. I roll over and see the name on the phone. My heart drops to my stomach.

KATIE AND I WALK into the rehab center together, hand in hand. I can't do this without her anymore. I've tried to keep her separate from this grief, this pain, but she's part of me now. And she's right. I need her. The nurse greets us at the door and walks us back to Dad's room. He's breathing shallowly, his eyes fluttering and rolling.

That tunnel vision is back, but I will it to stay away. Not now. I walk to the side of the bed where Dad lays, pulling up a chair so I can sit close to him. He's whispering a string of words, but I struggle to make them out.

"What is it, Dad? I can't understand," I tell him.

But my voice seems to strike some chord deep within his brain because he turns to face me. And I can see the awareness in his features. He knows who I am. Relief floods my body. This was all a misunderstanding. The doctor was wrong. Dad's not... No. He's fine.

"Hey, Dad." I force a smile to my face. "Hey. You gave us all a scare." I study his wrinkled forehead, the smile that always dances behind his eyes.

"I brought someone with me to meet you. You know that woman I'm always telling you about? The one I'm hopelessly, madly, terribly in love with? This is Katie. I turn, reaching for her, and she steps into my arm, hand sliding over my shoulders"

"It's wonderful to finally meet you, Mr. Edwards," she says. My heart warms, a glowing ember in the storm of fear and pain. The two people I love most in the world on either side of me.

Dad smiles widely at her, then turns to look at me again. I watch as he studies my features, taking in every line, every expression. His gaze is filled with fathomless love, and it immediately takes me back to the way Mom used to stare at me when she was sick.

He whispers something, but I don't understand him. So I lean in, and I hear him say, "I'm so happy for you, son. I love you. Your Mom is proud, too."

I pull back to look at him, shaken by his thready words. But the longer I stare, the more I realize he's not moving. And then I hear the heart monitor flatline.

Chapter 47

KATIE

I don't know what to do for Jacob. He's been a shell of himself since his dad died. I want so badly to make him smile again, to take away his pain, to bring back *my* Jacob. I've talked to my mom and dad about grief, and they've continued to assure me that the best thing I can do is be there for him.

On the morning of the funeral, a car pulls up outside of Jacob's house. I'm sure it's one of the Methodist church ladies with a casserole in hand, but when I open the door, Celia and Brian stand on the doorstep. Before I can exclaim my surprise, Cee is on me like a blanket, enveloping me in her affection. Tears run down my cheeks. God, I've missed her. Brian stands awkwardly behind her, giving me a small wave and a sympathetic smile.

Jacob walks into the room, and the dark circles of grief under his eyes are prominent. He furrows his brows in confusion.

"Well, there he is. Finally. Katie has been hiding you away from us all this time. We realized the only way we were ever going to meet you was to show up and walk through the front door," Celia says.

"I'm Celia," she says, sauntering up to Jacob. "And I know all about you, of course. You're Katie's Jacob." And before Jacob can stop her, Celia has her arms wrapped around him in a tight embrace.

Jacob flounders in confusion for a second, then returns the hug. A smile darts across his face, and, at that moment, I have never been so grateful to see my boisterous best friend.

"Now," she says, turning to take in the room.

I've tidied up in anticipation of my family coming over after the funeral, but I don't expect a big turnout.

"I've brought a tablecloth and some flowers to brighten things up a bit. Brian is going to cook dinner for everyone, so don't you two worry about a thing," Celia says.

Cee hops into action, as good as her word. She takes over Jacob's house like she's been there a thousand times. "Katie, music if you please. It's a sad day, but there is rejoicing in heaven, and we might as well try to make the best of it here."

Something about her words seems to shake Jacob out of his mourning reverie. "Now, here's what I need everyone to do. Brian, you start prepping the food for this evening. Jacob, honey, Brian needs help chopping the veggies, and Katie told me what a whiz you are at that." I hear her cheek, but it's just the right amount to keep Jacob and me from shoe-gazing for the rest of the day.

"And Katie, my queen, you and I are going to clean a bit. Scrub the toilets, wipe the windows..." Her gaze catches on Ollie. "And wash the dog. Actually, I think Jacob should probably handle that. Don't get me wrong, Katie, you know I love a furry creature as much as the next gal, but that one has a lot of drool sliding out of its mouth, and there really is only so much I can handle on any given day."

Ollie stares back at Celia and looks mildly offended, with his furry little eyebrows lifted.

We get to work. I turn on music, my favorite 90s jams blasting through the tinny Bluetooth speaker. Celia opens all the blinds, letting the sunlight in and sending the dust motes flying.

"We're airing the pain out of this house," Cee tells no one in particular. "It's good to grieve, but there's healthy grieving, and there's the curling up into a dead spider ball and letting food rot grieving. We don't want any of the latter."

And she's right. The sunshine cascading through the windows brings the worn home back to life. We wipe baseboards, clean dust off the fans, and discreetly toss the junk mail that had piled up next to Jacob's dad's recliner. By the time we need to leave for the funeral, the house looks fresh, and Jacob isn't carrying the cape of grief that's hung over him the past few days. It's more of a grief cardigan.

We all head to the church together for the funeral. Celia even joins us, leaving Brian behind to make sure dinner is ready when we walk through the door. Celia slides into the back seat of Jacob's car, and we sit up front.

"So, how's the job search going, Jacob?" Celia asks from the back seat.

I turn and glare at her. "Um, Cee. I love you, but this is not the time." I try to sound venomous, but it all comes out rather mousy.

"It's okay, Katie," Jacob says and slides his hand over mine. "I haven't had much luck. To be honest, when Dad's health started getting worse, I stopped looking. I thought..." his voice catches on the last word. "I thought I'd be here for a while, taking care of Dad."

Celia comes to her senses, thank God, and lets the topic drop. I'm terrified she'll bring up my job in Dallas, the one that I asked for a delayed start date on while I helped Jacob navigate his father's death and try to figure out our path forward. But she doesn't. Instead, she tells me about how much she dreads seeing her sister while she's in town. The two have never gotten along, and she just knows Jamie has been filling their mama's head with nonsense. Her prattle does the trick, distracting us the rest of the way there.

When we pull up to the church, Jacob gasps. The lot is more than half full. We get out and walk in, arm-in-arm, Celia close to my side. People from all over the city stop to offer condolences as we walk inside. Once we're through the doors, I'm nearly knocked over by a teary-eyed Amelia. Rhett embraces Jacob like a long-lost brother. We walk with my family into the sanctuary. The pews are lined with a surprising number of people... and they continue to fill the space.

Once the funeral formally begins, the minister says a few words. He asks if anyone would like to share some thoughts about the deceased. Jacob tenses, trying to muster up the courage to speak. But someone else beats him to it. We both watch in surprise as Mark Fisher, owner of the local hardware store, walks up to the church podium.

"George was an unassuming guy," he begins. "Although he mostly kept to himself, any time he came into my store, he'd always ask about me and my family. I know he struggled a lot in his life, what with losing his wife so young and raising Jacob here. But he always asked. And when my wife passed, George stopped by the store and invited me to talk. Said he'd been there and knew how awful it was. He wanted to listen, he said. And so I talked to him. He checked on me a lot after that, always making sure I was okay. So Jacob," he says, turning to look at the man sitting next to me. I'm here to listen. Stop by any time, okay?"

Chapter 48

JACOB

My heart thunders wildly in my chest as person after person walks to the podium and shares stories of Dad's quiet solidarity. How he'd show up, offer support, a listening ear, and the occasional chocolate chip cookie. I'm floored. How did I not know this about my own father? But Dad always thought about my comfort and happiness. Why would he share the grief of a community with his own grieving son?

Finally, the line of supporters slows, and I get up and walk to the podium. My steps falter briefly, but as I turn to face the crowd of supporters, my heart is filled with something else. Pride perhaps? All of these people showed up to support the man who supported them. To support me.

"This is not what I expected today," I begin. "I always thought Dad was a quiet, unassuming guy who didn't really talk to many people besides my neighbor Mary and me. But I'm so happy. That's a strange word for today. But, to be honest, I didn't think anyone was grieving his loss besides me. And to see the impact he made on the lives of everyone here… it's humbling to know that I am the son of such a man."

I look down at the piece of paper I've folded and unfolded a million times with notes about what I would say today. I didn't expect there to be many people here, and it now feels woefully inadequate. But then I think of Dad, how he simply listened, and I know that I don't need a lot of words.

"Thank you for being here today. For saying your final goodbye to a man who listened. He listened to bird song and music, my daily childhood chatter, and then stories of my young adult antics. He listened to me at the end too. He didn't say much in those last days, but I believe he listened. May you all honor him and do the same for others who need you. That's what Dad would want."

And with those final words, I return to the pew and sit next to Katie. Her hand finds mine and squeezes.

WHEN WE MAKE IT BACK to my house, I'm exhausted. I barely know Celia, but I can see why Katie loves her. The sheen of grief has been scrubbed from the house's surfaces. It's now full of life. Brian has a full spread of food waiting on us. There are two trays of lasagna, salad, bread, and homemade chocolate chip cookies. I can see a life where the four of us, Celia, Brian, Katie, and me, get together for dinner, and the thought takes me by surprise. I'm heartened to realize I can still have hope after everything that's happened this week.

As if reading my mind, Katie presses into my side, sliding her arm around my hip and holding tight. I look down to see her emerald-green eyes staring back at me. There's a promise in them, one that we can do this together.

OVER THE COURSE OF the week, people stop by to check on me, often bringing a meal. It frees up the time I usually spend cooking and meal shopping, so I decide to job hunt in earnest. Katie helps me, sending me links to listings, helping me freshen up my resume, and asking Celia and Brian to ask people they know. She starts her new job in a month, and I've promised to follow her, even if it takes some time. I have to figure out what to do with this home I've lived in my entire life, handle Dad's end-of-life stuff, and grieve.

But I know now that there is a future. One for me where I can grow and be madly in love.

The job search seems to be dry. I'm starting to wonder if my Ruston address is keeping employers from considering me as a real candidate. Or, my imposter syndrome yells, maybe I'm not good enough for any of these jobs. I haven't ever had to do a real job hunt before, and the whole thing feels like this amorphous unknown entity. It's like throwing a dart and hoping it hits a balloon fifty yards away.

After so many automated responses of "Thank you for applying. We'll be in touch after we review your resume if we think you are a good fit for this job," I'm strongly considering Katie's go-to of applying at a Dallas coffee shop. I've even started looking at some options near Celia and Brian. Just as I start to fill out an application, though, I get an email.

"Hi, Mr. Edwards. Thank you so much for applying for the job at Eagle Tide Media. I see that you have worked in traditional print journalism for some time. But are you, by chance, the same Jacob Edwards who was on a viral video at a crawfish festival? I'd love to set up a time to chat more. If you're the same Jacob Edwards, I think you have the kind of energy we are looking for in a new social media initiative we're preparing to launch. Kindly respond and let me know some days and times you might be able to talk over the phone. Sincerely, Cory Sanders."

"Hey, Bun, look at this," I say, sliding my laptop over to Katie. She's sitting across from me at my small kitchen table, sipping coffee and apartment shopping.

She pulls my computer to her, and I watch as her eyes scan the message. She looks up at me, eyes alight. Then she starts frantically typing. She spins the computer back around and has Eagle Tide Media pulled up on the screen. Katie scoots her chair next to me, and we lean in to look together. The company specializes in helping small businesses tell their stories and build their clientele. It looks exciting. Different but exciting.

Katie looks at me. "What do you think?"

"I think I'm setting up an interview," I tell her.

IT TURNS OUT THAT Cory really liked that Mudbug Madness video—so much so that he started following the other work Katie and I were doing together. They are looking for someone to be on camera for interviews with business owners and clients.

"We need someone approachable, someone who doesn't take themselves too seriously," Cory confides. "And that video has been viewed more than 50,000 times. Granted, a large part of it was going face-first into crawfish, but your subsequent work has done well, too. I think you would be a good fit for us."

When I tell him that I'm looking to move to Dallas to be near my girlfriend, the esteemed videographer of the infamous video, Cory, chuckles. "Perhaps it's fate, then?" he asks.

"Perhaps."

I get a job offer two days later. And the offer is solid. It's nearly double what I'm making now. Katie screeches when I tell her, jumping up and down like the wild bunny contained within her soul.

"Thank goodness," she says with relief. "That will make this next part far less awkward."

"What part?" I ask.

"The part where I tell you that I set up an appointment with three different apartment complexes this weekend so we can pick out an apartment we both like."

I stare at her. "An apartment for both of us? As in *live together*?"

She grins shyly. "I hope that's okay. Maybe I shouldn't have assumed," but I cut her off with a kiss. It starts off brief and flirtatious but quickly turns deep and searching. She pulls back from me, breathless. "So that's a yes, then?" she asks with a giggle.

"Hell yes," I say, then lean in to kiss her again. I reach behind her, grab her ass and lift her up. Her legs lock around my waist. I walk her to the living room wall, pushing her body into it. We've been intimate since Dad died, but our lovemaking has been comfort sex, two people seeking a distraction, a warm embrace, anything to keep from focusing on the horror unfolding around us.

This, though, this is the fire and passion that's been between us ever since that day at the college party so many years ago. Katie must feel it, too, because she's leveraging the wall behind her to connect our bodies in all the right places. I lean into her placing one arm above her head on the wall, caging her in with my body. My other hand slides up her side, over her breast, up to her neck until I'm lightly stroking the column of her throat with my thumb. She groans at the sensation. I replace my thumb with my lips, slowly trailing down her body with my mouth.

"Jacob," she gasps out.

I pull up the hem of her shirt, and move down her body, pressing a soft kiss to the sensitive skin just below her belly button. I reach for the button of her denim shorts. I undo them, and press a kiss there. I slide the zipper down, kiss again, lower, slower.

"You don't have to," she gasps out. I look up at her face above me, red hair curtaining her face, cheeks flushed with desire, lips swollen from kissing. I love all versions of Katie—singing Katie, laughing Katie, indecisive Katie, photographer Katie. But this version? The one looking at me like I'm her own personal piece of chocolate cake? This is the Katie I love most.

"Oh," I whisper, brushing my nose just above the line of her underwear. "But I want to." I wrap my hands behind her, grab her underwear and top of her shorts from behind, and yank it all down.

"Well, that was hot," Katie gasps out.

"Just wait. It gets better," I tell her wickedly, then I place my mouth where she wants it most.

The sounds she is making heat my blood and spur me on. I move quicker, more intensely, ratcheting up our mutual pleasure. When she cries out with release, I slow. I pull away, staring up at her, drinking in her satisfied expression. She looks down at me, lifts one foot, presses it against my shoulder, and pushes me until I'm laying flat on the ground.

"Your turn, Mister."

She doesn't give me a chance to protest as she starts pulling down my pants. Her mouth finds me, and the pleasure is an out-of-body experience. I watch, rapt, as she moves on me, deepening my pleasure, bringing me to the edge, and stopping.

"Katie…" I whine. "What are you doing to me?"

"Punishing you," she says.

"For what?"

"For making me think you didn't want to move in with me." And then she takes me in her mouth again. Over and over, she brings me to the edge and pauses. Until, finally, in an act of desperation, I hold her there, forcing her to finish what she's started. And then I'm seeing stars as I finally find my release.

Chapter 49

KATIE

Two Weeks Later

"Which one should I grab first?" Rhett asks, staring at the boxes piled around us. I turn my attention away from the moving truck that idles outside of Jacob's house.

"Maybe we should start with the big stuff, like the bed?" I ask him, not really sure and still unable to make a decision, apparently.

Jacob strides out of the back of the house. "Hey, Rhett, want to help me grab this headboard and get it loaded into the truck?"

Mom steps through the door, Dad close behind her. They have their work clothes on, always ready to lend a helping hand. Together, she and I work on continuing to pack up the kitchen, wrapping up mugs and plates, and stacking bowls. We're only bringing the basics for now, just enough to get us started in our Dallas apartment—the one we're going to share together. We found the perfect place. It's not too far from Celia and Brian, but it's also far enough that my bestie won't be able to walk over unannounced any time she pleases. Not that I would mind that too much.

"I'm proud of you," Mom says, still looking down at the set of coffee mugs she's carefully wrapping and placing in a box. I turn to look at her, studying her expression. It's tense with sadness, and it makes my heart jerk in my chest. I question for the millionth time if this move is the right thing. I hate seeing my mom sad, and her expression is chipping away at my resolve. A huge part of me wants to tell her not to worry about it. We'll return the moving truck. No harm, no foul.

She turns and looks at me, and I can practically see her reading my mind. "I mean it. I'm so amazed by your courage and determination to go after what you want." A tear runs down her cheek, and she reaches to quickly brush it away.

"Mom, I don't want you to be sad," I start, unsure of what to say.

"Oh baby, of course, I'm sad. I'll miss you terribly. But Katie, there's nothing a parent wants more for their child than to see them happy and successful, even if it means it hurts my heart a little." She pauses, turning to look as Jacob walks into the room.

"Hey, Mrs. H!" He calls out, walking over to press a kiss to her waiting cheek. "Thanks for coming to help us today."

"Like I'd be anywhere else. I packed some cookies for the road. They're in one of my old Christmas tins. Make sure to put them in the front seat before you go," Mom says.

"You're spoiling us," Jacob says.

"Nah, just buttering you up so you'll let me stay with you at least once a month," she says with a wink.

This whole packing thing has been harder than we realized. All of Jacob's dad's stuff is still in the house, and he's not ready to go through it all. Not yet. I can't blame him. He has enough money from his parents' joint life insurance policies to keep the house for a time. We'll travel back to Ruston on the weekends for a while and start sorting through it. He needs to decide what to donate, sell, and keep. Eventually, he'll need to make a plan for the house, but one step at a time.

As the day starts to wind down, Rhett, Amelia, Mom, Dad, Jacob, and I stand around a pizza box, taking slices and chatting. The conversation turns to how disappointed Lauren was when she found out that not one, but two of her employees were leaving the paper to move away, right on the heels of firing Carl.

"Don't be surprised if she shows up at your work and demands you come back to Ruston," Rhett teases.

"She won't need to with your promotion to managing editor," I tell my brother. He smiles shyly. "It's well deserved and shows just how smart Lauren is."

Finally, we start cleaning up, tossing pizza boxes, and grabbing Mom's cookies. Jacob deadlifts his hulk of a dog. Or, I guess I should say our dog now. I close the passenger side door and roll down the window. Mom and Dad wait, ready to see us off. Tears roll down Mom's cheeks, but she's smiling through them.

"We'll be back next weekend for more stuff, Mom. You'll see me then. Don't cry."

"A mother will do what a mother will," she says, waving me off.

We pull out of the driveway and make our way to I-20 West toward Dallas. I turn on the radio, and "End of the Road" by Boyz II Men comes on.

I look at Jacob and see the smile spread across his face. "Only the end of one road," I say, reaching for his hand. "And the beginning of the next."

Epilogue

JACOB

Ten Months Later

"Do you see Mom? We were supposed to meet her here fifteen minutes ago. It's not like her to be late," Katie says, staring at her smartwatch and scrolling through her text messages.

The sun is practically burning the flesh from my bones, and I'm jittering with nerves.

"Let's just meet her inside, Bun. I'm this close to shriveling up into a piece of fried bacon in this heat."

"Fine, but I do not want to go to the calf scramble," she says with a huff.

"I was thinking something more along the lines of the convention center and homemade peach ice cream," I say, reaching my hand out for hers.

The move to Dallas has been surprisingly easy, nearly as easy as falling into life with Katie at my side. Our shared apartment is decorated with a collage of both of our things. Katie has framed some of my sketches and insisted on hanging them up around the place. In turn, I've done the same with her photography. Katie even got Ollie his very own doggy bed, complete with a fleur de lis on the outside. "Because he's a Louisiana boy," she tells me.

But we both agreed that as happy as we are there, we'll always make a point to drive back to Ruston for the Louisiana Peach Festival. No one else grows peaches like they do here, and my soul yearns for the sweet taste of homemade peach ice cream.

"The Peach Pageant is about to start," I say, pulling her over to the stage.

"But wait, what about Mom?" She asks.

"She'll be able to find us," I tell her. "We might as well watch as crying toddlers are forced onto the stage in tutus while we wait on her."

She chuckles but turns her gaze back to her phone, brow furrowing. "I hope she's okay."

Kylie walks out onto the stage, serving as this year's pageant MC. Her magazine launch went swimmingly, and she and Lauren have, strangely enough, figured out a partnership wherein they can help one another.

"This year's pageant is unique! In addition to our usual categories for babies up to Queen Peach, we have a wild card category where anyone can enter. And I do mean anyone," she says with a wink. The crowd chuckles.

"First up, in the wild card event, we have Margie Murphy," Kylie announces.

I watch Katie. She stops scrolling her text messages and freezes, I watch as she tries to make sure she heard what she thought she heard. She glances up just in time to see Amelia's Aunt Margie strut across the stage. She's donned her usual overalls but has a purple and red boa wrapped around her neck and a wide-brim straw hat with a red bow on it for good measure.

"You have got to be kidding me," Katie says, bursting into light laughter. My heart squeezes at my favorite sound.

Margie proceeds to strut around the stage, pausing to flex her muscles. The crowd eats it up. She finally walks to the side and waits for the next contestant to appear.

"And it seems we have a family rivalry! Next up is Amelia Murphy!" Katie's full attention is on the stage now, and she's cackling as she watches her sister-in-law walk out in an outfit that mirrors Margie's own.

"I wonder why in the world those two agreed to this," she says, smiling.

"Next on the stage," continues Kylie, "is Lauren Bosch."

Katie's jaw drops as we watch our former editor-in-chief strut down that stage in a business suit and heels like it's her own personal catwalk.

"Coming in like a wrecking ball is… Kathy Hebert." Katie's mom walks out onto the stage, and Katie nearly doubles over in laughter. Her mom is donned in a gold sequined evening gown, crown, and all.

"No wonder she wouldn't answer her phone," Katie laughs. "This is the best surprise ever."

"Now I know I said before that this wild card round was open to anyone, and I do mean anyone," says Kylie.

"Keeping it in the family, next up, we have Brian Hebert!" When Katie's dad struts out in a suit and bow tie, grabbing Katie's mom by the hand and giving her a twirl, the crowd goes wild.

Katie is vibrating with laughter and shock at seeing all the people she loves on stage. "I can't believe them," she says.

"Two more contestants to go. Let's give a warm welcome to Celia Martin." Cee waltzes out onto the stage in a neon pink cocktail dress, hem up to her ass. Her strut matches Lauren's in confidence, but she outshines everyone in charisma.

"What the hell is Cee doing here?" Katie asks. She's beginning to realize that this is more than just a joke.

"And now for our last contestant," Kylie announces, spreading her arm to encompass the room. "Please welcome to the stage, Jacob Edwards!" My heart thuds in my ears as I let go of Katie's hand and walk to the stage. I swear even my vision thrums in time to its anxious beat. I focus on my breathing, watching my feet as I move forward. As I climb up the small set of stairs, I'm greeted by the smiling faces of all the people in my life who mean the most to me in all the world. I turn to Kylie, who's holding out a suit coat. I slide it on, then turn to find the love of my life looking at me like I just told her that I am a secret billionaire and she's just been faked on live TV.

I take the microphone from Kylie. "I know I have some stiff competition today," I say, nodding to our friends and family lined up along the stage. "So I know I have to do a little something extra to make me stand out from the competition." I grin and lick my bottom lip nervously.

I turn my gaze back to Katie, locking my eyes with hers. Slowly, I lower to one knee. I watch Katie as realization slowly starts to dawn on her. Her eyes widen.

"Katie Hebert, love of my life, my other half. I would not have survived this last year, heck, these last many years, without you. And I don't want to spend a single one without you by my side. Will you do me the great honor of becoming my wife?"

She stares and stares, tears starting to stream down her face. At first, I think I royally miscalculated, but then she's running toward me. She doesn't even bother going to the side of the stage where the steps are, instead opting to leap and haul herself up onto the stage. I start to stand to greet her, but before I can, she tackles me, literally. The two of us hit the stage, and she presses kisses all over my face.

"So I guess that's a yes?" I ask nervously. Everyone around us laughs.

"Yes!" She squeals. The entire room erupts into applause and cheers.

"I think we have a winner, folks!" Kylie announces. Kathy and Amelia walk over and hand us each a bouquet of roses and place crowns on our heads.

"Wow, I feel like Miss America," I say.

"And I feel like Mrs. Edwards," Katie says. She leans into me and presses a kiss to my lips. I hear the shutters go off around us and look up to see Rhett below us snapping photos.

"Front page news," she says with a wink.

I lean in and whisper to Katie, "And it's the story of a lifetime."

Acknowledgments

Some of the most common questions I get from people are: *How do you do it? How do you hold down a full time job, be a mom to four kids, and write books?*

I imagine the answer is the same for many writers: Because writing is my escape. Falling into someone else's story is my coping mechanism.

I wrote *A Picture Perfect Summer* during one of the most difficult years of my life. My son's chronic illness reached its peak and the scramble to find a solution to halt its progression dominated my thoughts and, unsurprisingly, found its way into my writing. Though it manifested very differently–in the form of Jacob's aging father–the grief in these pages came from a dark place within my own heart. But the sun continues to rise and we have found continued hope and healing, just like Jacob and Katie. Thank you to our doctors at Cincinnati Children's. You get so much of my love for seeing us through this.

This book would not have happened without the unwavering support of my husband, Mark. He always makes sure I have the space to write and edit when I need it. And my kids are always my biggest cheerleaders (even though they aren't allowed to read Mom's books just yet).

My mom and my sisters always know that asking about my books cheer me up. A special thanks to my Mom for sharing my book with all her friends, despite (or maybe even because of) the spice!

Book two was a chance for me to stretch myself and grow as a writer. I couldn't have done any of those things without my fabulous, knowledgeable editor, Kristin. She has pushed me and believed in me from the time she received my first ever manuscript.

Sometimes fate works in mysterious ways, and I will be forever grateful that it brought Sierra and I together. Partnering with The Bookery indie bookstore in Cincinnati allowed me to sell preorders and have the signing launch event of my dreams.

And to every single indie bookstore in Cincinnati and Indianapolis who took a chance on my book and agreed to stock it in store–thank you! You'll never know how much it means to me. The chance to find new readers without a personal connection to them is the stuff that dreams are made of.

Thank you to the Madams. You listened to every imposter syndrome meltdown, beta read, arc read, posted about my book, helped me decide book spine covers and, most importantly, you believed in me from day one. I love your salt. Don't you dare ever lose it.

To my beta reading and arc reading teams: Y'all are amazing. This book is what it is because of you (and I now know that Illinois doesn't have HOV lanes).

To every single person who bought *A Match Made in Autumn*, recommended it to a friend, posted a review, shared it on your social media, hosted a giveaway, told me that Rhett is your new book boyfriend: THANK YOU. Self-published authors need the help of their readers to get the word out, and you made it possible for my first book to be a grand success. I love you to the moon and back.

About the Author

Jessica is a lifelong reader and writer. She earned a bachelor's degree in communications and professional writing before making a career in journalism and editing. Jessica has always dreamt of writing books, and her love for novels spurred her into becoming an avid bookstagrammer. She loves stories that make people happy. Although she grew up in North Louisiana, Jessica now resides in Southwestern Ohio with her husband, pack of rowdy children, and a couple of hounds. They love to spend their time together visiting indie bookstor es, or outside digging up worms and transforming piles of sticks into castles.

Follow Jessica online:
www.jessicaboothauthor.com
www.instagram.com/jessicaboothauthor
www.instagram.com/readbelievelove